TEARING

THE VEIL

J. RODES

For information contact :
http://www.authorjenrodewald.com

Cover design by Roseanna White @ RoseannaWhiteDesigns.com
Images from Shutterstock.com and Lightstock.com
Party Seal by Kailynn Rodewald

ISBN: 978-0997850833

Published by Rooted Publishing
McCook, NE 69001

First Edition: July 2017

Do you know who you are?

one

Braxton Luther

"WE'VE GOT A STRAY SPARK ON THE RUN."

I wasn't sure who the voice belonged to as it came over my earpiece. All of us wore a vocal transmitter during a raid—it could have been any number of Jackals set on watch. My eyes burned as I stared into the fire we'd set. The roof was a black silhouette against the orange glow, and the walls groaned and snapped as the flames consumed them.

Standing across from my position near the front door, Hulk's anger contorted his already menacing face. "Where'd it come from?" he growled.

"West side," the voice responded.

Tristan's post. I forced an even breath and masked my hope with a scowl.

"I didn't see him," Tristan hissed over the intercom.

Hulk's contorted face smoldered as hot as the flames licking the house. "You'd better get 'em."

Heavy breathing rustled through the transmitter, and Tristan said, "I'm on it."

Run, kid. Although, if he got away, Tristan would end up with a trip to the Locker. Maybe worse. At least I knew where he stood though.

"He's headed to the trees," the other voice tattled.

Was Hannah there waiting to help? Maybe Miranda? *Run! God, let him run faster.*

I blinked against the searing heat in front of me—so I could remove the threatening tears burning against my eyes. I didn't know who lived in the house we'd torched, but I knew this family must have been faithful. Their home wouldn't be ablaze on this hot summer night if they hadn't been firmly against the Party. What had they done exactly? Arson was reserved for the people who posed real threats to the New Order. People of influence. They called them the Rebellion.

Or this kind of discipline came to the Cloaked. A shiver rippled down my arms despite the blaze. The Cloaked were the disloyal compliant, those who took the Party's seal only because doing so would keep their citizen status. Or, in my case—and Tristan's—those who became moles in the system.

"He's quick, sir!" Tristan spoke again, his breathing still heavy.

Hulk's frame bulged with rage. "Melzner, so help me, if you lose this kid, I will personally whip you with the claw. And trust me when I say your back will be nothing but ripped flesh when I'm done."

That was not an empty threat.

An image of my father surfaced as I continued to stare into the flames. Had they stripped his flesh before they'd clamped him on the table? With vivid clarity, I could picture his tortured face: blue lips, bulging eyes, pale skin. Dead. Murdered by the hateful hands of the Party because he'd refused to take their seal. Because he was a rebel Uncloaked.

Labored panting filled my ears as I listened to the chase. The sound of snapping twigs and then a thud rumbled over the transmitter.

"What happened?" Hulk demanded.

"Badger hole," Tristan gasped. "I didn't see it..."

A child yelped in the background.

"Gotcha." The other voice hissed like a demon from the pit of hell. Probably not far from it. "He's a small boy—six or seven. I've got him."

I couldn't breathe as I glanced down to my shirt—the same shirt every Jackal wore. The sledgehammer, the fist, and the creed were printed on the front. *Standing watch at home* branded the back. I hated every word. We were terrorists, not some kind of noble guard for the people.

Hulk crossed his muscle-bound arms over his bulldog chest. "Good. Bring him back." Flames gleamed in his eyes, chilling me through. The devil himself. "You're not in the clear, Melzner. I'll still see you in the Locker."

Invisible shackles tightened around my neck. I'd sold myself to the prince of hate. Now I was forced to watch the unfolding of his black heart. If only I'd listened before. To my father. To Eliza.

A crowd gathered on the sidewalk, which hit me as odd. That hadn't happened when the Jackals burned the Knights' home last year. No one had come then. No one had cared. Maybe this practice of torching the noncompliant was becoming a little too common to ignore.

My chest expanded as hope took a small breath. If people knew the truth...

"Can you tell us what happened here?" A woman, though speaking into her slender All-In-One (our government-issued everything device—communication, identification, currency—without it, no life), directed her question to Hulk.

Great. Exactly the wrong person for the truth.

"We got a call about some possible domestic violence."

Hulk talked as if he were actually law enforcement. Not hardly. We were a bunch of puffed-up guys given way too much power.

"It was already too late when we got here. But this wasn't domestic violence. This was a demonstration—a protest against our benevolent Party. This is why noncitizens are dangerous. Their nonconformist attitudes breed violence and destruction."

Liar. I ground my teeth, hardly managing to keep my loose cannon of a mouth glued shut.

"Were there any injuries?" the woman asked.

Hulk hung his head and shook it. "Unfortunately we were unable to rescue the family. The fire was already out of control by the time we made it to the scene. But one of our brave Jackals managed to rescue a small boy."

Heat surged white hot through my veins.

The woman tried to look concerned—just in case someone was running a video feed with their All-In-One, I was sure. "So sad. What will be done?"

"It is tragic." Hulk nodded, feigning empathy

7

as if he were on a Broadway stage. "But thanks to our new system, we have good homes for orphans. He will be taken care of, educated, and given every advantage of a Sealed Citizen. If there's any bright spot in this horrific violence, that's it."

How could a guy who mercilessly hunted the Uncloaked turn into this oversized man version of Mother Theresa without even a hint of regret? The things I saw as a Jackal would appall the average American. But they didn't know the truth. Apathy had given birth to a demented and ravenous son named Power, and Power had no moral compass at all.

I stepped away, balling my fists. Hot misery sunk into my body, pulling my shoulders low. I thought back to the night the Jackals had burned the Knights' house. Part of me had wished we had been lost to the flames.

I was living in the Den, yet I was among the hunted—the Cloaked. The cold, hungry breath of death brushed against my skin with every throb of my heart. But I had to survive. There were so many who needed help and so few who even knew to care.

I was there, in the Den, for such a time as this.

* * *

Hannah Knight

My hands trembled in the July heat. Dizzy waves crashed through my head, blurring the world around me and forcing me to stop. I slumped against a tree, fighting nausea and the blackness narrowing my vision. Food. If only Braxton could give us more this time.

No. If only we didn't live this life of the fearful hidden. Homeless, starving, sick, and worst of all, terrified. No one dreamed of this life. No one saw it coming. Now it was our everyday reality.

We grew what we could from the seeds that had been left in the barn, but only in little patches that we worked to make the plants blend with the rest of the forest. A few scattered potatoes here. A little grouping of onions there. A zucchini plant that hopefully mingled invisible with the wild gourds in narrow meadows. Nothing that would catch a hunter's attention.

One of the boys in our group had snared a rabbit the week before. One rabbit. For twenty starving people. It seemed more like torture than a blessing.

Maybe Reformation Camp wouldn't be that bad. At least they'd feed you. There would be a bed to sleep on rather than the damp earth, an actual toilet to use instead of a pit dug into the ground.

Or maybe Braxton's approach was the way to go. The Party had a group and a home for girls. The Pride. I'd turned fifteen last spring, so I was old enough to join.

Click, click...click.

Braxton. He and my sister had made up that call back when hide-and-seek was just a game.

Click, click...click.

I answered his call as the sun shifted, resting a ray of afternoon light on my cheeks. I ignored the warmth as it spread over my skin, concentrating instead on the irritation that spiraled in my stomach every time I used my sister's signal.

I loved her. Missed her. Envied her. That last part snarled around whatever it was that triggered things like irritation. Whenever someone spoke about Eliza, it was in hushed and hallowed tones. Because she was perfect. Smart. Strong. Always did what was right. And she—

Braxton's frame emerged from the barrier of trunks created by the dense forest. My breath snagged in my throat as he dropped to the ground near me. Did she feel like this with him?

He towered over me even when we were sitting, which made a girl feel like she could curl up next to him and (if he would wrap his arms around her) be completely safe. I looked into his eyes—light brown, the color of caramel, which I could stare at for hours. The dizziness returned, pouring over my body in tingling showers, and I slid my eyes closed, letting the image of his arms around me linger in my mind. I wasn't sure if it was the thought of food or that sweet fantasy that triggered the lightheadedness, but it also ignited irritation again.

I would never be in his arms.

Because of Eliza. Perfect, smart, good-to-the-bone Eliza. She always monopolized his attention.

"You okay?" His hand curved over my shoulder. Warm. Tingling again.

"Yeah." I fluttered my eyes open and looked back at him. "Just hungry."

Eliza wasn't there. I moved to cover the hand that still rested on my shoulder. He slid it away from my touch but curved his arm around me to give me a side big-brother kind of hug before he shifted to settle his backpack between us.

A chill replaced my lightheaded hope. It wasn't fair. He'd never notice me, even if we knew for a fact Eliza was dead. Not that I wanted her to be dead. That would be really, really sad. Honest. But I was there, and he was hurting... Even still, he only ever saw me as her little sister.

Not even as her interesting little sister—which I was. The only thing I had on my saintly sis was a personality. Eliza was utterly predictable. I, on the other hand, was more like Braxton...which was way more exciting.

I shook my head, heat flooding my face. Only when I was with Braxton did I think things like that. I looked to my knees as guilt poured through my body. Eliza had been shipped off to some cruel, fix-your-attitude-or-die camp, and here I sat beside her *best friend* (anyone with eyes knew they were definitely way more than friends), thinking about how I was better for him than she was.

"Here." He brushed my elbow with his knuckles and then handed me the bagel in his hand. "You eat all of this. You look smaller than the last time I saw you."

He noticed my size? I bit my lip, restricting a smile. "Thanks."

He nodded, his beautiful eyes serious, and then looked away at the forest, focusing on nothing. The threat of a smile on my lips died. He'd noticed that I was starving. That was all. I tore a bit off the dry bagel and shoved it into my mouth. As soon as it hit my taste buds, my stomach demanded more. Braxton's attention fell back on me, and I covered my growling belly with my free hand.

"Sorry," I said.

His mouth tilted in a sad smile. "No, I'm sorry." He ran a hand over his head and looked away again. "I'm sorry I can't get you guys more."

The ink near his shirt collar caught my attention, and I fingered my own neck. Girls in the Pride didn't starve. They weren't objects of charitable obligation. They were brave, intelligent, and admired. They didn't cower in the forest, forever afraid.

Bet they had their pick of the Jackals.

I shoved another bite of bagel into my mouth, forcing myself to chew completely before swallowing. Braxton sat wordless, still staring off into nothing—probably wishing he was sitting here with Eliza instead of with me.

Well, fine. I wasn't my sister. Might as well just settle that. I wasn't Eliza. I didn't do the things Eliza would do.

But I was willing to do what she refused.

I settled my gaze on his profile. Strong, set jawline, straight nose, distracting lips... My heart rate jumped. If he could only see me.

"I could help you," I said.

Braxton's head whipped back to me, the intensity of his eyes setting off an excited flutter in my stomach.

"What are you talking about?" His dark tone was like a dart pinning that foolish flutter, striking it dead.

I poked my shoulders straight. "What you did." I lifted my chin. "I could get sealed. I'm old enough to join the Pride."

His gaze turned into a glare. "No."

"What?"

"No."

I scowled. "You practically begged Eliza—"

He launched to his feet. "I was wrong." He spun to face me, anger sizzling in his look. "I was dead wrong, and Eliza paid—" His voice cracked, and he looked away. Both of his hands covered his head. After two long breaths, he looked back at me. "Don't ever say that again." His hand braced against the tree I leaned on as he glowered over me. "Don't even think it. Got it, Hannah?"

End of discussion. He actually scared me a little with that demanding, intense stare. I felt like a dumb little girl. So much for hoping he'd be impressed. Why did Eliza always have to be right? Why did Braxton have to...

I wasn't going there. Sighing, I forced my mind down another path.

"We're leaving soon." I tried to ignore that stupid, small feeling he'd provoked. I wasn't a little kid, and Braxton didn't keep charge over me. "The scout contacted Dad. The first group made it to the Refuge. We'll leave before fall."

"Good." Braxton pushed away from the tree and sat beside me again. "You'll be safe there."

"You think."

"Don't do that." A firm frown punctuated his command. "Cynicism won't do you any favors. Choose to hope."

I snorted. "This from Patrick Luther's rebel son."

One eyebrow on his face arched. "That's right. So I would know, wouldn't I?"

My cheeks grew hot, and I swallowed. "Sorry," I mumbled, looking at my feet. I swallowed again and drew a full breath. "You should come with us." I chanced a sideways look, though I didn't raise my head.

"I can't," he said.

Two words, but they said a hundred other things. He wouldn't—refused even to discuss it. He would never stop looking for Eliza. Wouldn't forgive himself for how everything turned out. Couldn't come to terms with all that had happened the year before.

"You really loved her, didn't you?" I whispered, staring at what was left of the bagel he'd given me. I could feel his gaze on me but couldn't make myself look. Didn't want to see his answer.

"I'll always love your sister."

Yeah, I knew that. The knot in my chest pulled tighter. Next to my sister, I'd never measure up.

* * *

Braxton

Why would she even think about the Pride? Didn't she understand that I lived in a nightmare? How could two sisters be so completely different anyway?

Hannah was headed for trouble. She needed to leave. Soon. Now.

But for the moment, I had to protect her. I owed Eliza at least that much. No, I owed her so much more than she understood, than anyone understood, and the guilt sat like a slow burn in my stomach every single day.

God, is she still alive? She had to be alive. She still called to me in my dreams.

My attention fell back to Hannah, who sat stiff by my side. The girl was spinning in her head like a tire on a bicycle, and because she was way too much like me, I could guess what she was thinking.

"It isn't better out there." I tipped her chin so I could see her eyes—something I usually tried to avoid. They looked like Eliza's, and I hated the ache that pressed into my chest. But I needed to make sure she was listening. "You've got to believe me on this. It's not what you think. Stay with your family. Go to the Refuge."

She stared back at me, but not like Eliza would have. Eliza would listen—hear what I was saying and process it intelligently, which was why she could always come up with a logical answer to my dumb schemes. Hannah...well, she processed with emotion, just like me. There was no reasoning with emotion.

I sighed and began transferring the food I'd squirreled away from the Den to her burlap sack. "You'd better get going. Remember, never the same place two times in a row, okay?"

Still stiff, she stood and, with a cool nod, took the sack. Not listening. Not good.

"Hannah, wait." I couldn't let this happen. "I need to speak with your dad. Tell him I asked for him to meet me next time. Okay?"

She dipped one curt nod.

Great.

"I really need to talk to him...alone," I said, knowing that last part was going to spark her defiance.

An icy stare was her only response. So not like Eliza.

I pushed my fingers through my hair, stuffing

a growl down into my chest. "Do you even know why you're mad?"

She spun on her worn-out tennis shoe, and I watched her shoulders, jammed straight and rebellious, as she wove through the trees.

Fine. Just as long as she was stomping back to the cellar. She had no business thinking about the Pride.

t w o

Braxton

I dropped to the metal runners of the rusted catwalk, inhaling the musty scent of the molded sawdust, damp earth, and decaying wood. Strange how this death trap—the broken old factory where I'd originally found my father after his first capture—had become my refuge. The other Jackals rarely went there anymore, and I could be alone with my tortured memories without having to put on a mask of unwavering dedication.

The boy we had pulled from the house fire haunted me. Why did they take the children? The cruelty of separation pierced me deep, because I knew the ache of having my family ripped away. Even with all of the resentment I'd harbored, I needed my dad. Children needed their parents. Was the Party really so vindictive that they'd separate parents and children just so they could torture the kids?

It didn't add up. Not because I thought there was any true kindness within the Party's leadership, but because taking on orphans was a burden. Why would they do that? Why not just let them die with their parents, or ship them to the camps, where they'd die anyway? What was their angle?

A creak in the metal joist snapped me from my questions. Though I was a Jackal, and thus relatively safe, my heart always crammed into my throat when something out of the ordinary filled my senses.

"Who's there?" I pushed up to my feet, my fists doubling and my mind going over the moves we'd been taught in combat training. *Sensitive areas—eyes, nose, neck, knees, groin. Use surprise. Inflict confusion. Cause imbalance. And show no mercy.* I eyed the sagging rail across from me. Wouldn't hold the weight of a guy my size, and the three-story drop to the broken cement floor below would be a death blow.

"Don't kill me." The whisper that drifted in the

semidarkness sounded feminine.

The muscles in my shoulders uncurled. "Who are you, and why are you sneaking up on me?"

A small shadowed figure stepped from the door to my left. "I had to make sure it was you."

The late-afternoon sun filtered through the grimy tinted window at the end of the long hall, backlighting the silhouetted curves of a young woman. The girls in the Pride were trained to fight just like us, but they wouldn't attack a Jackal. Who was this pixie making adrenaline race through my veins?

My chest expanded as my fists relaxed. "Come here. I won't hurt you."

She moved forward. "I know."

I couldn't make out more than her shadowy figure until she was next to me. A dark red fuzz of new hair covered the dirty skin of her skull, and her green eyes—eyes that had been hopeless and terrified when I'd first met her—met mine with a hint of strength.

"Miranda," I whispered. "I thought you'd have gone to the Refuge."

"No." She didn't hide away in shame as she had eight months before. Standing her full height, she looked more like a woman than the girl Tristan had set free.

Our first act of treason. Followed by...sadly,

not much. Food for the Uncloaked, and that was about it. Something painful jabbed my chest. I was failing.

"Why didn't you go?" I asked, feeling the panic of the darkness we lived in. "You're not safe here."

Her jaw moved. "There are more captives." Her look penetrated through the dingy light, a determination that held undertones of familiarity. Quiet resolution. A characteristic I had both hated and loved in Eliza. Mostly loved.

"So many more," she continued. "Why haven't you done anything?"

"They quit bringing in the Purge girls. There were others, like you, who got away." I knew, even though what I said was true, I wasn't off the hook. I'd never be off the hook.

Miranda wasn't satisfied either. "But the families they're taking? The fires? The kids they're capturing? What about them?"

My gut clenched as if she'd sucker-punched me. Eliza would be that direct, and she would ask me those exact questions. I didn't have an answer. I'd seen them. Agonized over them. But... "I'm under scrutiny right now. It isn't safe."

"For who?" she asked.

Ouch. I swallowed and looked away. "I mean, I don't know if we can pull it off."

"They're dying while you and Tristan are

laying low."

She stepped closer, and I could feel the warmth of her body against my bare forearm.

I wanted to slide away from her, but my legs suddenly wouldn't respond. "Have you talked to Tristan?" I asked, hoping she'd let it go.

"No, I'm talking to you."

She gripped my elbow, and her touch stung. "You're here. For such a time as this."

Eliza's words. I jerked away. "Don't." I pivoted to face her, scowling into her challenging eyes. "You're not her. You can't say things like that to me. You don't know anything about it."

Without flinching, Miranda straightened her shoulders and held my gaze. "I know she loved you. And I know that she was right. There are so many more who need your help. Don't waste what you've been given."

"I haven't been given anything." I seethed, blinking against the burn in my eyes. "I'm here because I was stupid and blind. That's all."

Her eyebrows tilted up. "Will you stay stupid and blind?"

Eliza's last whispered words floated into my memory. *Free our people.* I shut my eyes. How could I? I was just one guy, and not a very impressive one at that. What was Eliza thinking?

"I don't know what to do," I said.

Miranda's weight shifted on the catwalk, and I could feel her presence backing away. "Doing nothing is still a decision."

I opened my eyes and pinned my attention on her. "Doing something rash is stupid."

Miranda nodded, but her determination didn't waver. "I'm staying here. I'll be in the shadows, waiting." She took one step and then looked back at me. "I wouldn't be alive if it weren't for her. I won't ignore that."

Noble reasoning. But Miranda didn't understand. Eliza wouldn't be gone if it weren't for me. I didn't know how to live with that.

"She believed in you," Miranda continued. "Doesn't seem right to ignore that either."

* * *

Hannah

My pulse throbbed through my limbs, causing my hands to quiver with every pound of my heart. I clenched my fists and tucked them close to my chest as I pressed against a tree trunk. Dumb adrenaline. Not like I was spying on the Jackals. Just my dad and Braxton. Not that big of a deal—except I really wanted to know what they were going to discuss.

With practiced moves, Braxton scrambled down the rocky bank. Dad had struggled quite a bit—he'd never actually been to the mill before—but he'd reached the old wood structure long before Braxton had emerged from the forest. Not really surprising. Sometimes Braxton didn't even show up. These meetings were dangerous and unpredictable, and more than once I'd gone back to the cellar empty handed.

Dad stood from his crouched position as Braxton approached the mill. Without hesitation, Dad engulfed Braxton with his strong arms. Tall and more muscular than he'd been the year before, Braxton looked like a man, not a boy. But he leaned into my dad's embrace like a kid. His eyes squeezed shut, and I thought I saw a tear roll off his nose.

They stood locked in a father-son hug, though they were not related at all. I shifted, turning my eyes to my shoes. Spying on such a raw guy moment felt wrong.

"I'm sorry." Braxton's ragged whisper reengaged my attention.

I peeked around the tree again, finding that they hadn't moved, though Braxton seemed to have tightened his hold.

"I know." Tears clogged my dad's voice.

Braxton sniffed, and when he spoke, his voice came strained. "I'm so, so sorry, Evan. It was my fault."

Dad pulled away and gripped Braxton's shoulders. "No it wasn't."

Head shaking, Braxton looked to the ground. "You don't under—"

"I don't have to." Dad gave him a little shake. "It doesn't matter what happened. I know the last thing you wanted was for her to get caught. And I know she doesn't regret what you did for Miranda."

The air seemed to hang in a long, heavy pause. I watched as my dad cried, pulling Braxton back into a hug.

Some people were perfect and never did anything wrong and would remain the icon of goodness far after they'd gone. Some people could do the dumbest things possible and still come out as the beloved, after all their stupidity.

Some people were just middle-ground rejects who never got noticed at all.

"It's forgiven, Braxton," Dad said. "You'll always have a place with us."

Braxton pushed away, pulling himself straight, and motioned to the mill. "We can talk inside. It's safer."

Nodding, my dad disappeared through the black opening. Braxton took a step toward the entrance and then paused. Turning toward my section of the woods, he scanned the trees with a look of concentration. Listening.

I tucked my arms in tighter and pressed my forehead into the bark of the tree. My breath held. I demanded my heart to stop pounding so thunderously and wondered why I had this great urge to bawl. Why should my dad's easy forgiveness bother me? I liked Braxton—more than I should—and wanted him with us. What was this resentment that balled up in my chest?

Sniffing, I stuffed all that stupid junk down into a place I couldn't feel and peered around the tree. Braxton had disappeared, and I could hear nothing of their covert meeting. The only thing I'd accomplished on this spy mission was more tangled-up emotions.

Turning away from the mill, I pressed my back against the tree and tipped my face toward the graying sky. My eyes closed, and a gathering of moisture warmed my lashes. What had I hoped for?

Hannah has been so brave. And clever. She always finds a covered spot to meet. Had I hoped Braxton would speak of me with that kind of praise? That was a dumb wish.

Hannah has lost so much weight and strength. Make sure she eats before she comes back to the cellar; the worker is worth her wages. Silly. Dad didn't know that except for the last time, I never touched the food Braxton brought for us before

I delivered it to the cellar. Perhaps he assumed I did, which would explain why sometimes I would go without altogether.

For months I'd tried to find my place in this game of hide-and-seek. I didn't have one. A pack mule could do what I did, and no one would know the difference.

"God be with you, son."

I froze, the sound of my dad's voice breaking my pity party and sending warm adrenaline back into my veins.

"You too."

There was a breach in their talk, and I imagined them hugging again.

"Don't let Hannah come back." Braxton spoke in that demanding, way-too-sure-of-himself voice. "She's too much like me. Send Miranda if you need something before you leave."

My skin prickled, as if someone had just thrown ice water in my face. What was he talking about? I'd done a good job. My heart squeezed, and sharp pinpoint pains made it hard to breathe.

Rejected. Flat out rejected because I was *not* like my sister.

Determination gripped my mind and filled my body. Standing straighter than I had in months, I tilted my chin up so I wasn't looking at my feet. I wouldn't stand in my sister's shadow anymore. They would see me for me. Respect that I was not her.

I swallowed hard and locked my jaw down tight. Staring at the montage of leaves and sky above, I shut out Braxton's condescending speech. I had a place. Somewhere. Even if it wasn't with the Uncloaked.

* * *

Braxton

We'd been watched. Every nerve ending sensed it, but somehow the alarm that kind of danger set off felt dull, as if the eyes that had spied our meeting were harmless.

I stopped at the top of the bank, turning to watch Evan move through the forest in the opposite direction. Dusk was fading, and a breeze stirred up the moist, earthy smell of the woods. I inhaled, hoping to pick out why I felt off, while letting the familiarity of this spot soothe my edgy nerves.

That kind of breach in my defenses was exactly the kind that would end this operation. I scanned the narrow openings between trees across the creek, seeking anything that looked wrong. Carelessness had cost me the girl I loved in this very spot. I couldn't allow it to rob Evan and his family their shot at safety too.

Folding my arms across my chest, I planted my feet like we did in drills every morning. Habit. The whole volunteering-for-military-school-type living and loving it was still a mystery to me. Waking up at four every morning to run, pushing my body until it screamed during combat training, spending late afternoons in team exercises, which were basically war games, and then squeezing in school somewhere between shaking muscles and belly crawls...none of it appealed to me. At all.

But I had to admit, the physical challenges had their perks. I'd filled out over the last few months, and the bulk in my shoulders and chest as I stood watch over the ravine bolstered my confidence. Plus, and probably more significant, a plan was coming together. At least the beginnings of a plan.

Still alert as the gray faded into soft black, I allowed my conversation with Evan to replay.

"We're going," he'd said. "Next week there'll be a new moon. We'll leave then."

"How will you travel?" I asked.

"The scout left instructions." Evan shifted, his look darting to his feet. "I can't tell you, Braxton. Secrecy is one of the conditions. I'm sorry. But we're leaving, and I wanted you to know. We should cross the Vacant Plains when the moon is full. The scout will tell us where to go from there."

Breathing deep, I pushed emotion away. I'd already cracked earlier. I couldn't let Evan see how desperate I was to go with them or how terrified I was for them. I cleared my throat and squared my shoulders. "Is there any way I can know if you get there?"

Evan scratched his chin. "Miranda insists that she's staying here. The scout will make his rounds again, so I could send word with him, but it could be months."

I nodded. It was what I needed. "She came to see me this week," I said.

"Miranda?"

"Yeah. She told me she was staying." I took a breath. "She wants to help..."

Evan gripped my elbow. "What are you planning?"

"The kids..." I pulled my chin up and focused on his eyes. "The Jackals take them, put them in the Party foster system, and there's something going on with that. Last week though, Tristan almost got a little boy out before he was taken. If we can do it again—only be successful—we can get them to the Refuge, away from whatever the Party is doing with them. But I need you to do something."

Evan shook his head. "You'll get caught."

Probably true. But I couldn't live with Eliza's memory whispering her confidence in me, and now Miranda demanding that I stop doing nothing. *To go against one's conscience...* Eliza's voice whispered to my soul. I couldn't continue to fail. She'd believed in me too much.

"The risk is less if you're gone." I stuffed my hands into my cargo pockets. With Evan and his family safely tucked away at the Refuge, I could afford more risk. "If I can get them out, it'd be best if they can get far away from here. Fast. I need info. Or some way to get them to the Refuge, to safety. You can get that to Miranda, right?"

Evan's jaw moved as he thought. The silence in the mill allowed the past to echo in my mind. Eliza's warm eyes had melted the fear that had hardened my heart, and yet becoming the man she'd seen in me was proving harder than anything I could imagine. Especially without her.

"I'll have to talk to Jude." Evan finally broke the spell of quiet. "It'll be his call." He crossed his arms, his eyes probing my face. "It may be too risky. In fact, it probably is. Jude is careful—he'll probably say no. If the Refuge is compromised..."

"I know." I straightened my posture. "You

know I won't allow that to happen. But I have to have a place to send the kids. I have to have a plan."

Evan's head bobbed once. "We'll work on it. Perhaps Jude will help. They say he is quite the strategist—the Umbrella was his invention. Maybe together we can come up with something."

The Umbrella was the satellite interference mechanism that covered the Refuge. It was the whole reason it existed undetected by the government. The guy who invented it surely could help fill in the gaps of my mental aptitude. Because so far, this wasn't much of a plan. I'd give just about anything to speak with Jude. Heaven knew I wasn't that smart.

Darkness shrouded my vision as I continued to stare into the woods, and I thought about the Party's strangling grip on this nation. The giant force of its power seemed irrepressible. If I was going to make any kind of difference, I'd need all the help I could get.

three

Hannah

Stars winked from the sky between the swaying treetops before Braxton finally left. His intense stare unnerved me, as if he were looking straight at me and challenging my resolve. Didn't matter though. I wasn't changing my mind. I'd heard enough, and I wasn't going to continue to live in Eliza's shadow.

I waited until the rustling of leaves under his boots no longer danced in my ears. Pushing off the bark of the tree, which had left jagged gulfs imprinted on my arms, I pulled myself to full height. Now what? How does an Uncloaked go about becoming sealed? And what did I need to do to become part of the Pride?

If only Braxton had listened to me, he could have helped me. As it was, I had no idea where to go, what to do. But if Braxton Luther could figure this out, so could I.

I crept toward the creek, stopping a few feet from the bank. The fall line made the water swift and a little intimidating there, but farther upstream the waters flowed at a gentle, playful pace. I'd be safer crossing nearer to town.

Picking through the forest in the dark had become a normal part of life since we'd been hiding. My eyes adjusted to the limited light of the waning moon as I moved. Following the beams reflecting off the water, I wove steadily north until the artificial lights from the LiteRail station blinked through the trees. A little bit farther and I'd be directly parallel to the heart of town. The perfect spot to wait until morning.

I found a downed tree a bit off the bank and settled against it for what remained of the night. Though I dozed on and off, sleep didn't take me under as I listened to the forest's nocturnal life play out in its star-lit theater. The trees moaned as they swayed in the ever-moving air, setting the background for the faint crackle of leaves stirred by the movement of raccoons and possums. A chorus of frogs called out their good fortunes from one side of the bank to another, assuring me I was fine in their company.

As dawn pried under the black horizon, lifting the dark lid to reveal its deep oranges and cool pinks, an owl sang from a tree nearby. The nighttime symphony paused, and I held my breath against the sudden eerie stillness. Only the strong thud of my heart filled my ears as I waited for the play to resume. From a tree deeper in, another owl called, his *hoo-hoo-hoo* answering perfectly to the first.

My heart squeezed, and a single tear cut a trail down my nose. I brushed it away, noticing my hands in the pale light. The swirls of my fingerprints stood out with brown earth pressed into their tiny valleys. Sooty black outlined my fingernails and cuticles. Who knew what my face looked like.

Pushing to my feet, I stretched the tight muscles in my back and then moved to the bank of the creek. Cool water covered my hands as I plunged them deep enough to scrub to my elbows. Goose bumps erupted along my neck when the breeze brushed my wet skin. I continued to work at the ground-in dirt, determined that I wouldn't show up at Party headquarters looking like a forest troll.

"Are you bathing?"

A merry, deep voice ripped me out of my

thoughts.

I jerked my hands from the water and scrambled from the bank into the shelter of the trees. My heart kicked hard against my chest, and my breath shook.

"I'm sorry." A young man spoke from across the creek. "I didn't mean to scare you."

My hands trembled. I tucked them close to my stomach as I huddled next to the tree I'd leaned against during the night. A rustling of ground sounded as he moved, his white shirt like a dot of snow against the dark bank of stone. He backed from the shore across from me, took two quick steps, and then leapt over the spread of water.

Oh no. What had I been thinking? I was caught already. I shouldn't have snuck out on my own. Shaking, I tucked my chin close to my knees, covered my head with one arm, and waited for a blow.

"Whoa. Hey."

He stopped near enough that I could imagine his feet sinking into my stomach. His presence towered above my bent form, making me feel like a cornered mouse.

"I'm not going to hurt you," he said.

Something in his voice washed over my terror, and when he squatted to my level, the warmth from his body convinced me to uncurl mine. I peeked at him. Dark-blue eyes studied me with confused alarm.

"Hey," he repeated, his low voice soft. "I promise I won't hurt you." He laid his hand against my shoulder, provoking a fresh shiver. His palm moved up and down my arm, and then he cupped my elbow. "Come on now. Let me help."

Before I could answer, he was tugging me to my feet with one hand and wrapping my frame with his other arm. My heart thundered explosively, and I stiffened again.

"Wow," he whispered, "what happened to you?" He guided me back to the bank and let me crumble to the ground, but never loosened his arm around me. "Shaking like a caught bunny. Why are you so scared?"

I turned my face back up to his. Could he really not know? "I'm Un-Uncloaked," I stuttered, certain I'd just proclaimed my own death sentence.

The arm that rested around me moved, and he pushed my hair off my shoulder to expose my neck.

"So you are." His voice didn't change—still soft. Kind.

I sat a little straighter. "I was coming...going to get sealed."

His gentle eyes didn't change—like it didn't matter. "Okay. I can help with that."

He could? I moved my gaze from his eyes to his neck. Inked. Not surprising. Why did it seem like he didn't care that I was Uncloaked?

"I'm Quinn."

I looked back at his face. Those blue eyes still studied me. All of me. Heat bloomed in my middle, and I studied him back. He had thick dark-blond hair that had been styled with a small amount of gel into a preppy, all-American-boy look. He was fairer skinned than Braxton, but his handsome appeal rivaled any boy I'd ever seen. The compassion radiating from his expression added to his attractiveness. I guessed him to be a little older than me—eighteen or nineteen maybe.

"Does the scared bunny have a name?" His playful grin teased a tiny smile from my own lips.

"Hannah," I croaked.

"Hannah..."

"Just Hannah." Dragging my family into this wasn't part of my plan. Dad and Mom had been through enough losing Eliza. Besides, maybe Quinn had heard of us—the rebellious Knights who refused to cooperate with the Party. That could bring an end to his compassion in a hurry.

"I see." His hand settled on my back. "Orphaned?"

"Yes." My stomach burned. *Thou shall not lie* slithered in the back of my mind. I looked to the ground, wondering if Quinn could tell when someone was not telling the truth.

"Poor thing." He tucked me under his arm and squeezed. "How old are you?"

"Sixteen." Almost. Well, in another six months. Did it matter? Two lies were just as easy as one.

"You're tiny." With his arm still around me, he ran his palm down the length of my arm. "You must be starving. How long have you been hiding in the forest?"

How long? Through the worst of winter, all spring, and then summer. Fall had just begun its yearly repainting of the landscape. "I don't know. Since my house burned down."

Oh no. That was too much information. Quinn's arm tightened, and his other fist clenched. "Protesters." He stared across creek, incensed. "They don't care who they hurt."

I pulled away, afraid he'd know who I really was.

"Hey." He looked back at me and rubbed my arm again. "It's okay. Honest. I won't hurt you. I can help. My mom, she's got a lot of pull. We can take care of you." With his free hand, he touched my chin, bringing my face back to his. "Will you let me help?"

His mom had pull? That meant she was with the Party. The Party killed Braxton's dad. Sent Eliza to a Reformation Camp. Dad said they burned our house down—except Quinn just said that had been protesters. My stomach squeezed. Something wasn't right. My dad didn't lie. But Quinn—I looked back into those eyes. Kindness. Real concern. Maybe something had been misunderstood.

Did I dare trust him?

* * *

Braxton

Safe. Do what you must.

Words I had waited eight weeks to read. I stared at the note, scrawled on the heavy, grainy kind of paper that hadn't been used in my generation. Air left my lungs like I'd been holding my breath for months—because in many ways I had—and I looked back to Miranda.

"They made it," I whispered.

Her eyes darted away from mine. "Yes..." She looked to the ground, littered with the yellows and reds and oranges that had drifted from the branches above.

"But?" I waited. The spot in my chest that had just relaxed began to knot up again because there was something she wasn't telling me.

She bit her lip, stalled for another moment, and then pulled herself straight. "But nothing. I just miss them."

I exhaled again and put my hand to her shoulder. "You should have gone. You didn't have to stay here."

Her green eyes flickered back to me, tragedy and determination mixed within their depths. Yes, she did. Because she felt a debt, just like I did.

A northern gust rushed through the trees, raining more colors around us. The chill pressed against my neck and ears; winter wasn't far off. What would Miranda do during those frigid months? Hunker down in the cellar and live off whatever I could provide. Not much promise there.

She shivered, and I took inventory of her clothing. An old button-down shirt from two or three decades before. Probably something scrounged from the collapsing barn near the cellar. Attached to the waist of her pants—no, not pants like I knew them—were straps that draped over her shoulders. Something you'd see in aged photographs with farmers wearing them. What were those called? Coveralls? Overalls? Weird—

that was what I'd call them. But Miranda had gone to the cellar with a torn blanket and not much else, and the straps kept the oversized pants from falling off, so I couldn't laugh.

She hugged herself as another blast of wind pushed through the trees. Come winter, she'd freeze.

I slipped out of my jacket and tugged off my sweatshirt. The full force of October's chill seeped through my T-shirt, provoking a shiver. "Here." I pushed my sweatshirt into her hands, ignoring my goose bumps. "I'll bring something warmer next week. And a hat."

Her hand grazed over the fuzz of reddish hair slowly trying to cover her head. She didn't look at me, but I could see her eyelids flutter. I'd embarrassed her.

"I didn't mean it like that." With one hand, I lifted her chin. "Honest. You're—" My words halted as her look begged me for...something. The sheen in her eyes poked pain into my chest. Robbed of dignity by heartless people, she'd been abused more than I could imagine.

Suddenly my eyes stung. "You're pretty, Miranda," I whispered. Without thinking, my palm slid over her shoulder and across her back. I pulled her into a long hug.

She stood frozen for a moment, and then her

arms curved around me. A shudder rippled over her shoulders, and she sniffed. Her head turned, and she nuzzled her face into my chest.

Eliza's eyes flashed through my memory. Soft and full of love, she'd looked only ever at me. Here I stood, in our forest, cradling another girl while she cried. What was I doing? Thinking? I stepped away, nearly pushing Miranda from my arms as guilt punctured my gut.

"I'm sorry." I pushed a hand through my hair. "I—"

"It's okay." Her head hung as her timid voice floated up. She sniffed again, and her fingertips swiped at her cheeks. "I know. I shouldn't have done that."

My heart's dull thud filled my ears as an awkward silence hung between us. How could I have done that? Dead or alive, Eliza was everything to me. And Miranda had already been to hell and back. How could I betray one to hurt the other?

"Stop." Miranda's demanding tone forced me to look back at her. "Stop agonizing. It was just a hug, and you're just lonely. We both are. Let's not make more of it than it is."

I nodded, but the knot inside me didn't unravel. I was lonely—I missed Eliza like a fish would miss water. Everyday her voice would whisper in my heart—*Everything I see is inside you. God made you to be this man*—and I wanted desperately for it to be true. But living without her, or worse, wondering what they were doing to her at the camp, was like suffocating under the press that had taken my father's life.

Eliza was my greatness. I didn't think I could do this without her.

Miranda gripped my elbow and shook it a little. "She saw *you.*"

Were my thoughts written on my forehead?

"And we need you," she continued. "Evan is working on his end, so you can't quit on us now. Every life that you save honors hers. You have to do this."

I did have to. I'd landed myself here because I was too stubborn to listen. I couldn't be blind and stupid forever. "Do you know how to get to the Refuge?"

"The scout will be around," she said. "We can get them out, to safety, if you can get the kids to me."

I nodded. "I can't until after the rally next week. Everything is tight right now, but after the rally, when the approval numbers surge back up, the Party should relax."

Her lips tightened. Every week that went by meant more kids put into the system. Taken for a reason that still didn't completely register in my brain. But it was something, a start.

Not the whole of it though.

"I need you to do something." I stepped a little closer, dropping my voice low, as if afraid the trees might be listening.

Miranda didn't hesitate. "Anything."

How could she trust me like that? She wouldn't—not if she knew what a total failure I'd been. The sellout. The weak link in the Luther lineup. The reason Eliza was gone.

Miranda was right though. Every life I could change would be a tribute to Eliza's. That mattered more than my failures. I gulped, studying Miranda. She was strong and determined, but... My request was like asking her to step back into the fire when she had yet to heal from the scorching flames that had scalded her soul. But I needed to know.

"Tell me about the camp."

She stared at her feet, her shoulders caving inward. "There is not human heart there, Braxton. They strip us of our dignity—clothes, hair...virtue—they take away any trace of human likeness, and they keep us trapped with the electronic tags. They're buried into our backs, deep enough that the electronic pulse that can be sent through them goes to our hearts. Like an electric fence you would use on a dog."

She stopped, and I waited, knowing there was so much more stuck in the memories that must haunt her. The chill of her agony seeped into me.

"That's not what you need to know most though." She again pushed her shoulders straight. "Those kids—the foster system—it's not what you think. There's a reason they're taking the young ones, and the homes. The communities they put them in are specific. Selected."

The mystery of this compounded in my head. "Why? There's so much effort there. So much cost? Why would they do that?"

"They're building a new nation, Braxton."

Yes. I got that. "And?"

"If you want to win the heart of a nation, you start with the hearts of the young. Loyalty can be bought. Minds can be trained. But both usually require the moldable heart of a kid."

f o u r

Hannah

Filtered light warmed my face, and I turned, my eyes still closed, to soak it in. I inhaled the morning. Scents of clean sheets and fresh cucumber mixed in my nostrils. Gathering a fistful of bed coverings, I buried my nose into the linen and drew another long breath. I released the clean bedding and let my eyes flutter open before I finger-combed my hair and pulled a handful to my face. Another whiff.

How glorious to feel clean. To smell clean. To be clean.

I sat up and ran my manicured hand over the white duvet. The fabric slid under my palm like the soft fur of a rabbit. A scowl creased my forehead. I didn't like thinking about rabbits. We'd eaten rabbit—the pungent dark meat had often been our only source of protein. I hated it.

With one quick flick of my hand, the covers flew up and I set my feet against the plush, intricately carved rug. White. Only the wealthy used pure-white rugs to soften and warm their solid cherrywood floors. I scanned the room I'd been given, ignoring the tiny burn of guilt in my gut. The dark wood, the white carpet and bedding, the carved headboard and matching dresser. Every scrap of trim and every carefully chosen article of décor screamed luxury. Comfort. Security.

Before the reformation, before my family ran from the Party, my father had done fairly well. But this was beyond even our dreams. And now...now I lived in it. Had for almost two months.

I could never go back.

The burn in my stomach intensified. With a glance to my right, I studied the girl in the heavily framed mirror and remembered what she looked like the first time Charlotte had brought her to this room. Shallow cheeks, thin, pale skin, dull eyes, and filth. Everywhere, filth. How laughable that I had thought a quick splash in the creek would clean up months' worth of ground-in dirt from living in an earthen dugout.

Charlotte, Quinn's sweet mom, had pushed me toward a full steaming bathtub, the size of which allowed for my entire body, including my head if I slipped in low enough, to be submerged.

"Stay as long as you like," she'd said, her voice gentle. "The tub will keep the water warm. Use any of the soaps that tickle your fancy. This will be your bathroom, so make sure it suits."

My bathroom? It was the size of my old bedroom, complete with a separate tricked-out shower, double sinks, polished chrome fixtures, and marble on the counters and floors. This would be mine?

I had turned to her, probably looking like she'd just told me I'd won the Miss Universe pageant, and she'd smiled.

"Quinn insists we keep you." She chuckled. "He's been waiting for the opportunity to do his part—to be a part of something good." Her smile softened and turned proud. "Such a good heart, that boy. He's everything wonderful about the Party."

Wonderful? I'd turned that word over in my head as I soaked. My world had turned a one-eighty in less than twenty-four hours. From leaving the forest as a starving little wretch, to boarding the LiteRail for the first time in my life, to catching my first view of the state center. The trip hadn't taken nearly as long as I'd thought it would—a little over an hour—and I wondered why Eliza and my parents had made such a big deal about her going when she'd taken the Career Track exam.

Wonderful... That word had never been used in relation to the Party in my world. My world had been dark. I'd been wearing blinders. In that moment, I was convinced. My family had been wrong—something just didn't add up, and we'd been hiding for nothing. Who knew—maybe if we hadn't run like guilty fugitives, Eliza wouldn't have been sent away. We made ourselves the nation's enemy, when really, we should have been supporting the new, promising order.

The girl in the mirror continued to stare back. She looked...beautiful. Bright brown eyes; soft, healthy skin; full not-chapped lips; and long wavy chocolate hair. Beautiful. I smiled, and the girl smiled back. She was me.

Knuckles rapped against my bedroom door, followed by Quinn's morning voice. "Hey."

My grin spread full, and I caught his eyes in the mirror. Oh so blue. Oh so handsome.

"Good morning," I said.

"One of these days you're going to have to get out of this sleeping-in habit." He crossed his arms and leaned against the doorway, amusement dancing in his eyes. "Maybe even start going to school again."

School... Eliza's department. Charlotte hadn't pushed me to test for placement, and I was grateful. Quinn didn't need to know how smart I wasn't.

Then again, Eliza wasn't around, and I was living in *this*... Maybe book smart wasn't everything.

I smiled into those happy eyes still resting gently on me. "Your fault." I turned, grabbed a light cashmere cardigan from the bench at the end of my bed, and moved toward the door where he waited. "I've never been this spoiled."

His merry expression faded just a bit. "After what you've been through, I figure..." He reached to stroke my hair and then pressed a kiss against the top of my head.

A flutter danced in my stomach. I didn't know what exactly we were, Quinn and me. He never did more than what he'd just done, but somehow, under his kind and intense gaze, I always felt as if there was so much more waiting. And I liked it. Craved it.

Quinn Sanger was nothing like what I would have imagined. The son of one of the Party's top officials, he didn't act anything less than a humble and sweet gentleman. Charlotte served as one of President Asend's closest advisors, and she and Quinn had come to our state center on official business. What that business was, I couldn't say, but they lived in the apartment above Party HQ and had opened their home completely to me.

It must have been fate that I left the cellar that day. It was the only day Quinn and Charlotte were in Glennbrooke, and Quinn had happened to be out for his morning trail run when he found me. Charlotte didn't blink when her son brought home a scraggly forest troll.

"Is she an orphaned Uncloaked?" she'd asked.

"Yes." Quinn held his mother's eye, and something unspoken was understood between them. "Not orphaned anymore. Right, Mom?"

"Right." Her soft, beautiful face resembled Quinn's. Not just physically—Quinn's mother was darker in both skin and hair, but she had the same compassion in her expression. "We lead by doing."

Not sure what that meant, except that I had a home. And what a home it was. That made me grin as I stood there in the doorway, warm and clean and happy.

Quinn's hand dropped to my shoulder, and he gave me a playful shake. "Come on, now, sleepy girl. Mom's got cinnamon rolls waiting."

I slid my downy-soft sweater over my tank top, and then he caught my hand and pulled me alongside as he walked down the bright hall. The dark-cherry plank floor set off the beautifully pearled wall coverings. Images framed in gleaming nickel lined the wall, each one with a printed saying to remind us why we were there.

By our hands...others know love. A soldier carrying a child away from poverty.

By our hands...we build a brighter future. A woman helping a small girl with her letters.

By our hands...we give hope. A smiling couple holding their hands out to a child who was clearly not their own.

An awkward feeling unraveled deep inside me. It always did when I read those prints. I remembered eavesdropping on my sister and Braxton the year of the reform. Fear had laced Eliza's voice as they spoke; she'd been trying to get Braxton to see why.

Don't you understand what the Progressive creed means? By our hands. It's defiance. Rebellion.

Eliza had made a mistake. It wasn't defiance. It was a statement of purpose. Where had Eliza come up with her fear? She was too smart to be so dumb. And yet...she'd been duped. If only she'd cooperated—tried to understand. The Party was for our good. They wanted equity and progress and safety. Why had she twisted their agenda into something ugly and frightening?

Rebellion? Against whom?

"Inspiring, aren't they?" Quinn's voice drifted from above my head.

I pulled in a sharp breath—his nearness and attention tickled my spine, even though it had been this way since the day he brought me home.

"Yes," I breathed. Actually, they confused me, but I didn't want to share that with Quinn. As far as he knew, I was an orphan, my family was dead as a result of one of the rebel's careless demonstrations, and I was completely grateful to him and his mother. The last part was actually true.

I pointed to the last picture, the one with the couple and the orphaned child. "Is this why you brought me here?"

Quinn winked, but then his study turned deep and serious. "Only partly." His fingers left my hand and twined lightly in my hair. He traced my jawline with his other thumb while his gaze held me captive.

My pulse throbbed. Every moment I had ached to be noticed came together and found their answer in his unwavering stare. He saw me. Just me. And I met the measure of his esteem.

"Come on." Both his hands fell away, but his heated look stayed on my face. "Mother is waiting."

* * *

"There is a Pride in Glennbrooke." Charlotte looked over her delicate espresso cup at me, her smile, as ever, there, but somewhat plastered. "Your hometown, yes?"

I swallowed the bite of cantaloupe I'd been savoring. Fruits like this had been a rarity in my world, and though a feast of such had filled my plate every morning since Quinn had brought me there, I hadn't grown tired of them.

"Yes." I nearly squeaked. A sense of caution—of protectiveness—still stirred deep within me. I clung to the assumption they'd had of me, that I was an orphan. Alone. It was safer that way.

Across the table from me, Quinn cleared his throat, and when I glanced at him, he darted his attention away from Charlotte. He'd been glaring at her though. I could tell by the scowl still engraved on his forehead.

My breakfast turned, suddenly unsettled in my stomach.

Her smile still fixed, Charlotte's eyes remained settled on me. "I have an early meeting today." She turned her chin toward Quinn. "We shall talk more later. Have a lovely day." She rose, setting her cup in the china saucer resting above her breakfast plate, and strode to Quinn. Bending, she squeezed his shoulders and said the same thing she'd said to him every morning. "Do well, my delight and hope. I will see you tonight."

Quinn sat stoic, and for a moment his eyes seemed glazed, as if his mind had gone elsewhere. When he blinked, the lack of emotion remained constant. He was unmoved by her affection, her praise. He didn't typically respond with gushy emotion to his mother's endearments, but neither did he often let them slide off a frigid shield of indifference, allowing her fondness to fall flat and unwanted.

Confused and a bit alarmed by his unusual demeanor, I kept my eyes on Charlotte as she floated across the room to the door and then out of the loft. She seemed entirely unaffected. His silent rebuff—rejection—didn't appear to touch her at all.

How could it not? I'd crumble. My eyes wide, I turned back to him. There he sat, still angry about something, stabbing the door his mother had just exited with a hard stare.

"Quinn?" My voice barely lifted from my lips as I sat there dumbstruck.

His Adam's apple bobbed, and his chest rose

and fell with a deep, controlled breath. "Let's go somewhere today." The words were out of his mouth before he looked back at me.

Determination made his eyes seem intense as they held me. Suddenly I felt gripped by him—by everything about him. His gentle ways, obvious compassion, and now this strength of resolve that both surprised me and sparked a deeper connection. Though opposites in many ways, we were not completely unalike.

"What about your classes?" I asked, though a smile tickled the corners of my mouth, certainly giving my answer away before I ever spoke it.

He grinned—the knowing kind. "I'm first in my class. By a mile. One day gone won't hurt."

Tipping my head, I molded a sassy expression. "And where will we go?"

"You'll see." He stood, flicking his cloth napkin to the table, and came around to where I sat. With his hand held out for mine, he stood. "Let's go."

"I haven't said yes."

A deep chuckle rolled from his chest, the sound and the look that came with it causing my insides to twirl.

"Yes you have."

My lips tingled again, and I slipped my fingers into his palm. His hand closed around mine and held secure as we walked to the door. I wondered for a moment what Charlotte would do if she found out. Thought maybe I shouldn't be the reason her son skipped school when it was so clearly important he do well. Succeed. But when I turned my face up to his to speak those thoughts, I found those blue eyes already studying me.

Determination still there. Along with a new depth. I swam in it. Soaked in the silent, steady warmth. And let the small arguments drown.

One day wouldn't hurt.

Quinn led me down the stairway and out the first-floor door. Crisp air caressed my face, and I gathered in a lungful. A promise of snow hung in the air, a draping of something white and fresh and lovely.

I glanced down to the hand that still held mine. Gentle pressure squeezed my fingers, and I looked back up to his face. He grinned, and I wondered at the newness I saw there. Almost as if he'd just stepped beyond a barrier that he'd feared and a fresh sense of freedom had welcomed him.

Fresh and lovely.

Like the snow. This day. This life.

He led me to a transport station, and we waited for the approaching bus. I didn't bother to look at the route destinations. With my palm warm against his, it didn't matter to me one bit where we went, or why.

"Mr. Sanger?" A man stepped off the transport while we waited to board.

Quinn nodded at him, the edges of his smile fading. "Good morning, Mr. Smith."

Mr. Smith looked back at the bus he'd just stepped off. "Taking an alternative route this morning?"

That determined glint took over Quinn's expression. "Some days require a variation. For perspective, yes?"

One brow on Mr. Smith's face lifted. "Perspective?"

"Have a good morning, sir," Quinn replied, his voice stiff and rushed, and then he stepped past the man and onto the transport, his hand still in possession of mine.

I looked back, catching Mr. Smith's scowl. A sinking ache replaced the delighted swell in my chest.

"Quinn, maybe—"

"Don't." He cut me off with a harsh whisper. His look settled on me. Determined. Deep. Now almost pleading. "My life isn't theirs."

I felt my eyebrows pull in as I turned his resentful words about in my mind. The boy who had everything. Who could do anything. Except perhaps make his own choices. My expression eased, and I relaxed my mouth into a small smile. His hand turned against mine until his fingers wove with my own, and he tugged me closer to his side.

"One day. That's all I want," he whispered above my ear. "One day to live outside of their shadows. Without their expectations."

I tipped my head to his shoulder and nodded against it. His breath felt warm against my hair as he pressed a kiss there. In silence, we remained like that, and I felt safe tucked against his arm. Useful as he found the freedom to be himself with only me.

The bulk of the state center passed by the windows of the transport, and when we came to a break of buildings, Quinn guided me off the bus and toward a wooded park. A walking path wound through the trees, beckoning us deeper into the unknown beyond the edge. We walked, letting the breeze that stirred the leafless trees and the dormant grasses fill in the easy silence between us.

When a hillside opened before us, covered only by the soft brown of winter grass and patches of white from the last snowstorm, Quinn directed us off the trail and into the natural amphitheater. Close to the middle, he stopped at a large stone, laid bare to welcome and keep the warmth of the weak sun poking through the heavy clouds. Releasing my hand, he lowered onto it, his small grin inviting me to join him. When I did, he reached a hand behind me, leaning it against the stone.

I studied his face, which was not set on me but on the scroll of grass leading back into the woods below us. He seemed both thoughtful and relaxed, though a longing filled his expression. I felt the warmth of his body, so close to mine, and the strength of his arm solid near my back. Boldness gripped me, and I leaned into the curve of his shoulder. He glanced down. One side of his mouth tipped up, and then he laid his head against mine.

"I like it here." His voice rumbled against my back.

"I didn't know this existed." I pulled my knees up and wrapped my arms around them. "The city seems so big. Covered with buildings and people." Unbidden, the images of my childhood flashed, days spent in the woods behind our house. Playing alone or chasing Eliza and Braxton. "This reminds me of home." My voice caught on that last word.

"You miss it." His hand came off the rock and curved over my shoulder. "I'm sorry. I'm sorry for all that you've lost."

A painful concoction of resentment and grief

roiled through me, and I was startled to find that some of it was aimed at him.

Not him. His mother. The Party.

I reshuffled the misplaced emotions. Dealt them back where they belonged. My parents. The Luthers. The stubborn Uncloaked. Braxton. Eliza. Those hissing thoughts made me shiver, the blackness of what I really felt lodging an iceberg in my soul. I pushed them away, focusing instead on the boy whose arm warmed my shoulders.

He still studied the open space around us, his face tilted up toward the sky, angled at the spot where the sun fought to break through above. As if he could feel me watching him, wondering about his thoughts, he shared. "It's open here, you know?"

"That's why you come?"

He nodded. "Mother thinks I come here because I like to run. But really, I like the quiet. And the freedom of not being watched. Measured."

No shadows he didn't want to live beneath. The sky was open, and Quinn could be himself. Unsupervised. Unguarded.

"Your mother has big hopes in you," I said, scanning the sky and then coming back to his face.

"For me." He looked back down at me. "And even that..." His voice drifted off on the chilly air.

"What?"

"I'm not sure of the words—how to explain what I feel. Deep down." His expression pinched, as in pain. "Something feels off. Has always felt off."

I waited, hoping he'd share more but wishing he wouldn't have to. His life seemed perfect to me. Adoring mother. Opportunities most don't even dare to dream about. He shouldn't feel...

"Because you feel alone?"

His shoulder moved against me in a shrug. "I don't know. Used, maybe. And like my life has been set out before me—I don't have a choice."

I bit my bottom lip, understanding that helplessness, knowing how caged I'd felt at the cellar, feeling like I didn't have a say about my life. Or, really, that my life didn't matter.

His gaze settled back on me, and he leaned closer. "Sounds spoiled, I'll bet. My rich life, with everything spread before me, and I don't want it."

A small laugh slipped from my mouth before I could stop it. "Maybe a little. You definitely don't want the life I had."

He sobered, then dipped a slow nod. "I'm sorry, Hannah. Truly, I am."

Emotion surged hard through me, and I

looked away.

"What were they like?" he prodded with a whisper.

I focused on the trees again, not wanting the memories to replay.

Quinn's body stiffened behind me. "Were they bad to you?"

"No." The word came out harsh. I breathed in and tried again, softening my tone. "No, they weren't bad. They were good people. I just..."

His hand slid down my arm and back up, and then his thumb began kneading my shoulder. As the moments beat by, the silent invitation to continue, to share what lay splintered in my heart became irresistible.

"I had a sister." I drew a shaky breath.

Quinn waited, but I didn't know what to say. There twisted too much confusion, too many contradicting emotions about Eliza to put my voice to words.

"You loved her."

"I did."

"What happened?"

I raised my face to his, the secrets I held close threatening to break free. Could I trust him? With even the ugliness inside?

"She wouldn't take the seal, and she was sent to Reformation Camp."

His eye pinched slightly, but when I thought that he'd tell me that she would be fine, that all would be well with that situation, he looked down. Unease sank into my heart.

"This is why you're angry now?"

I opened my mouth to argue, but he lifted his hand and traced the furrows that must have been lining my brow. Proof of his claim. I shook my head and shifted so that I could look away again.

"She was perfect." I couldn't control the wobble of my voice. "I loved her. Looked up to her. But I could never *live* up to her. I hated living in her shadow."

His hand draped over my neck, thumb tracing a line up and then down. I leaned against the gentle touch.

"Were you expected to?"

The question indeed. Had I been? Felt like I should, every bit as much as I knew that I couldn't. But I couldn't produce an honest answer for Quinn.

With gentle pressure, he turned my head into his chest and spread his fingers through my hair, holding me safe against him. "I'm sorry she was taken from you."

That was all. No reassurances. No more questions.

But with a sure sense of his understanding. He didn't like the shadows cast over his life either.

For different reasons, we both remained trapped within them.

"I see you, Quinn. Not your mother or the Party. Just you." I dared the words pressing into my heart. "And you are good."

He looked at me with an appreciative smile, then lay back and tipped his face toward the faint imprint of the sun.

five

Braxton

"No Commons tonight." Tristan launched from the floor to his shelf bunk without much effort. His dark skin rippled with toned muscles under his T-shirt, and I wondered—not for the first time—why he didn't have the highest rank under Jed, rather than Hulk. Tristan had the bulk, the skills, and the leadership that the position required. What he didn't have was simmering rage.

Who decided these things?

"Is that a bummer?" I couldn't resist a little poke. Tristan with a crush was actually a tad amusing. Had I been like that with Eliza?

He didn't respond.

"Come on...I know you want to see Skye."

Those two had been glued together for the past few months—but it wasn't like the other hookups that happened at the Commons. They would find a corner, huddle together, and make it look like something hot was going on. It never went sultry though. Tristan wasn't that kind of guy. With her on his lap, his arms locked around her, they'd spend the whole time talking in whispers.

"You don't know anything," Tristan said. His flat voice made me shiver. The things I didn't know were usually horrible, and that tone, when employed by Tristan... I swallowed the bitter taste of my anxiety, and suddenly I didn't want to talk about Skye anymore.

"Why aren't we meeting tonight?" I asked.

"Doesn't matter."

I sat on my mattress. "How do you always know about this stuff?"

Silence. Above me, Tristan shifted without a word. That meant I'd asked a question I wasn't supposed to, which also meant that Tristan was telling me something I was supposed to read something else into. Didn't he know I wasn't that smart?

Fine. I'd try a different question. "What are we

doing instead?"

"Jackal stuff." His hand slipped over the bed and then dangled above me, palm facing my way.

Annoying. I ignored it as irritation began oozing into my thoughts because of his not very informative answer. Drills? Running? War games? Raids...

Raids.

I glanced back to his hand. The pink skin of his palm still faced me. Tiny, subtle markings lay in the wrinkles of his digits.

Numbers.

3185511

What did that mean? Time to try my own version of coded messages.

"Should be warm out tonight, don't you think?" Fires made stuff hot, right? I cringed. I was so not good at this.

"Depends on where you stand." Tristan's hand left my sight as he pulled it back to himself. "Hear the birds are flying south these days."

Birds? 3185511, and birds?

"Migrating?"

He shuffled, and then his feet dangled next to me, and with a small launch forward, he was on the ground again. "Maybe." He looked at me like I was supposed to get this. "Maybe just finding a place to gather. Storm's moving to the east."

He turned away and moved out of the bunk room, his fists closed, before I could slip in another question. I watched him walk down the hall until he turned into the bathroom. To wash his hands, no doubt.

3185511. What was I supposed to do with seven numbers...aha. Phone numbers are seven digits. I regrouped the numbers in my mind into two sets. 318 5511. Definitely a phone number—but not one that was local. Our district only had two prefixes, 368 and 237. Didn't fit the number Tristan gave me, which meant I needed more information. Or a translator.

Pushing from my bed, I moved to the window at the far end of our room while forcing my mind to switch into puzzle-piecing mode. Storm equaled raid, that one I was sure of. The numbers I had figured, but they didn't help. That left me with east and birds.

Our window faced west. What was opposite our window? Wait, he'd said birds were flying south. Did he mean south or east?

I snagged my jacket and left the room. Walking the opposite direction Tristan had gone, I wove through the Den, avoiding eye contact with the other boys who were littering the larger gathering areas. The front doors were in sight when a hand snagged my shoulder.

"Where are you running off to?" Hulk leaned in to speak as he held his grip on me.

"Outside. That a problem?"

He crossed his arms. "Where's your sidekick?"

"I thought all the dumb monkeys hung around you."

Hulk's hand lifted like he was about to let me taste his knuckles. I disciplined my expression, not allowing the urge to wince surface. He held his form, glaring into my face. "Where's Tristan?"

I shrugged, like I wasn't afraid. Pretty sure that was a dumb move—he'd be determined to give me a reason to be scared, but that was how I rolled. "Just passed him in the bunk room. Don't know where he went."

"Why were you in the bunk room?"

I lifted my jacket. "To grab this."

His hand drifted back down to his side. "Where are you going?"

I rolled my eyes. "Out. For a walk. Would you like to come?" Sarcasm came natural to me, so I fluttered my eyelashes as I continued. "We could tell each other our dreams. It would be cozy."

Someone snickered behind me. Oh good. An audience. That should definitely make this encounter end well.

Hulk's face twisted into his trademark rage. He pointed a death finger at whoever was behind me.

"You," he barked, "move along. It'll be five miles for your pack in the morning and then a trip to the Locker."

I glanced over my shoulder. The guy was just a boy—barely fifteen. A new pledge—we called them pups. Poor kid.

"And you"—Hulk's voice drew my attention back to his smoldering face—"it'll be you and me on the center mat tomorrow. Jed's coddled you long enough."

I flung a wilted salute at him. "It's a date."

He sprang at me, murder in his eyes. But I wasn't the same bean-pole kid I'd been in high school, thanks to the intense training of the Den. A quick duck, an upward jerk of my shoulders, and his momentum did the rest. Hulk landed with an *oomph* flat on his back.

I stood straight and glared at him sprawled on the floor. "I look forward to that match. Sir," I said without any effort to hide my disdain.

Hard silence froze everything in the Den. Except me. I stepped away from the dazed beast at my feet and moved to the doors.

The chilled air cooled my hot face as soon as I stepped outside. Hulk was suspicious of Tristan, which wasn't good for either of us. Once I figured out what Tristan had been trying to tell me, I'd have to figure out how to do whatever needed to be done without implicating him.

Frustration blew from my lungs as I approached the end of the parking lot. I had a phone number that wasn't local, two possible directions, and a warning that a raid was going to happen. What was I supposed to do with that?

Tell Miranda.

No problem. Because communication through the woods when she didn't have an All-In-One wasn't a big deal. I didn't even know where she was at the moment. Possibly at the factory—

The factory was south of town. Birds fly south. Storms go east. Tristan had already told Miranda. I needed to warn the birds.

Where were the birds?

318 5511...I needed an area code. I couldn't go calling a nonlocal number without knowing what area code to use first. Why wouldn't Tristan have given me the first three numbers?

And east? East of what?

I growled into the wind. Tristan would have to give me more. I couldn't work with this. After pivoting back toward the building, I marched through the Den, ignoring the whispers slithering through the halls—no doubt about my recent tussle with Hulk—and went straight for the bunk room.

My steps stalled at the doorway. Tristan's bunk had been stripped and his stuff cleared out. I had no idea what that meant, but my stomach knotted with sickening suspicion.

* * *

Hannah

"We have something to discuss." Charlotte set her fork, tines down, against the lip of her china plate.

Quinn eyed her as if he were warning her to hold back whatever she wanted to talk about. I swallowed, which was tricky with the lump of anxiety stuck in my food's path. I hadn't witnessed a verbal conflict between them yet. Everything was polite and friendly and perfect in this home, even if I'd glimpsed an undercurrent of resentment.

Quinn dropped his napkin onto his place setting. "Mother, you and I have—"

"No, we have not." Her sharp tone sliced the air.

Whatever their issue, I didn't want in on it. "I'll just go—"

"No." Charlotte's voice glued me to my chair. "You will stay here. This involves you."

Me? Oh no. That meant I was on my way out. She was tired of me. My unpracticed manners.

My political ignorance. Maybe my social history. Imagine, she, who was not only a close assistant to our president but also in some way related to Kasen Asend, taking in an orphaned Uncloaked. It must be unheard of, not to mention embarrassing. I was a stain on her home.

Or worse, she'd found out about Quinn's truancy the day before.

I fingered the ink branded into my skin. I looked like I fit with them now, except that my skin tone was light brown—darker than either of theirs, and my Hispanic heritage set me distinctively apart from them both. Was that the problem? Was this all because I wouldn't pass as her own flesh when they went back to DC?

"Mother, I don't think she's ready." Quinn leveled a determined look on Charlotte. "This doesn't have to happen now."

Ready for what?

Charlotte didn't blink. "She is absolutely ready, and we must all fulfill our civic duties."

My attention bantered between Charlotte's expression—a stone of resolution that took me by surprise—and Quinn's scowl. I felt my eyebrows pinch and focused my gaze on Quinn. "What am I not ready for?"

"The Pride," his mother answered. "You are of age, and we must set the example for the people..."

Quinn stayed silent, the possessive desire in his eyes pouring warmth into me. I stayed locked in that moment with him, letting Charlotte's practical decree fade into the background.

"...it's not as if you'll be too far away. Of course, you will come home anytime you wish..."

Tell her no.

I wondered if I read his thoughts correctly.

He wants me here... Energy oozed through my limbs. If I could belong to Quinn—oh goodness. The thought made my pulse throb.

"...and when we go back to DC..."

DC. They would go back. What if they left me? Suddenly, life in the cold forest without having ever met Quinn seemed more appealing than a life apart from him now.

Quinn broke our silent connection, spearing his mother with a frown. "We're not going back to DC without Hannah."

"Of course not, son." Charlotte reached to touch his arm. "We will wait until she has completed a year with the Pride."

He set a determined look on her again. "Why does she need to join? The Pride was established for orphans. To give them a home and a purpose. She has a family, has she not?"

Air seemed to become scarce as I waited for

Charlotte's response. Quinn had a point. With a few exceptions, the Pride was populated largely by parentless teen girls, same as the Jackals for boys. Why would Charlotte send me there when she'd given me a home?

"Responsibility comes with our position." Charlotte moved her attention to me. "Surely you must know coming from a common background, dear Hannah. If we subvert the system, does it not look bad to the public?"

Uh, was I supposed to answer? I didn't know how these things worked.

"It would not be a permanent arrangement," Charlotte continued.

So I was not expected to respond. Massive relief.

"A year is all, my dear. A year to show to our people that our system is reliable, that our leadership trusts the strength of the reform."

How did the Pride reflect the strength of the reform?

"Mother"—Quinn leaned back and sighed—"you speak as if we have something to prove."

She dipped one firm nod. "Always, son. Leadership is a precarious position. We must never take it for granted. If Hannah joins the Pride for a year, it will affirm our approach to social welfare to the people. We are a results-based society, so we must deliver results." Her attention fell back to me. "What do you say, Hannah? Can you support the Party? Will you embrace your social responsibility as a part of this household?"

I bit my lip and looked back to Quinn. He didn't return my gaze, his focus falling to the floor instead. Charlotte had made a compelling argument. If I refused, it would reflect badly on her. How could I do that to the woman who had given me a home?

But how could I leave the boy who had rescued me, who was quickly becoming my life?

I looked to my hands, which were busy twisting my cloth napkin. "C-can I think about it?"

"Of course, dear." Charlotte's smile floated in her voice.

I looked back to her and found approval.

Quinn still stared at the ground.

"We'll discuss it again tomorrow morning." She pushed to her feet and sidestepped from her chair. "Until then, you both have a lovely day." Two steps took her to his side. She rested a hand on his shoulder. "Do well, my delight and hope."

Charlotte left the room, and a chill settled in her absence. Quinn sat stiff across from me, that distant look filling his eyes again.

Looking away, confused by his strange

reaction, I concentrated on the napkin I'd twisted like an old rag. When I finally raised my gaze to him, I was startled to see that not only had he returned to himself, but unmasked anger locked on his expression.

"Quinn," I whispered, "why are you mad?"

His jaw moved as he looked past me out the doorway his mother had just walked through. "You don't have to go." His voice cut hard. "That wasn't an ultimatum."

An ultimatum? Like if I wanted to be a part of this family, I had to join the Pride? I didn't hear that from Charlotte. Why had he?

"I know that." I held quiet until he focused on me again. "But maybe she's right. It would look best to the people if I did. Like she wasn't pulling favors or something."

Something passed through his velvet blue eyes. A look that made me shiver. Fear. What would Quinn have to fear? There was nothing scary in the Pride.

"Explain this to me, Quinn." I pushed my hand over the polished wood table but stopped short of reaching his. He glanced to it and then shoved back his chair. Confusion swirled in my head as he jumped to his feet. He had pulled me into his arms every morning. Pressed a kiss against my hairline just as often. Just yesterday we'd practically snuggled together on the hillside in the woods for hours. But my first forward move angered him?

He stalked around the table, and without hesitation his hand curled around my arm, pulling me up. Suddenly I was pressed hard against him, his arms clutching me as if he were drowning and I was his only hope.

"I can't lose you." His low voice mixed a demand for compliance with a frantic plea.

What was this? His passion was almost frightening, but it also filled that vacant spot deep inside. The place that longed to be wanted just as I was. Quinn did—he saw me, not anyone else—and he wanted me. Tingles spread over every inch of my body, and I curled myself into him.

His hold loosened, and he stroked my hair, keeping me close. "I don't want you to go, Hannah." His voice was gentler but not any less sincere. "I need you with me."

Amazement broke through my dizzy euphoria. I tilted my chin to speak up to him. "Why would you need me?"

"You see me. Just me—Quinn. Not Charlotte Sanger's son. Not—" He cut the thought short and swallowed. A tender smile pulled on his lips. "You were the prettiest thing I'd ever seen, even while you were trying to scrub the forest off your arms in that little creek. And there was something about your big brown eyes..." One large hand cupped my face. "You have to know that you were never a charity project to me."

I wasn't? I knew he'd been kind—sweeter than any boy had ever been to me. But why would he have brought me, a forest troll, home to his mother if it had not been at least a little bit out of pity? He was the only son of a highly respected government official. Handsome, smart, and nice on top of that. Any girl with eyes and a hint of sense would make herself silly just to capture his glance. Why would he settle for me?

His hold dropped altogether, and then he gripped my shoulders. "I know you have questions." The chilly darkness eclipsed his eyes again. "But I can't answer them right now." One hand moved, and his fingertips brushed the outline of my jaw before they spread over my cheek. "Just know that I don't want to lose you. I could give you the world, Hannah. Truly I could. You don't have to join the Pride."

My face burned, but it was nothing compared to the fire in his eyes. I did have questions, mostly about why he was being so cryptic, but in that moment, I couldn't remember a single one of them. The throb of my pulse made me feel alive, igniting a fresh boldness in me. I reached to frame his face with both of my hands and drew him down until his forehead touched mine.

"I don't want the world." I closed my eyes and brushed my nose against his. "Just a place in it."

His lips skimmed mine. Too light, not enough. I pushed on my toes to reach his mouth again.

My first kiss—full and deep and breathlessly wonderful. With a boy I was falling for fast.

He pulled back before I'd had my fill.

"With me."

His breath fanned over my mouth. I cuddled against him, and he wrapped me close.

"Your place is with me."

Falling for? No way. I was gone. I'd found my place. With him.

six

Braxton

Gray shadows rolled over the landscape outside the bunk-room window. Night would be on dusk's heels. I was running out of time.

Shifting back to the room, Tristan's empty bunk demanded my attention. Where had they put him? What reason did they have to take him? I'd gone to the restroom down the hall, knowing he wouldn't be there. He wasn't, and I could only pray that he'd removed the ink on his palms before they got to him.

My gut burned. Whatever Tristan had been up to had caught up with him, and he must have known they were on his heels. He'd trusted me with his secret, but I couldn't unravel his code.

318 5511. I dug in my back pocket for my All-In-One. Pointless to dial, but maybe something would come up. I pressed my right thumb against the microscanner to unlock the device, and the option grid lit up.

Citizen Status: B. Luther, good standing. Jackal, Den 368.

Citizen Benefits: Full. Distributions made through Den.

Academic Progress: Satisfactory. Career TBA.

Currency: Credit balance positive. All debts settled.

Options: Communicate. Maps. Games. Entertainment.

The cursor blinked, waiting for me to tap my selection. My fingers slid over *Communicate*, and the dial-out grid bloomed on the screen. I moved to select the numbers Tristan had given me, still knowing the sequence would be insufficient. I needed three more digits.

Why would he give me a nonlocal number in the first place? My hand hovered over the screen, frozen. We didn't go outside of our radius. This was our territory, and we didn't interfere with another Den's.

Tristan wouldn't have given me a phone number anyway. All calls were subject to monitoring. It wasn't safe. I'd been on the wrong track. I turned the All-In-One over, and it vibrated, indicating it had closed the program and gone into locked mode.

Not a phone number. I regrouped the numbers again in my mind, putting them all back as a single unit. 3185511.

Not an address.

What else could it be? I moved back to the window, pressing my head against the cool glass. It was a code for something. Surely Tristan would have clued me in on a code only if he expected me to understand it. I squeezed my eyes shut, going over what had been said that afternoon. Storm. Heat. Birds. South. East. And a number.

Nothing. He'd given me nothing.

Okay, how did codes work? Something represented something else. Symbols for ideas. Pictures for events. Letters make words. Numbers sequence to...

Numbers. Letters. Numbers for letters. Was that it? I pushed away from the window and walked back to the bunk, dropping onto my mattress. Numbers to letters.

Three...I ticked off my alphabet, tapping my fingers for each letter. A-B-C.

C.

One... A.

Eight... A-B-C-D-E-F-G-H.

H.

Five... A-B-C-D-E.

E, and then another E.

One...A, followed by another A.

CAHEEAA.

That meant nothing. I was messing this up. What other kind of code did Tristan mean to use? I slammed the side of my fist against the wall. I couldn't do this. If God wanted me here for such a time as this, He should have made me smarter. How was I supposed to unscramble a bunch of numbers, decode them into understandable letters? Twenty-six letters in the alphabet—that could...

Wait. Twenty-six. That meant that maybe I needed to combine some of those numbers to find a different letter—one with double digits if it was transposed into numbers.

Which numbers needed combined? I shut my eyes again. First two numbers—31. Too high. So, the first number had to be three. The first letter had to be C.

Next...one and eight. A and H, or...I counted the letters as I went through the alphabet again. Eighteen landed on R. C-R. Could be.

Next number—five. The letter E. Twin Es, because 55 is too big. C-R-E-E.

Last two. One and one, or eleven. My fingers tapped against my thigh again as I went to the eleventh letter. K.

C-R-E-E-K. I sat up, smacking my head on the bunk. Growling, my hand covered the spot above my eyebrow that I'd slammed. East Creek Drive. I pushed off the bed and strode for the door, grabbing my jacket as I moved. East Creek Drive—had to be. And I knew exactly where it was, two blocks over from our old school.

Now to warn the birds. Shouldn't be too hard to find them. The house would be dark—no electricity—which would be easy to spot at night.

* * *

Hannah

"No!"

Quinn's shout jolted me out of sleep. I sat upright, my head cocked, waiting for more.

"Son, stop being juvenile about this." Charlotte's cold voice echoed down the hall. "She has to go, and that's final. You're too old to throw temper tantrums. And look at what having her here is doing. Skipping classes, Quinn? That's not you."

"I *don't* want her in the Pride." Quinn punctured every word with hard precision.

"Whyever not?" Charlotte laughed. "You're

acting like a lovesick boy. She'll be fine, son. They take good care of the girls, and she'd survived the forest for who knows how long. If I'd known you'd go all puppy dog about her, I—"

Silence swirled in the house. She what? My heart pounded, and I concentrated on keeping my breath silent. The last thing on earth I wanted was to leave Quinn, but being the chisel that split his relationship with his mother didn't sound like a good thing either.

"Look." Charlotte's voice took on a softer tone. "I understand you're worried about her. Your compassion is one of the things I love most about you. But the Pride is a good place for her. And, Quinn—"

I imagined her framing his face in her hands like he was still her little boy.

"She's very young. You're nearly grown, a man ready to take your place in the world. Be wise."

"What does that mean?" Irritation stamped Quinn's response.

Exactly. What did that mean? Suddenly every moment that Quinn had brushed a tender touch over my skin replayed...always outside of his mother's presence. Had he been intentionally hiding his affection?

"It means just what I said. She's young. At least four years beneath you, and miles under your status—"

A chair screeched across the floor. "I knew it." His angry voice billowed. "I knew this was about her social status. You preach equality, but you don't really believe it."

"How could you say that?" Charlotte matched his outrage. "I took her in, no questions asked. Made sure she was sealed and immediately granted every privilege of a citizen. I protected her from the inquisition process. She never had to tell who her family had been or what they had done. She is absolutely equal to us, which is why she must do this."

My shoulders wilted as I looked down to the white duvet, which glowed in the full moonlight. An unexpected slice of regret stung my heart as my thoughts traveled back to my family. A full moon meant that they should be to the Vacant Plains by now. Close to the Refuge, wherever that was. Charlotte said she'd protected me from inquisition. I didn't know there was questioning involved with getting sealed. What if they'd asked me about my family? Could I have pulled off a lie?

I had. With Quinn. Guilt festered in that fresh wound. What would happen if I stayed, if I defied Charlotte's wish and refused to join the

Pride? Would I lose her protection?

What about Quinn? What would he think if he knew who my family was—that they were rebels, and worse, that we were closely connected with Patrick Luther and his family?

What if that changed everything for him?

I would lose him. I would lose my place with him. That couldn't happen.

* * *

Quinn didn't tap on the doorframe the next morning, nor did he wait for me to come to him when our eyes met in my mirror. For the first time since I'd become part of this household, he entered my room, walking straight to me and wrapping me close.

I breathed deep, soaking in the feel of his arms, the strength of his chest. In some ways, I'd lose him either way. I'd lose this every morning once I was part of the Pride. But maybe—hopefully—not completely, not forever.

"Quinn"—I put some space between us so I could see his face—"we need to talk before breakfast."

His lips drew a tight line. "You heard us last night."

I looked away and nodded.

He released a long breath. "Hannah—"

Raising my hand, I skimmed the smooth skin

of his freshly shaven jaw with my fingertips. "You know I have to."

"No, I don't." He caught my hand and pressed it to his cheek. "I know I don't want you to. And you don't have to. There's nothing in the rules that say you do."

"But your mom—"

"I don't care."

He leaned close, and I felt the heat of his breath against my forehead.

"She may have power, but she doesn't control everything." His mouth brushed over my temple. "She can't micromanage this."

Would she, if she could?

"You—" I took another small step away because his kiss made me fuzzy...being so near him seemed to slow down my brain. After a cleansing breath, I looked into his blue eyes. "You're not like this with me in front of her, like you're...afraid."

He didn't blink. Silently his head moved back and forth.

I wanted to believe him—didn't really have a reason not to. But. "Would she disapprove?"

"Don't care."

Not the answer I'd wanted. "Would she?"

He removed the space I'd put between us and pulled me close in one motion. "Hannah, trust me. Okay?"

Back to cryptic again. What was I not understanding?

"Tell me why you don't want me with the Pride."

The muscles in his arms pulled tight, and he only stroked my hair. "I told you why."

"That can't be all of it." I slid my palms over his crisp button-down shirt until I reached his shoulders, and then I tilted back. "You have to talk to me. I trust you, but you're acting afraid. What are you afraid of?"

"I already told you." His eyes connected with mine again. "I don't want to lose you."

"Not possible." I traced an eyebrow with two fingers. "And I'm pretty sure you know that."

Emotion flooded the eyes that continued to hold me. I'd never seen emotion like that. Deep and fierce. Love. Not just love, though. Fear.

Love casts out fear.

I wasn't sure where that came from. Didn't matter all that much in that moment. Quinn loved me. Every thread of my being knew it, felt it in that undivided intense gaze. Did loving me make him afraid?

His gaze darkened until he was nearly scowling as he bent to rest his head on mine. "I won't let them touch you."

What?

He meant it—and that was definitely fear, not only in his eyes but his voice.

"Who, Quinn?" My pulse throbbed, and it wasn't because I wanted him to kiss me again.

His mouth closed tight, his lips forming a thin line, and then he closed his eyes. "Just stay with me, okay? No one will hurt you if you're with me."

Suddenly I remembered how every nerve screamed in terror the day Quinn found me. How every movement in the forest whenever I neared the edge of the woods sizzled panic through my veins. Life as the Uncloaked, always the hunted, never safe. That was all supposed to end when I got inked. I was protected now. By our country. By the Party.

But Quinn still felt that he needed to protect me.

A chime drifted from the hall outside my room, and Charlotte's heels clicked against the wood floor as she strode to answer the door. Quinn straightened, but his fingers stayed tangled in my hair.

"Quinn," Charlotte called, "you're needed early. Take breakfast with you."

Needed early for school? My forehead scrunched as I searched his face.

His look held firm, as if he'd known this would happen. His lips brushed mine, and then his fingers slid from my hair. "See you tonight."

I watched him leave, his shoulders straight, his stride confident. Nothing seemed rumpled, until he paused at my door and settled one more look on me. Pleading oozed from that glance.

His footfalls echoed in the halls, leaving me with an empty feeling of finality. I listened while my stomach twisted as he left the apartment with a muted click of the door, and then I took inventory of this room—this life I'd been given.

Comfortable. Pretty. Easy.

Probably not what life would be like with the Pride. But I didn't need it. Did he think I did? Was that why he was so adamantly against my going? Surely not. He knew where I'd come from, that I was a survivor.

"Hannah, dear?" Charlotte's voice again drifted from the hallway. "Are you eating this morning?"

"Yes, ma'am."

What was Quinn afraid of? The mystery twisted through my mind as I pulled my hair back and secured it into a ponytail.

"Did you sleep a bit later this morning, dear?" Charlotte passed a plate of cut fresh fruit from her place at the head of the large table.

Was she serious? She really didn't know? "Yes, I guess I did."

"A lot on your mind, I'm sure." She stirred sugar into her coffee and tapped her silver spoon against the cut crystal cup before she set it on the silver saucer beneath it. "Let's talk about that, shall we?"

I swallowed, feeling like a bug caught in a jar.

"Did you know Quinn is on an accelerated Career Track?"

Wait. I thought we were talking about me—about the Pride. "No. I guess I didn't know there was such a thing."

"There is." She sipped her coffee. "Very uncommon. Academic test scores, personality indicators, coping abilities...these things are all factored together. However, rarely we find some students who can not only keep up with the high demands of accelerated academics but who possess markers for professional success at a young age."

She paused, cut a delicate piece of her poached egg, and slipped it between her perfectly glossed lips. After swallowing, she continued. "You can imagine how proud I was that my son fit into that extremely small category." Setting down her fork, she zeroed her attention in on me. "He is destined for greatness. Certainly you must see that."

"I do." My voice sounded like a mouse's.

"Of course you do." She smiled. "And you

must also know with President Asend being his uncle, his place in our society will be both public and influential."

I hadn't figured this relation to Kasen Asend. Quinn never spoke of a father. Charlotte never mentioned a husband, so the relation must be through her, but the names wouldn't be different then, would they? How exactly did this work? I nodded, leaving one part of my mind to work on this puzzle as the other part continued to listen.

"Oh, Hannah, dear." Charlotte leaned toward me. "I can see how much you care for Quinn. After he pulled you out of the forest the way he did, it would be only natural for you to carry deep affection for him."

I shifted in my chair as my stomach coiled.

"That is why I know you want to do what's best for him."

I stopped fidgeting and raised my eyes back to her. "I would never do anything to stand in his way."

"I know that, dear."

Pushing my shoulders straight, I narrowed my gaze. "Then why are you insinuating—"

Charlotte tipped her head back and giggled. "Oh, my sweet girl. You misunderstand me entirely." She moved to reach across the large space between us and squeezed my hand. "This is not a threat, not an ultimatum. I simply wanted you to see why I think your going to the Pride is for the best. For you and for Quinn."

Sitting back in her chair, she sipped her coffee again. "The people will be looking at his life—picking it apart. Looking for inequities, things that he took advantage of because of his social and political position. We can't let them find anything they would deem unfair, can we?" Her crystal cup clinked against the silver platter as she replaced both on the table. "That is all I want you to see. I feel it is important for you to understand where I am coming from, because I know that Quinn has been blinded by emotion where this matter is concerned."

She did see. Much more than either Quinn or I could have guessed.

"Why is he afraid?" I asked.

Her smile drew loving and proud. "Compassion is his biggest asset. And unfortunately, his greatest blind spot. He only wants to make sure you're safe, especially given your past. He fears what he cannot see when it comes to your safety."

A charity case. That was what I was to her.

"He also doesn't understand the difference between his compassion and...deeper things." Charlotte's smile vanished, and her eyes narrowed. "You and I, my dear Hannah, must guard his blindness. We must do what is best for him, even when he doesn't see what that is. Don't you think?"

A chill swirled in my chest, while blood throbbed through my veins. Doing what was best for Quinn, that I could agree to. But this subtle...threat? Was it a threat? If it was, who was she threatening? Me. I could lose my citizen status with a snap of her fingers. Quinn. Would she really ruin her own son?

I was going to the Pride. I couldn't afford either possibility.

seven

Braxton

Sweat pooled in between my shoulders, but I kept my fast pace. I'd ducked out before dinner but made sure I'd been seen at the Juice Shop on Main. Acting didn't come natural to me, but I'd smoothed the panic rumpling my gut and came across to the people I made conversation with as if I didn't have a worry in my head. It took measured movements not to stuff my turkey and Swiss wrap down my throat and take off from the joint at two-alarm speed. But once I passed the lights at the LiteRail station, I pushed myself through the woods at top speed.

Raids usually happened around midnight.

Usually. But if I knew anything about the Den, it was that they capitalized on the atypical—which kept the ignorant Americans from suspicion just as well as it kept the Uncloaked locked in fear.

Once I crossed the creek, I broke north again. I had a good two miles in front of me. Holding this pace would be a miracle. But they needed a miracle, so I kept pushing. When the vein of water elbowed east, I veered west. The school would be in a clearing about a quarter mile from that point, and East Creek Drive would be a few blocks west of that.

The thick trees opened, and I slowed to a walk as I circled the well-lit school building. I left my Jackal coat behind, tucked carefully next to a downed log, and wore an old sweatshirt I'd found in the lost and found pile in the Den. *Glennbrooke Wrestling* was printed in orange on the front of the hoodie, with a wildcat's face screened on the back. Perfect. I hadn't been a wrestler—hadn't been much of anything actually—so if anyone saw me walking across campus, they wouldn't suspect it'd been me.

When the school was at my back, I slid the hood over my scruffy hair and hunched my shoulders, as if that could hide my six-three frame. With a casual stride, I walked the suburban sidewalk like I was any normal eighteen-year-old heading home from practice. As I turned right on East Creek, adrenaline shook my legs. From the corners of my eyes, I scanned every front window I passed, looking for the dancing yellow of candlelight.

A two-story house three blocks north of the school captured my attention. Still as death and as dark as the inside of the mill. But I needed to be sure. I turned west at the next corner and walked into the alley behind that row of houses. One, two, three... I passed the houses clearly running on electricity. The fourth...the backyard was a bleak as the front. Not a single electric light burned inside or out. But something did flicker in one of the second-story windows. The glow moved as if it had life—not the static white light from an LED bulb. Yellow, it danced in the lowest part of the window, and its light didn't even reach the top of the room.

A candle. This was the place. These were the birds.

I scratched the ground with the sole of my shoe until a pebble the size of a dime rolled under my foot. One rock probably wouldn't do it, but I picked it up and flicked it toward the house. My aim needed work—the stone hit about four inches to the left of that upstairs pane. Continuing to scruff around, I finally collected five more rocks and, one at a time, pitched them toward the dim glow of light.

By the fourth stone, a shadow moved to across the view and stopped in front of the light. I tossed my last pebble, hoping my aim had warmed up.

Not a bull's-eye, but I'd grazed the top corner, and the shadow leaned into the glass, hands cupped around face, peering my direction. I grabbed for a bush nearby, quickly brushing over the branches until I found one that was loose. After I snapped the weak twig, I ran it against the metal fence separating the road from their yard.

The shadow shifted.

I pulled in a long breath of air and scoped out the alley in both directions. Nothing moved. No shadows, no sounds. Then a door latch clicked in front of me, and a man stepped across the yard between us.

"Who are you?" His voice was low, cautious.

I searched for a clever response, a code name that would make sense. Tristan would've had one ready.

"Are you one of them?" This time a defensive growl rumbled in his low tone.

Too much to explain. Too dangerous to try. "You have to go," I said, keeping my voice low but firm.

He took another step toward me. "Why?"

"You're not safe." I slunk back into the shadows. Surely an Uncloaked wouldn't turn me in, but then again, I'd been sure that all of my father's fears about the Party were dumb. No more certainties.

He followed my movement along the fence line. "How do you know?"

I swallowed, pressing my lips together. "You have to go. Tonight. You don't have much time."

"Is this a trap?"

"Take only what you can carry. Food. Warm clothes. Go to the creek, and follow it south, past the LiteRail station. When you get past the light, stop. Someone will find you."

He stopped moving, and the shadows of his face held steady on mine. The soft hiss of his breath passed through the night air. I wondered if anyone had warned Evan or my father the night of our fire. Probably not. The Knights had been the first to have their house burned in our area. At the time, I'd thought no one cared, that they all supported the way the Party was purging the Uncloaked. Wasn't true. The way Hulk fed the media, I was sure that everyone had stayed away out of fear—and they had believed my father was to blame. That was why they did nothing when he'd been murdered. In their minds, he deserved it.

The outspoken pastor had become a violent rebel. That was the lie they'd been fed, and though it still baffled me, the people believed it.

Flames blazed across my memory. The unforgettable smell of charred wood irritated the back of my nose, and the tight burn of smoke in my lungs made it hard to pull in a full breath. Over a year had gone by, and yet the memory was so powerful I actually wheezed when I inhaled deep. It would all happen again, right here, and I couldn't stop it. But these people didn't have to die.

"You have to listen." I leaned forward, gripping the fence. "Go. Now."

"How can I know that I can trust you?"

I bit my lip, suddenly realizing that it quivered. "They'll take your children while you die in the flames. They'll be reeducated. Trained for Party loyalty. Is that a risk you're willing to take?"

"The flames..."

His voice dropped until he was so quiet I had to lean closer to hear.

"They aren't what we're told, are they?"

"No."

"The Party?"

"Just go. Don't look back." I slid my arms out of my sweatshirt and pulled it over my head.

"Take this. Leave it in the house. Someone will find you south of the rail, and they'll show you what to do next, but you have to go now."

I didn't wait for him to respond as I shoved the hoodie into his hands and turned away. I walked into the gray shadows of the ally, forcing my legs to keep a calm pace. Goose bumps raced down my exposed arms. My black T-shirt did little to protect me from the late-November chill. But it would conceal me until I made it back to the woods.

Weaving through the quiet streets until I came to the school, my mind whirled. If I got caught...

No. I wasn't going to get caught. I'd make it back to the Den before ten. If asked, I'd been downtown—first to the Juice Shop, and then I sat and watched the LiteRail. If asked why...because I was bored. No Commons tonight, and my bunkmate had mysteriously disappeared.

I would make sure someone downtown would see me in my Jackals coat, hanging around the LiteRail station. I'd find some detail to remember—how many people got off the last set of cars—or something to give weight to my story.

It'd be okay.

My coat waited right where I'd left it. I pushed my arms through the cold sleeves and wrapped it tight around my body, willing heat to replace the icy chill. Running would warm me up—but only until I reached the lights of the LiteRail station. I'd need to cool down before I got back to Main.

Everything went according to design. I reached town as a set of railcars stopped at the station. Seven people got off and scattered in different directions once they hit the platform. I shoved my hands into my pockets and walked north on Main. A couple of turns, a few blocks east, and the church building I'd grown up in loomed as a dark shadow against the gray night. The Den. The Party's perversion of my father's life and work, its mockery of everything he believed.

My current home.

Hardness gripped my chest. Regret wasn't something that you could ignore. It was like a giant zip tie that slipped around your heart. Every reminder of each stupid act notched the bindings tighter. I had done a lot of stupid stuff.

I squeezed my eyes shut as a question swirled through my heart before it lifted to heaven.

Can you still use a sellout?

* * *

Hannah

The queasy rolling of my stomach wouldn't go

away. It'd been there every minute of the hour it took to travel from the state center back to Glennbrooke, from the moment I'd stepped off the LiteRail platform, and the entire time it took to register with the Pride.

I looked at myself in the reflection of the window—sturdy boots, formfitting pants tucked into those boots at the ankles, and a black shirt— also fitted—with the Party's symbol embroidered on the front. Every girl in the Pride wore the same thing. I was among them. One of them.

Wasn't that what I'd wanted when I left the Uncloaked?

I turned from the building and walked across the expanse of grass toward a group of three trees that grew a little way from the Pride's Hall. Interestingly, they used what looked like an old church building to house us. I glanced at it over my shoulder. Single-story, sprawled-out brick building with a set of colored windowpanes at the front. Baptist maybe?

Weird. Wonder why I cared. Clearly it had been abandoned, and the Party had made good use of the vacancy.

Wrapping my arms around my stomach, which still rolled painfully, I continued toward the piles of winter-dead leaves scattered under the dark trunks. Splotches of brown-crusted snow dotted the landscape here and there, pathetically hoping for more white to cover up their dirty survival. Supper hour would come soon. The other girls were still out for evening drills. I'd missed them on this first day because our commander had been showing me around, getting my uniform. Making me official. Likely trying to impress Charlotte, who'd come with me. "To see you settled, my dear."

Wasn't so sure about that anymore.

"You'll bunk with Skye." Commander Knott had put a hand on a shelf bed.

Guess I get the top.

"She's been with us since we moved in here over a year ago, so she knows the life. Listen to her."

Skye. I had imagined blue eyes and blond hair. A bubbly personality. But, *please*, not too perfect. I'd already lived with too perfect.

Reaching the trees, I picked the middle one and eased to the ground at its base. Tipping my head back, the rough channels of its bark pressed against my hair. I closed my eyes, picturing the home I'd left that day.

Quinn had been at school. I didn't even say goodbye. Couldn't. If I'd waited, I wouldn't have been able to do it. Charlotte had been around though, which was a little off. She was always gone during the day, doing whatever important business Party leaders did.

I had made my bed, making sure the sheets were tucked squarely like my mother had shown me, and smoothing the duvet. My room had been pristine, just the way I'd found it when I'd first come home with Quinn. I stood at the door and inspected the elegant space. It looked like I'd never been there.

With only the hairbrush and a spare shirt tucked into a small bag, I had slipped down the hall toward the front door. Charlotte had been sitting in the front room, working on something on her government-issued tab.

"Are you going out?" she called.

I stopped, my hand raised for the door handle, and looked at her for two heartbeats. "I'm going."

She stood, smoothing her hands down her designer pants. "Going? To the Pride?"

"Yes."

Her smile beamed. She'd won. "Oh, my dear. I'm so proud of you for making this decision."

Her eyes moved to the small bag in my hand, and heat crawled over my neck. Would she accuse me of stealing? In reality, the things weren't mine. I didn't have anything. Even the clothes I came with were gone, because they'd been putrid.

She pointed to the bag. "Is this all you're

taking?"

I exhaled. "I don't have anything to take. This is just the brush you gave me and an extra shirt."

With four quick steps she covered the space between us. "Sweet Hannah. Everything in that room is yours. Take whatever you like. But I do believe the Pride will supply everything you need, so perhaps this is wise." She squeezed my shoulders.

For some reason, her show of affection sent a chill over my body.

"But if you find there is something you lack, feel free to come back for it."

Quinn. Could I come back for him?

We left. Charlotte saw me safely into the Pride, and with a proud pat on my back, she left for the state center. For Quinn. The pecking of her pristine heels against the sidewalk had hammered in a finality.

I was out of the way, no longer the distraction threating her son.

That was that, and there I was, sitting under a tree with my heart beginning to crack. The shaded grass seeped coolness through my pants as I pulled my knees up to my chest and wrapped my arms around them. Emptiness settled over me in the quietness of the yard. I'd found a place to belong, and it had been ripped out from under me. Would I see him again?

I leaned my head down on my arms, and moisture lined my eyelashes as I shut them.

"Hannah."

See, already I missed him so much I was imagining him there.

"Hannah."

Not imagining. I sat up and turned my head toward the sidewalk edging the street. He stood, hands in his pockets and a mix of anger and regret in his eyes. Mad at me. Disappointed in me. A teardrop slipped over my eyelid before I could blink it back. Still planted in his spot, Quinn held out one hand. I scrambled to be near him.

Rather than wrapping me close, which is what I had hoped for, he took me by the hand and started walking, leading me away from the Pride. His grip was firm, and I had to nearly run to keep pace with his steps. Confusion and disappointment sank heavy in my chest. Why had he come? He could have stayed home to fume. And where were we going?

After two blocks, he rounded the corner, led me another block, and then turned into an alley. We passed an old truck—the kind that had been outlawed twenty years before because it used too much fossil fuel—and he tugged me toward the building the rusty dinosaur had been parked next to.

His hand left mine, and he tipped my chin so that I would look at his face. "What have you done?"

I blinked. *No crying.* Big girls didn't cry. Pride girls didn't cry. "It was necessary."

His eyebrows pushed together, and the betrayal on his face made me feel sick.

"Why?"

I reached for him, gripping his dress shirt. He hadn't even changed before coming to find me.

"Your mom is right. You have a future, and I can't get in the way."

A hard, cold mask covered his face. "My future is what I want it to be, Hannah. It doesn't belong to my mother or to anyone else. I get to choose."

"Quinn." My heart pounded. "This shouldn't make you this angry. Your mother loves you and wants the best opportunities for you. Why are you going to school? Why do you work so hard in your studies? You're the only nephew of our president, the son of a government official. That kind of life isn't given to everyone. I can't let you throw it away because of me."

His hands perched on his hips. "Who says, besides my mother, that it really matters if you're with the Pride or not?"

A point I'd questioned as well. But if people

found out I was an orphan and didn't go through the Progressive structure like every other orphan, they would likely question the system. Which would lead to questions about the government. Eventually the lines of doubt would find their way to Quinn.

"Quinn, you're too smart not to see this."

"I see plenty." He took a step closer, hot anger radiating from his body. "And I know more. You don't know the things I know."

My body froze. Even the breath in my lungs turned to ice. "What don't I know?"

He looked away and blinked several times. I watched the Adam's apple in his neck bob. "This can't be undone, Hannah."

"I know."

My lips quivered. When his eyes fell back on me, the sheen over them undid my stoic resolve. A tear slipped down my cheek. He followed its trail with his gaze until it spilled over my lips, and then with a feathery touch, he wiped it away with his thumb.

"I have to go." With one hand, he cradled my face.

I wondered, because of the heavy emotion in his hushed voice, if this was goodbye. Like the goodbye, goodbye kind.

He bent down and brushed my mouth with his. I gripped his elbow, silently begging him not to let it be that kind of goodbye.

The sorrow in his eyes held for a moment longer and then gave way to the anger he'd come with. The hand that still warmed my cheek moved to grip my chin.

"Don't go to the Den, Hannah." Heat surged through his command.

I scowled. "It's expected."

"I don't care." The fingers that held my jaw sank deeper. "Don't. Go." With that, Quinn turned and strode away.

He didn't look back.

eight

Braxton

"Sir, there's no one here."

As a young recruit reported his findings, I trained my breath to remain even, though my muscles longed to sag with relief. The birds had listened.

Hulk's massive build went rigid at my side. "What do you mean there's no one here?" He stepped forward into the pup's space. "Where would they be?"

The pup pulled in a shaking breath. Hulk was the epitome of perverse power. Where did his long leash end?

"I don't know." The kid eked the words out.

"All I know is the house is empty."

The muscles in Hulk's neck bulged. "Melzner." He turned fiery eyes to me, rage masking his face.

I drew straight. "I don't know where Tristan is. He was gone when I got back. Bunk cleared."

"You think I don't know that?"

I knew he knew. He'd done it. He'd taken care of Tristan.

"What'd you do with him?" I said.

"None of your business." Hulk stepped closer to me. "What'd he tell you?"

I scowled. "About what?"

The anger on Hulk's face took on a feral quality. The guy was possessed.

Shouting from across the dark street distracted our heated discussion.

"Sir, I said you need to stay back!" one of the Jackals demanded.

"No." A growl from an older man surged forward. "I am an American citizen and a resident of this street. I want to know what is going on here." The man, built like he could handle himself despite the wrinkles around his face and the silver in his hair, pushed past the ring of three Jackals and strode toward us.

Operation miffed. On multiple levels. How had Tristan known about this? I glanced to Hulk and was surprised to see panic cross his face. Mister confident-on-his-feet had just landed on his backside.

Interesting.

My focus bounced from Hulk to the concerned citizen and back again. Opportunity had just bloomed in the cover of night.

I stepped forward past Hulk and toward the riled bystander. "I'm sorry, sir." I reached forward as if to shake his hand.

He stopped, glancing at my hand as if he expected a viper coiled around it, then glared back at my face.

"We're just trying to protect the people," I explained. Lied. "We had a tip earlier. A firebomb threat. We're doing our best to defuse the situation before any damage occurs."

"Firebomb?" He sneered. "You boys seem to be in on all sorts of action. Usually involving fire."

Hulk stepped forward, confidence—arrogance—refaced in his demeanor. "Yes, sir. The situation with the rebels has been fierce. We're doing our best. I think this time we made it before anyone or anything could be harmed." He pressed the spot by his ear that would turn his communication mic on. "Bring the bomb out, boys. Make sure it doesn't detonate."

That ought to thoroughly confuse the Jackals

who had been placing the explosive.

Hulk continued his charade with manipulative skill, gripping the man's shoulder with a convincing sense of camaraderie. "I know things get twisted, and with the intensity of the attacks growing, people have questions. But you'll be glad to know this time everyone was evacuated. The Prestons are safe, and the bombing has been averted. Perhaps that will allay your fears. We *are* the good guys."

The Prestons. I hoped they were safe. Prayed that they'd found Miranda and that she'd been able to see them to the dugout.

Dropping away from us a step, the man examined first Hulk's face and then mine. Sweat rimmed my hairline as I fixed a blank stare. I wasn't as good at acting as Hulk. And the truth was I didn't want to lie to a man who was figuring out the truth. But if I outed the Den, the Party, right there, right then, I would be useless to those who would follow.

And there would be more. Without a doubt, so many more birds would need to fly, because this storm was only going to get worse.

The man cleared his voice with a garbled sound. "You understand the people being nervous. No one expected the violence that is rising up. It doesn't make sense."

Hulk followed the man to the street. "Of course, it's understandable. Don't misplace your fear though. Anger, targeted rightly, is useful. Make no mistake—this is the rebels' work."

A familiar grip of anger squeezed my insides. Someday the truth would rise. But not before the veil of darkness could be torn.

Not that night.

Hulk pivoted to face the target house again. "Pack it in, boys." He looked at me, still pressing the mic. "Nice work."

The last thing I wanted was a compliment from him. I turned to march the opposite direction, but his massive hand caught my shoulder, stopping my escape. In the next heartbeat, I felt his bulk push against me, and the heat of his acrid breath spilled onto my ear.

"Don't think for a minute this is done, Luther."

Oh no, not by a long shot. I wasn't done—this little hiccup was only the beginning of his troubles.

"Sir?" I spat.

"You and I have a meeting in the Locker. Tonight. And if I have to drag your sorry carcass in there, it'll only be worse."

I drew a long breath. The Locker...hadn't made it there yet. But I'd seen Tristan's back after he'd had those kinds of meetings. Beef Jerky came to mind.

The wave of defiant resolve I'd just surfed moments before crashed around me, leaving only the churning waters of fear. But fear—anger—rightly aimed...

He could tear my back to ribbons of flesh, but he wasn't going to turn my purpose.

* * *

Hannah

"You'd better not snore."

The girl's voice penetrated my deep focus on staring at the ceiling. Didn't matter how hard I looked at the white tiles above my bunk, I kept seeing Quinn's back as he walked away from me.

"Hey, new girl." The voice gained a body, and that body used her hand to smack my arm. "You hear me? I like my sleep, so don't mess it up."

I rolled my head to the side and examined the girl with an attitude. For her forceful words, she was a small thing. Dark hair, dark eyes, and skin even browner than mine.

"Skye?"

"Yeah, that's me." She smirked. "Guess you've already been told."

"Told what?"

Her eyebrows peaked, and her gaze hardened. "About me. Stay in line, little kitten, or you'll answer to me."

I snorted. "Yikes?"

That hard gaze gained heat as she leaned in close. "That won't be a question if you keep pushing. The Party believes in order, unity, and strength. Don't think for a moment that we aren't prepared to enforce those ideals."

Questions swirled in my head as I compared Skye's statements to the pretty framed colloquialisms hanging on Charlotte's walls. Not quite linear. I kept my faltering opinions off my face as I continued to look at Skye.

She stared back.

I pictured us as two lionesses prowling in circles as we deadlocked in a face-off. I could hold my own. I'd survived living in the forest as an enemy of the state. Little miss big talker was nothing.

"Get up," she barked.

"Why?"

"Because you just challenged me, and I don't back down. From anyone." With a decisive pivot, she showed me her back. "Now, get up. We're going to the training center, and you can show me exactly how stupid you are."

Fine. If I had to establish myself on my first day, so be it. Good to know I hadn't joined an idiotic sorority club. Wouldn't be singing in harmony while we fluffed each other's hair. No squealing about boys while we waited for them to call.

No thinking about boys.

Actually, come to think of it, think of him. I pictured the anger in Quinn's eyes right before he turned his back and left. Captured the hurt he'd pushed into my heart.

My muscles ignited with boldness as I shoved off the bunk and landed on the floor. Skye's dark hair flared as she spun out the door, and I followed her into the hall and toward the exit.

Stopping, she turned back to the hall. Her attention landed on me for a moment before she called out, "Pack it in, girls."

Scuffling suddenly filled the rooms, and the four closed doors that I'd passed all opened within moments. Out spilled the Pride, two dozen girls ranging from age fifteen to twenty.

I glanced at Skye, just then wondering how old she was. Petite, dark, and confident, she gave me contradictory impressions. If she led this group, it wasn't by seniority—her face hadn't left adolescence yet, although she probably had a couple of years on me.

How did this system work? Someone had to decide leadership.

Commander Knott wandered into the space from a hall adjacent to our bunk rooms. "What's this, Skye?"

"A challenge, ma'am." Skye's eyes didn't waver from me.

"Ah. From the new girl, yes?"

"Yes."

Knott glanced at me, a slight smirk tipping the corner of her mouth. "This is a surprise. Hannah came from special circumstances. I didn't think she'd want...attention."

Special circumstances.

I became certain that letting these girls know where I'd been living over the past months would be a mistake. So would allowing them to know about me and Quinn.

His retreating back flashed through my mind again. There wasn't a *me and Quinn.*

Anger surged with rekindled strength through my limbs. "You're wrong, ma'am. Nothing about my circumstances was special. I'm an orphan. But I won't be kicked around."

Commander Knott's smile grew, and she looked back to Skye. "What shall we do, Skye?"

"The mat. Now."

"No dinner first?"

"Dinner can wait."

One eyebrow cocked upward as Commander Knott turned to the other girls. "Dinner can wait." She motioned toward the door with her hand, and the ranks broke away from the walls. As soon as they crossed the threshold from the building into the yard, the girls ran with poise and speed, well formed and conditioned. I followed, my legs pumping to keep up, my mind whirling to understand their unspoken arrangements. They migrated into a clearly established order and didn't break formation as they maintained a pace that made me breathless.

We turned left at the first side street, me still on the fringe of the group, not having a place within their system.

I was back there again. In the hollow spot where misfits see where everyone else belongs just as clearly as they see that they don't have a place with them.

Quinn. A lump swelled thick in my throat. I was supposed to belong with him. He said it. And I left him.

So he left me.

This was what I had chosen. Now I was left with only one option. I would fight for a place to fit in.

My lungs cried out for respite when we reached the training center. Sweat lined my warm face and trickled down my back, but as I looked at the other girls in the Pride, they barely seemed winded.

We spilled into a large room—no doubt a place set up for wrestling practice for the high school. The girls wordlessly formed a circle around the red mat, breaking their formation only in the spot in front of me where the two who would have blocked my path separated to give me access.

I swallowed. The lump remained, but I shoved my shoulders back. I would fight for the right to fit in. If I couldn't have the place I ached for with Quinn, I would carve out a place where I would not be hurt by rejection. I would measure up. I would not be broken.

The Pride would be my home, and I would not regret it.

As I passed through the break of girls, I saw Skye standing in the middle with two three-foot wooden poles in her hands. Splitting them, she held one in her left palm and tossed the other my direction. I reached to snag it from the air. It hit the tips of my fingers and then fell to the floor as if my touch had rendered it dead.

Muffled snorts surrounded me.

Keeping my posture stiff, I bent to retrieve it from the ground.

Skye jabbed my chest with her pole and then anchored it under my chin, lifting my face to hers. "She who loses sight of her target has not fully committed to the goal."

I locked my sight on her, feeling the floor near my feet for my weapon.

Skye raised her eyebrows. "How committed are you?"

"To what?"

A single laugh came off her snarling lips. "That is the question, isn't it?"

My hand found the pole, and the cool feel of smoothed wood filled my palm, reminding me of the ax we used to cut fire wood back at the cellar. Confidence revived my noodled muscles. I was a survivor. These girls invented battles to fight. I had fought real ones.

This Skye was nothing more than a conditioned mercenary bent on my humiliation. She knew nothing of survival and had nothing on my purpose.

I stood straight, and as soon as my other hand wrapped around the pole, Skye came at me, her hands spread in the middle of her pole with enough distance between them that they would not encounter impact.

So. We were not playing swords. I positioned my hands to match hers and raised my weapon to deflect her strike. Her eyes widened as I caught her attack and shoved against it.

She caught herself with one step back and grinned. "The kitten isn't so dumb."

I stepped forward with the pole in front of me, grabbing the advantage of the offensive position.

Her smirk vanished, replaced by cold determination, and suddenly we lit into combat.

The crack of wood against wood rang up to the high ceiling room as she first deflected my attack and then engaged her own. Her hands moved with a speed I could barely follow, and her small, agile body, very close to my own size, prowled with a strength I hadn't guessed she could possess.

Still, I fought back, matching her moves as my heart rate spiked. I pictured chopping into the flesh of wood as I moved in this bizarre dance. With every strike, wood would splinter, and eventually the whole log would give way, allowing me to split it in two.

Eventually Skye would give way.

My arms quivered as my breath drew fast and heavy. Skye, too, gasped for air, and I realized we both grunted or shouted with every strike.

I am not beneath her.

The thought must have played on my face. Murder passed through her eyes, and then she launched a frenzied attack that left my ears ringing and my vision blurry. More than once, she landed a blow on my fingers, and I felt them swell, making my grip loose and clumsy.

Not wanting to lose my determination, I looked at her fingers. Blood dripped from every knuckle, satisfying my competitive thirst.

I did not see her body crouch before she flew at me with a force that knocked me off my feet. I landed on my back, legs sprawled, and before I could elbow my way up, Skye had a knee in my chest and her pole pushed flat against my neck.

Her chest heaved as she measured her breaths, regaining a natural rhythm. "You lost sight of your target."

I'd been distracted, yes. It had allowed her to attack without fear of deflection.

The pressure against my neck eased, and she lifted her knee from my chest. Nearly back to a normal breathing rate, she stood in one fluid motion and reached her bloodied hand to mine.

"Stay focused." She pulled me to my feet and leaned in close. "Your life may depend on it."

I said nothing as I wondered if she was truly done with me. What now? Did we shake hands? Say "Good match?" Hardly seemed like the Pride's way. Like Skye's way.

"Fall out," she barked.

Every girl turned, though some paused to settle a smirk on me.

Nice. Way to fit in, Hannah. I glanced back at Skye, who remained beside me. She met my look and then dipped a tiny nod.

Approval.

Maybe that was what I'd wanted in the first

place.

"Let's go." She took off without another word, and I forced my quivering legs to match her stride. Completely breathless, and my legs numb, I kept up with her all the way back.

Commander Knott looked me over and then turned to Skye. "Dinner, yes?"

"Dinner."

So condescending. Like they couldn't get a meal without her permission. Once again I wondered about this ranking system.

The rest of the girls broke the stiff stance they'd taken while waiting for their leader and clustered to the doors. Skye remained rooted, overseeing them. My dislike for this arrogant cat ballooned, and I decided her approval meant nothing.

It shouldn't mean anything.

"Clean up." Skye took a step away from me. "Nobody wants blood on their food."

Dismissed. And apparently I'd waited for it, which meant that she'd gained rank over me. I felt like growling.

I tried two doors before I found the bathroom. My hands shook as I turned on the water faucet, and I stared at the flow for several seconds, cringing. Raw and bleeding, my knuckles were already screaming. Water against those wounds...my stomach lurched.

Skye pushed through the door, a box tucked under her left arm. She paused as our gazes met in the mirror, and then she looked to the running water.

"Wasteful." She moved forward, nudging me to the side, and shut the valve off. With quick movements, she plugged the sink with a folded rag she'd tugged from her shoulder and ran the water again, but only until the sink held two inches of water.

She turned back to me. "Waste nothing. Not a drop of water. Not a word from your mouth."

She was like this dark-skinned little Yoda, spouting off random bits of wisdom as if she'd mastered the Force.

I muffled a snorted chuckle. Her eyebrow quirked, and then she grabbed one of my wrists and shoved my hand into the water.

Screaming shots of sharp pain sliced through my hand. With a quick intake of air, I clamped my jaw as tears flooded my eyes. Blinking, I forced them back and withdrew my hand.

She pushed it back into the water. "Pay up."

"What does that mean?" My voice quivered, which was irritating.

"Next time you'll count the costs, won't you?"

I glared at her. "Maybe it's worth it."

A tiny smile poked one side of her mouth up.

"Maybe." She stepped away, moving to another sink. After plugging it with another cloth, she ran enough water to soak her own hands. She didn't hesitate before plunging both fists into the water, though she did suck in a sharp breath when her wounds met the liquid.

Satisfaction swelled in me. I stuck my other hand in, controlling my reaction to the pain.

Guess she'd count the cost next time too. Or pay up.

nine

Braxton

Hulk circled around me like a hyena, his fiery eyes both amused and hungry. He'd been waiting for this moment for a year. Now here I was, right where he'd wanted me, in the center of the Locker. Defenseless. Alone. And yes, scared.

I eyed the leather strip in his left hand. It hung in a single braid for two feet, and then it split into three talons of painful discipline. Tristan's scarred back and shoulders flashed through my mind. How many times had he met Hulk in here?

Mastering control over my limbs, my arms

hung at my sides. But my chest and stomach quaked within me as I imagined the balls of sharp spikes fastened to the ends of those leather strips eating the flesh on my back.

Who thinks of these things?

Hulk stopped circling and squared to me. "You know something, Luther?"

"We both know I don't know much of anything."

"Shut up!" He took one step toward me. "Don't think that I won't use this on your mouth, idiot."

I clamped my jaw shut.

"Where were the Prestons?"

"I don't know."

"Liar. They were supposed to be home tonight. They had nowhere else to go and no reason to think that they should be anywhere else. Someone warned them. I'd bet anything it was you."

Masking indifference, I stared at him in silence.

"Where are they?" His voice boomed off the walls of the small room.

"I don't know."

Hulk surged at me until our noses nearly touched. "You know something about it. What did Tristan tell you?"

"Tristan?" I pushed my eyes up, working at incredulity. *God, help me here...* "When would I have talked to Tristan? He disappeared. Maybe this inquisition should be about that, and I should be asking the questions. Where is he?"

Fire blazed from his stare. "Where traitors belong."

I stumbled back, my shock not completely an act. I'd suspected, but hearing that Tristan had... What did they do to traitors? I'd seen what they did to those who were outright defiant, but traitors?

"Don't act like you didn't know."

"I didn't," I choked. My shoulders, which I'd held stiffly, caved inward, and I leaned against the wall. I prayed my emotion looked like betrayal.

Hulk snarled, taking a ready stance. "What did he tell you?"

"Nothing."

The sound of leather snapping shattered the hot, heavy air, and in the next breath, a sharp, sizzling pain started in my right shoulder and followed a trail down to my left hip as the metal spikes dug into my skin, tearing the flesh in its path. I couldn't bottle the pain as a loud cry escaped from my chest. Trembling, I turned into the wall, my hands bracing against it, as I fought a wave of dizziness.

"Where are the Prestons?" Crazed intensity

laced Hulk's thundering voice.

I swallowed. I was going to die. This was what had happened to Tristan. They let Hulk beat him with a clawed whip until he was nothing but ribbons of agonized flesh.

What kind of people did this?

The whip cracked again, and another bite seared against my back. My knees buckled, and I hit the concrete floor, coming face to face with layers of blood stains. Tears burned against my eyes. *God, help.*

Hulk squatted beside me, and his voice came at me low and dead calm. "This can end right now, Luther. Just tell me what Tristan told you."

I inhaled, grasping desperately at self-control. "I told you," I gasped, my voice a harsh whisper. "He didn't tell me anything. I don't know what happened—I don't even know where he is right now." With a slow turn of my head, I stabbed him with an accusing look. "But you do, don't you?" I glared in the pause. "If you know everything, just tell me what I'm supposed to tell you, and we can be done with this."

His mouth exploded with a vocabulary fit for a devil, and he jumped to his feet. The whip shattered the air and tore my back with repeated fury. I lost count after six strikes, and the sounds filtered into a bleak silence. Eliza's tear-stained face surfaced in my mind.

I'm sorry, Liza. God, I've failed. Please, just let me die.

Pain-riddled blackness stole her image, and I hoped God was answering my prayer.

* * *

Hannah

My hands felt stiff and useless as I dropped from my bunk the next morning. In relative quiet, the ten girls around me readied for their day with proficiency and purpose. They knew exactly what they were doing, where they were going, and why. I compared that to the life I'd lived with Charlotte and Quinn. I never knew what each day would bring... Sometimes Charlotte had me delivering rations with her. Sometimes we went to the Community Tribes, the foster system the Party had put into place even before Kasen Asend took the presidency, and I was put to work with the children. Others, I was left at the apartment with plenty of reading material about the Progressive Forward Policy and was asked about my opinions concerning those advancements at the dinner table.

I was told what to do. These girls didn't need told. They simply did. I wanted that.

Skye straightened from her bed and looked from me to our bunk and back again. "Your bed is pathetic."

I glanced at hers. The brown covers had been squared and pulled as tight as a trampoline. Looking around, I found every other girl's bed looked exactly the same. Military style.

Maybe I *didn't* want that.

I looked back at Skye, who lifted one eyebrow. Did I dare challenge her again? My fingers curled into my hand, the stiff ache growing into real pain as my grip tightened. I wouldn't be able to hold the pole. I wasn't even sure I could grasp the bedding to fix my bunk.

Eyeing Skye's perfectly made bed, I lifted my chin. She did it, and her hands looked every bit as bad as mine. She wasn't going to outdo me. In anything. With what I hoped was a fluid, confident move, I swung back up onto the bunk and began tucking the backside of the ugly brown covers under the thin mattress.

"Morning drills start in three minutes. Don't be late."

I looked up, catching sight of Skye's back as she strode out of the room. I scowled.

"Seriously," said a girl in the bunk two beds away as she finished pulling her hair into a ponytail. "Don't be late. We'll all pay, and after we're done owing up for your laziness, a pair of sore hands will be a pleasant memory."

I tucked faster, making sure as I went the

covers were tight and straight. "Do you like it here?" I asked the girl.

"Better than nowhere," she said.

Memories of life in the forest, starving and scared, flashed in my mind. I hoped this was better.

"Is that where you're from? Nowhere?"

"You don't need to know where I'm from."

I hopped down, gave two final tugs, and moved for the door, catching up with ponytail mystery girl.

"No questions asked, is that the policy?"

"No. Only important questions."

"Okay. What's an important question?"

"Do you know where you're going?"

"Breakfast, I hope."

She snorted. "Not yet. Drills. Then we eat. Discipline for excellence."

I put a hand to my turning stomach. Great. More starving. I thought I'd left that life. "Excellence, huh? Is that where you're going?"

"I'm going with the Party. And yes, excellence is part of the destination. A country transformed. By our hands, we will become the excellence of humankind."

"How long did it take you to memorize that?"

She stopped and set a hard, examining look on me. "Only as long as it took me to figure out where I belonged. If you only want food and shelter, the Pride isn't for you. If you want to be something, then you'd better figure it out. You can't keep sight of a goal if you don't know what it is."

We had reached the door, and she pushed it open. Girls stepped into formation in the dim light of early morning. Not one of them complained—they didn't speak at all. Their faces seemed focused, determined. Like every one of them knew where they were going.

...become the excellence of humankind.

That would be something. No longer Hannah, Eliza's little sister. Not even Hannah, Quinn's little project. Hannah...the excellence of humankind. Or at least part of it.

Ponytail mystery girl moved toward the ranks, and I stepped with her. "What's your name?"

"Analise." She moved into formation, glanced my way, and nodded to the spot next to her.

I took quick inventory of our group and molded my position to match the rest of the girls. Two breaths after I'd locked my posture straight, we began moving.

Running.

This time, I'd keep up.

My lungs burned as tightness in my chest gripped its familiar squeeze. I pictured the trails

I used to run in the forest. The damp earth was littered with roots and ferns, nature's obstacle course. Back then, I would keep pushing, even through the wheezing that shuttered my lungs, because I didn't want to be away from the cellar after dark. I didn't know my way around the forest the way Eliza had.

But always, when I would return to the dugout, my recovery would take a long time. My chest would feel like liquid fire, and every breath drawn had been painful. Once, after an unusually long run, I'd collapsed before I reached the cellar. My dad found me and brought me back. I woke up near the pond feeling as though boulders had been stacked onto of my chest.

I pushed my legs to stay with Analise. My body quivered as my breath continued to grow short.

Next came the wheezing. *Don't panic.* My command fell on a rebellious body. Panic is natural when oxygen won't penetrate the thickness clogging your lungs. Air. I desperately needed air.

Analise dropped beside my struggling pace, her form still perfect and her little puffs of breath controlled.

"Are you okay?"

I looked at her as I drew another stuttered

breath.

"You have asthma, don't you?"

I nodded, hoping it wouldn't disqualify me from the Pride. And also hoping that I wouldn't have to explain that my condition was fairly new, a result of smoke inhalation that had damaged my lungs. It didn't always act up, but the cold air of the morning was aggravating the problem. All of that would demand a much longer explanation—one that I didn't want to give to anyone in my new world.

She eased her pace. "You should have told someone before. Did you bring your meds?"

"No. There..." *wasn't any meds for me. My mother needed them more.* "There wasn't time."

"You should have told Commander Knott."

I drew a breath to answer, the effort shaking my body.

Analise reached to steady me. "It's okay. We have medical access. She won't be mad. Next time, just be honest."

Honest? I hadn't been honest with anyone— not completely—since the fire changed my life. I wasn't even sure how to be honest, because I didn't know what was true.

She slowed us down to a walk. "We're almost there. Just focus on breathing."

My shoulders curled around the fire in my lungs. *Breathe. Breathe.* My damaged lungs wouldn't cooperate. The air filled my mouth but was denied access deeper into my body. Panic took over as I fell to my knees.

"Skye, new girl has asthma. She's not good. Get Commander Knott."

I glanced up, seeing Analise pushing two fingers against her ear. Nothing of a response reached my hearing, and I wondered if anyone actually heard her—or cared about me.

Analise nodded. "Knott will be here in a moment. I'll stay."

Were they actually talking to each other? I saw nothing attached to her ear.

I struggled for three more breaths, and then a quad turned up the street toward us. Those had been outlawed at the same time the other cars had been. Fossil fuel waste.

Guess some rules were bendable. At the moment, I was thankful.

"Hannah, you should have said something." Knott came off the ATV and squatted beside me.

She pushed a pin-like stick against my shoulder, and a sting shot through my arm.

"Just a steroid. It will help open up your airways. Now..." She pushed an inhaler into my hands. "I assume you know how to use this. Three puffs."

I didn't know for sure. I'd never used one.

Couldn't be that hard though, right? I closed my mouth around the opening, pushed the tube on the top, and tried to breathe deep as a metallic-tasting vapor filled my mouth.

The thickness in my neck began to dissipate. Panic eased away, and as I drew the next two puffs, the tightness in my chest loosened its grip. I dropped my head back, pulling deep gulps of air.

"Better," Analise said. "The blue is leaving your lips. You'll be fine."

I recovered, and we both caught a ride with Commander Knott the final half mile to the training campus. Tables lined a rectangular room attached to the side of the wrestling-arena-turned-Pride-combat-training-central. As we entered, I inhaled a clear breath, allowing the aroma of coffee and pancakes to sink in deep.

My stomach rumbled. Loudly.

Analise laughed. "Guess you're fine now, right, new girl?"

"Yes." I grinned. "But I'm Hannah."

She nodded. "Well, Hannah. This is your new life. Let's begin."

Eight hours later, I climbed up on my perfectly made bunk and sank into the thin mattress. This new life might be every bit as demanding as the forest life. But at least I had a bed. And my fill of hot food. The hours in between meals had been spent at school, academics being important to the Pride. Doing mediocre with the books wasn't acceptable, Analise had informed me. I had gulped. Eliza was the smart one between the two of us. Mediocre pretty much defined my whole life.

Or maybe I'd defined my life by hers.

I didn't have time to examine that. Instead, my focus narrowed on the studies. The usual lineup followed: math, English, science, social studies. And then they added some new twists. Values class. Huh. I wasn't sure what to expect of that one. That day we discussed loyalty. *What does it mean? Give an example of loyalty. How do you feel when someone betrays your trust? What should happen to those who are not loyal?*

While most of the questions the instructor had asked were for class discussion, the last question was an essay question. Silently, every girl in the Pride wrote out her answer. I had scanned the group. They all looked so confident. I wasn't sure what the teacher was looking for. Were we talking about friendships here, or something else? Because I knew what the Party did to those who were disloyal.

Queasiness rolled through my gut while I considered what to write. The Pride an establishment of the Party. And in fairness to them, they did take care of us. Maybe they had the right to demand citizen loyalty. After all, I wasn't sure exactly what had happened at the fire—Patrick Luther may have been the instigator. That was what the Party claimed. And Eliza...

I didn't know what happened there for sure. She was stubborn and wouldn't get inked, but maybe there was more to it than that.

Loyalty is essential for a complete and sustainable society. Mutual trust cannot be undervalued between a people and their government...

I had typed those words in the minutes that ticked by for the remainder of that class. I went on to describe the collapse of a society that did not have loyalty among its people. Revolution. Warfare. Poverty. Death.

The instructor glanced over my tab as she passed my row. Her lips tipped up, and she nodded.

My relief stayed with me until that moment I allowed myself to review what I'd written as I lay on my bunk. I really didn't remember much of history. It was boring and seemed completely irrelevant. But didn't the early American people have a reason to rebel? I couldn't quite grasp it, so maybe they didn't. Maybe they'd just been spoiled, disloyal, power-hungry people who simply didn't want a king.

Did that mean absolute loyalty was essential for any successful society? Where did personal conviction fit into that scheme?

"New girl, get up." Skye bumped my bunk with the side of her fist. "We leave in ten."

"Hannah," I said, sitting up. "My name is Hannah."

"Whatever." She spun away, her ponytail swishing. "Just get up. Commons tonight."

The whole loyalty debate disappeared from my mind. Suddenly I had a much more pressing issue to deal with. The Commons was at the Den—I'd overhead as much at supper. Quinn told me to stay away from the Den. I didn't even know what the Commons was, but I remembered with vivid clarity the fierceness in Quinn's eyes when he told me not to go.

I glanced around the bunk room. Every girl was getting ready to go—perfecting hair, applying lip gloss, which was the only makeup allowed in the Pride, and checking the one mirror we shared in the room.

Didn't seem that I had a choice. Loyalty demanded obedience.

Quinn or the Pride. Obedience to whom?

It was really a nonquestion. I wasn't ready to take up another battle with Skye, and I had no explanation to offer for not wanting to go. She didn't need to know about my *special* situation. Not really caring what I would find, I glanced in the community mirror and tussled with my hair as if it mattered.

Analise eyed me from her spot on the other side of the looking glass, her inspection drifting from my head in the mirror, to my chest, and then back to my eyes.

"First time at the Commons." Her eyes gave away nothing of her intent. "Best stay close."

Why? My stomach churned.

"Remember you're from the Pride. You're not one of the Purge girls they used to bring in. Don't act like one."

What was a Purge girl? How did such a girl act?

"Carry yourself with pride. Demand respect..." A sly grin settled over her mouth. "And only give what you want."

The rolling in my stomach turned to a tumultuous storm. Quinn's warning sank hot in my ears. *Don't go to the Den.* It was like overhearing Eliza beg Braxton not to go to the rallies. Like she knew something we didn't. Understood more than we could grasp.

What did Quinn know about the Den, how would he have acquired such a knowledge, and why wouldn't he just tell me straight up why he was afraid?

More irrelevant questions. I nodded at Analise in the mirror, even attempting to fix a grin to match hers.

"Got it." I stepped her direction, and then we both filed out the bathroom door. "Anything else?"

She snorted. "Be back in time for morning drills."

Fire burned in my gut.

The climate surrounding us seemed to grow heavy as we stepped into line with the rest of the girls. I wondered, as we waited our turn to climb onto the bus, why we were going at all if it seemed none of the girls really wanted to. Glancing at Skye, I noted her stoic expression. Concentration glazed her eyes as she stood expressionless near the back of the line, not speaking. Not smiling. Nothing. She seemed to fortify herself behind a wall of a superhuman level of unfeeling.

As Quinn's warning continued to hiss in my mind, I began mimicking her resolve. Whatever lay at the end of this quick bus transport, I was certain I could not let it affect me.

The bus pulled up, and the doors slid open. I drew a breath, hardening my face as I folded my emotions and tucked them in an iron box. The line moved forward, and I followed in step, my heart rate spiking despite my resolve against feeling.

"Hannah."

My heart lurched as Commander Knott barked my name from behind. With a hand on the grip rail of the transport and one foot on the first riser inside, I stalled and looked back.

"You need to stay."

Called out. Singled away from the group. *Misfit.* I glanced at Skye.

Still with a glazed look of indifference, she met my look with merely a slightly raised brow. "Step out of line, new girl. Let the rest pass."

I didn't want to go, but I didn't want to be singled out either. Stuck in the spot with my mind gripped in a tug-of-war, my look slid from Skye to Commander Knott and back again.

"Move," Skye said.

Her bark commanded my compliance without me even thinking about it. My foot and hand both dropped, and the line of girls passed in front of me. Skye paused in the space right before me and waited until the last of the girls loaded.

"Next time." Her expression remained unreadable.

I was left wondering if that was a consolation or a threat.

t e n

Braxton

I'm not dead.

A cold, hard surface pressed against my face as I vaguely processed that thought. Pain registered with Richter-scale strength as I blinked into consciousness.

Why didn't I die? I wanted to die.

Pushing against the solid block beneath my body, I groaned as the pain in my back and shoulders flared. My arms quivered, and I dragged my knees forward to brace my shredded torso.

God, why didn't you let me die?

"Easy, Luther." A gentle voice, hushed and

regretful, sounded from a dark corner of the room. "Ten lashes will take the strength out of a man, but you'll recover."

Wasn't Hulk. Not Tristan. Who was speaking and now draping a cool blanket over my shoulders?

"Just stay still. You've got a little time before you'll need to make an appearance."

"Where?" I mumbled, the pain of breathing, let alone speaking, nearly taking me into the blackness again.

"The Commons. The Pride is coming tonight, and you'll need to show your face." His voice carried authority and yet compassion. And it was familiar.

"What if I can't?" I could hardly move, and nothing really registered with me beyond the flames of pain.

"You will."

Liquid touched my mouth. Instinctively, I licked my lips, thinking nothing of the danger until after I swallowed.

The gray light of the dark room faded again. I was slipping into a haze I was familiar with and didn't want to experience again. But I could do nothing to fight it away.

* * *

A familiar rhythm jarred my senses as lights

flickered through my hazy vision. I began to struggle through the fog of persuasion, knowing even in the fuzziness of my mind where I was.

I almost didn't want to leave persuasion's gentle cloud. At least there I didn't have to shield my mind and heart from the reality playing out around me.

"Where's your friend?" A female voice punctured my solitude, dissipating the wispy comfort of the surreal.

I had to roll her question around my brain for several breaths before I could make sense of it. Still numb and clumsy, I flickered a look at the girl near my right side. Her stoic face, sharp eyes, and confident posture glimmered with familiarity.

Skye.

"I don't know where Tristan is." I fought the temptation to fold my arms against the table and tuck my head into them. "His bunk was cleared yesterday. No one knows where he went."

I felt her unwavering gaze on me, but I refused to meet her stare. I didn't know what exactly, but there was something between her and Tristan. I hated that I had nothing more to give her.

"No warning?" she asked, her voice low and still cloaked with indifference.

"None." I looked the opposite direction. "Just

gone."

A long pause passed as the music pounded between us, and then her hand touched the back of my shoulder. I flinched, darting away from the contact before I could stop the reflex. Her hand snapped away, and then she leaned closer.

"Did they take you to the Locker?"

I turned my neck, angling my face toward her. "Do you know what that is?"

Her hand gripped mine, and silence met my question. I knew little of the Pride, but I couldn't image the girls having a Locker like ours. I couldn't imagine a young woman forced to endure the claw. It was almost as unthinkable as...

No. Nothing was beyond the boundaries when it came to the dark side of the Party. Unimaginable was their specialty.

Skye squeezed my fingers and leaned in close but was careful not to touch my shredded back or shoulders. "He trusted you." Her warm breath danced against my ear. "Don't let us down."

She vanished into the array of strobe lights, loud music, and crude laughter.

* * *

Hannah

Wordlessly, I followed Commander Knott back into the Pride quarters. Knowing enough to not let my disagreement air in front of the others, I determined once we were out of earshot I'd voice my protest.

Knott stopped just outside the door to her quarters, turning to face me. Her mouth was drawn in a tight line as disapproval radiated from her expression. Yet she said nothing. Her measured stare drifted away from me, directing me to look down the hall opposite her doorway.

Prepared to tell her I was one of the Pride and should be on that transport, I followed her silent look to my left. At the end of the long, dim corridor stood a rigid man, arms crossed, shadowed by the limited light.

I knew that form, and part of me turned to mush. The other part snapped in anger.

Quinn. He was going to ruin me before I even had a chance with the Pride.

I was going. After pushing my shoulders back, I turned to inform Knott that I would be getting on that transport. She was gone.

How had Quinn acquired this much power?

Didn't matter. He was not going to rule over me. With my posture snapped straight, I pivoted backward and stalked toward the door.

"You're not going, Hannah." Quinn's voice cut through the long space between us. "The transport is gone."

I froze. I'd left the forest to get away from people telling me what to do and when to do it. To prove that I was more than a stupid pack mule. Not to fall under the palm of a manipulative man who apparently had a control-freak side well hidden behind his compassionate smile.

I glanced over my shoulder, setting a cold stare on him. He'd moved toward me, cutting the hall between us by half. My heart rate spiked as I watched him continue to prowl my way, and I wondered if I'd known this boy at all.

He would not know my fear. I wouldn't allow it. He'd already torn my heart in two. I wasn't going to let him take my dignity into the wreckage. I moved away from him, not at a run but at a solid, anger-stamped pace of self-determination. The glass door met my hands, and I shoved, leaving the heavy stale air of the old church building behind. Betrayal and anger throbbed through my veins as I stalked into the grass, and I drank them in as fuel while I clenched both fists at my side.

When his hand caught my elbow and pulled me to a stop, I whipped around, my left fist flying with all my body strength behind it. Quinn leaned back, and my hook missed his neck. He kept a grip on my right elbow and with his other hand caught the punch I'd thrown, spinning me around so that my arms crossed as he pinned me to his chest.

The tamping of his heart kicked against my shoulders. His hold tightened. For a moment, I was too stunned to fight. Where had he learned such a move? He was on the accelerated academic track, for something political, I assumed. Hand combat moves shouldn't be a part of that course.

Irrelevant at that moment. I arched my back and tugged to one side, lifting one booted foot to slam into his shin.

He grunted when I made contact, and I felt the momentary slack of his grip on my elbow. I pulled forward, one side free, but he recovered before I could muscle a backhand toward his nose. Once again, he caught my hand midair, and now both my wrists were captive in his iron grip. He tugged me forward until I was pinned against him. His eyes burned into mine as his scowl lowered toward my face.

"You need to trust me," he hissed.

I refused to cower. "Why?"

"Because I know stuff you don't."

"How?" I glared at him. Why would he think I would trust him now, especially since he *still* wasn't telling me the truth?

Those blue eyes glowed with a passion I wasn't

sure about. My heart thundered as, unbidden, the memory of his kiss flooded through my body. It must have played in my expression, because his expression softened, and his look dropped to my mouth, making my lips tingle.

His grip loosened, but his stance didn't change as his face continued to hover near mine. "Please, Hannah." The fingers around my wrists uncurled as he leaned so close that his warm breath brushed against my cheek. "Trust me."

As his hands fell away, I realized I was trembling. Fear had doubled, but not of *him*, and dark questions sowed into the furrows of my mind.

What were they hiding? If going to the Den was bad—and me being a part of the Pride something that made Quinn afraid—then what about those Reformation Camps?

My heart still hammered, and my lungs burned as I studied him. His expression had turned to a plea, though the demand for compliance still heated his stare. He stepped back, opening the space between us, and reached into his pocket. When his hand came free again, he'd produced an inhaler.

"Use it."

I eyed him, confused. "I'm fine."

"Don't care. Use it. It's our cover. It's the reason you didn't go tonight."

I frowned. "They kept me back so that you could give me an inhaler? That was legit to them?"

"You had an attack earlier today. I told them your asthma was severe and that you needed to recover tonight if they expected you to train tomorrow."

He'd heard about that? "You lied to them."

"I did what I needed to do. Now use the inhaler, and make it look real."

I continued to glare at him, part dumbfounded and part livid that he'd used such a pansy excuse to keep me out of the Den. I'd never live it—

"Now, Hannah. Unless you'd prefer I kiss you right here where Knott can see, and everyone can know the real reason I kept you out of it."

That would be so much worse, and I wouldn't be the only one who would pay for it. Quinn's reputation would be jeopardized, and by extension, his future.

My attention fell to the inhaler I held in my hand, and after a few shakes of the canister, I breathed in two long puffs.

"Now what?" I asked, searching his eyes.

So much there. Fear, pleading, calculating. I couldn't understand any of it.

"Please tell me, Quinn."

His lips pressed hard together, and a slight shake of his head cut me off. He stepped away, turning as he moved. With his head angled toward me over his shoulder, his low voice drifted my way. "Just trust me."

eleven

Braxton

Something bumped my arm as I dozed. I opened my eyes, catching movement by my side.

"Braxton." Panicked, her voice whispered in the gray light.

Where were we? I pushed my hands against the solid ground beneath me. It was cold and damp and very hard. My eyes began to adjust to the filtered light, and my surroundings slid into a distant familiarity. Bulging wood planks, dark from age and water damage, hard-packed dirt floor...we were at the mill.

"Braxton." Her hand shook my shoulder, fear

animating her voice. "You have to wake up. They're coming. You said you would protect me! They're coming!"

I jolted straight. The Jackals were coming. With one motion, I scrambled to my feet and took her by the hand. "You're mine," I promised, pulling her close. "They can't get you, because you're mine."

She trembled against me. I bent to kiss her, and the warm, metallic taste of blood smeared on my lips. My muscles locked tight as I hovered above her face. "Eliza, what happened?"

"Braxton..." Her shriek tore into my chest, ripping my heart. "Help me!"

Suddenly she was gone. I stood, shaking and alone, left only with her terror-filled scream.

"Eli—"

Cold water splashed against my skin, and I recoiled against the wall. Except it wasn't a wall.

"Braxton, wake up." A hand, small and yet insistent, shook my shoulder as a low voice hissed. "You can't be dreaming out loud. Wake up."

I blinked again. Reality had changed. Skye hovered above me, her hand dripping with water ready to flick at me. I sat forward, catching my head in my hands. "What did I say?"

"Nothing." She let her hand fall to her pant leg and wiped it against her uniform. "Just mumbled, but you were going to cry out."

I rubbed my eyes, which were wet. "Did anyone else hear?"

She dropped into the booth seat next to mine. "I don't think so." Her tone hovered just above a whisper. The movement of our LiteRail car hummed almost unnoticeably while I gathered myself in the semidarkness.

My heart continued to clang against my ribs, and Eliza's scream echoed in my mind. Same dream. Hadn't changed since the day they'd ripped her from my arms eight months before.

I rubbed my forehead and glanced out the window. "How long until we get to the state center?"

Skye eyed me like she knew I didn't really care how close we were. Didn't want to go to this hyped-up rally in the first place. "Ten minutes. Maybe a little less." She turned her focus forward, settling it on the window across from our cushioned chairs. "You know you'll have to look like one of us," she muttered, her lips barely moving.

"What does that mean?" I hissed, keeping my voice low. "I am one of us."

Skye was like those shadow puppets you could never identify. A bunny? A lioness? What was she?

She'd known Tristan, and I was fairly certain she knew where he'd been sent. But just like him, she refused to show me her hand.

"People still talk about you." Skye tossed a quick glance at me. "You can't do what you're here to do if you don't look like one of us."

My heart stalled. Tristan and I never talked about these things. We couldn't. Which meant Skye shouldn't be doing so either. And what exactly was I there to do?

She cleared her throat and leaned her elbows against her knees, clasping her fists together. "Participate. Blend."

The hair on my neck prickled against my collar. Tristan's words. The last time he'd said that... Heat swirled in my stomach as images I couldn't push away demanded my attention. Eliza, held in the fierce grip of the boy who'd antagonized her since we were twelve. Eliza, bleeding, and a bruise darkening under her eye, caught. Eliza, pulled from my arms and ripped out of my life forever. Gone.

No. She couldn't be gone. Not forever. She had to be alive. I wouldn't have these dreams night after night if she were dead, would I?

I glanced over my shoulder. Two Jackals sat on the bench behind us, both with their heads tipped back and their eyes shut. Across the aisle, a pair of girls from the Pride slept against their foam-padded backrest.

I settled my gaze on Skye. "What are you getting at?"

One eyebrow hiked. "Nothing. Just don't let emotions rule your actions."

My stomach clamped hard. "You know something."

"Just remember I've been to one of these before. Put on your loyal mask, and you'll be fine." She pushed her back against the seat and crossed her arms.

A shadow dropped across her torso and over my face. "Who'll be fine?" Hulk's growl descended from his Sasquatch-sized frame.

I forced myself to bypass Skye's face as I sought Hulk's, keeping my expression neutral, if not a little irritated. "Bored, Hulk? Don't you have puppies to oversee?"

"I don't babysit, Luther."

"You sure hover over me." My mouth. Not something I'd tamed yet. "Maybe just a man crush?"

"Some people require a little more supervision." Hulk sneered. "Because they think they're smart."

I shrugged. "Not me. Remember? I was among the dummies at school—didn't make the Career Track. That'll let a guy know exactly how smart he isn't in a hurry."

It was true. I wasn't smart. All the brains my father had possessed, which were quite a few, had been passed on to Jamis and Annyon.

Hulk, however... Now that guy was a complete and baffling mystery. He wasn't that smart. I could take him down in verbal spar any day of the week, and I preferred to do it as often as possible. But he'd tested into the Career Track—was on course to become a Technology Engineer. Couldn't figure that.

He'd also managed to score high rank within the Jackals Den. That was maybe a little less of a mystery—he was a fanatic when it came to the Progressive Reform Party and their take-over intentions. But still. Who would put a steroid-hyped twenty-year-old in charge of a Den of boys with the expressed motive of giving them vision, purpose, and excellence? Hulk had brawn, fury, and control-freak issues, none of which would lend to the Den's purpose. Someone goofed—and it hadn't been Stevens.

"You excited for the rally?" Hulk's question didn't actually sound like a question.

Why was he still there? I glanced back up to scrutinize his face.

Hulk crossed his arms over his chest, waiting for my answer.

"We can't all be cheerleaders." I tipped my

head back and closed my eyes as if I intended to take nap. Nothing irritates ego-heads like an uninterested audience.

A fist gathered my shirtfront and pulled me forward. My eyes popped open, and Hulk, stretched across Skye and pinning her against the seat back with his shoulder, hovered in my space. "I suggest you find some pom-poms, Luther."

My jaw set hard, and I glared straight into his blazing eyes. "Or what?" I cocked an eyebrow. "You don't have anything on me. What do you think you can do?"

His fist uncurled, and then he shoved me back. "You think I've shown my hand?" He snorted. "You're right. You're not that smart."

* * *

Hannah

The throb of patriotism pulsed through the gathering crowd. Never before had I felt this surge of energy that rushed around me from every side. It bordered on hysteria.

Easy, Hannah, I thought. *Take it in. Become part of it.*

With a purposeful gulp of crowd-stale air, I pushed the creepy sensation away. I was a part of this. Wore the uniform of the Pride. Bore the seal of the loyal. Had chosen, beyond my family's resistance, to be immersed in the Party and all that it stood for. Which included patriotism—even if it felt out of control.

"By our hands, we built a new nation."

The cry echoed from the center of the arena, the words belonging to a distinctly familiar voice. More than one hundred thousand gathered in this space, most of whom were within ten years of my own age. Heat from packed-in bodies radiated upward, sautéing the emotion of the gathering. The cheer following the proud proclamation drowned out the woman speaking from center field, sending a sensation of ice over my skin.

"By our hands, we have defined life over these past three hundred years. Right. Wrong. Direction. Purpose."

The gathering began to move, shift, jump. Hands raised, fists curled. As a unified choir, voices rose until the vibration shook the center of my chest.

"By our hands, we are rebuilding this great nation. We are taking back what has been our destiny. Greatness."

As the roar increased, the frenzy causing my soul to quiver, my memory glimpsed the serene images secured to the walls in Charlotte's home. The contrast pierced me. This crowd was nearly feral. Those images whispered peace. This crowd made me afraid. Those images breathed hope.

What was true?

Quinn... I felt my breath tremble as I whispered his name. *What is real?*

In the space of one quivered breath to the next, that thought turned away from Quinn and found redirection toward heaven. *I don't know what to believe.*

Did that matter to God? Eliza had been firm in her conviction—she would not sell herself to the Party because she saw them as opposed to God. Her stubbornness—her conviction—cost her. She was gone. Reformation Camp. Why did the thought of such a place come with a rush of fear?

My inward thoughts quieted, and I focused on the woman in the middle of our gathering, her hand raised, face turned up with resolution written over her entire posture. The crowd around me settled, the movement stilling like a hive of bees suddenly ceasing in their flurry of work. As the view before me parted, the clear glimpse of the woman center stage confirmed what her voice had already hinted.

Charlotte Sanger addressed the gathering. She fanned the flames of nearly out-of-control patriotic explosion. With an effortless command of stage presence, she held the massive audience captive while at once feeding them more fire. Given her hospitality to me, I thought I should feel proud to know the woman commanding center stage.

Shame curdled inside, with a healthy dose of trembling alongside it.

"We are evolving to what we should be." Charlotte's passionate voice settled over the crowd. "It has taken time. Struggle. Persistence. But now that we are in motion, nothing can stand in our way."

"Yes." The single word, hissed in waves around me. "Power to the Party, man's glory revealed."

Whoa. What was this chant? It began on the ground, among the highest ranked people who stood on the field.

"Power to the Party..."

The words continued, a mantra that felt as though it carried the weight of everyone's fate within the four words spoken. Did it? What fate would this be?

"Power to the Party..."

My knees and hands shook, and I glanced to my left and then my right, searching every face for any misgivings. Among the strangers, all of whom bore masks of that same resolution and zeal, one face grabbed my full attention.

His lips did not move. His stare did not

consent. He was not among the faithful.

And I knew him.

I darted my attention away, suddenly fearful that my stare might point him out. If others saw what I'd just seen, they would know.

Braxton Luther was among the hated Cloaked.

Still at center stage, Charlotte changed her stance, locking her posture rigid and turning to face the massive screen on the south side of the field. Following her lead, every last person in the gathering turned to face the same way, and the air became thick with somber devotion. On the screen, the Party seal stood in bold black against the digital image of the American flag behind it.

"This Party, which is established on earth, we give power and honor, as is due."

I swallowed. The cadence of the pledge hit me with twisted familiarity, the true words curling unbidden in the back of my mind even while the perverted version continued to rumble all around me. *Our Father, who art in heaven, hollowed be thy name...*

Dear God, this cannot be right. There was no way the Party would have—

"Our kingdom *has* come. We will do what must be done. By our hands. Power to the Party, the glory of humankind revealed."

The words were barely finished, when every

soul surrounding me touched two fingers to their inked seals, then tapped their hearts with those same fingers and finally held their hands forward toward the emblem covering the large screen.

The depths of who I was curled inward, as if I'd just sold myself to some kind of secret evil I couldn't comprehend.

A voice hissed over my shoulder, the owner's hot breath colliding with my already burning skin. "Salute, new girl. Show your respect."

Skye. I would pay for my show of disloyalty. I hoped I could beg ignorance and gain grace. I didn't pray for it though. Didn't have any right to seek God now.

As I stretched out my hand, I secreted a look toward Braxton.

He stood, arms down, face cast toward the ground. Certainly his show of insubordination would not go unnoticed. I wondered if I'd just caught my final glimpse of the boy who had loved my sister.

* * *

Braxton

It was as though my soul bled. My body ached. My spirit shriveled into a dark cocoon of disbelief and shame.

God, I didn't know.

How many times had I thought those words, whispered them in the stolen moments of solitude over the past year? So many, and yet not enough. This price was so steep, the payment for my faithlessness. To stand and watch the Den act as terrorists to our own people, to swim into the conscienceless practices of the Commons, and now this rally at the state center.

I couldn't say why it shocked me to hear the perversion of the Lord's Prayer. I had seen so much of the Party's darkness after I'd bowed to their demands. Sin let loose, unbound, was sickening, terrifying. But even so, with all that I knew by then, my gut split at hearing the crowd united in their rage against heaven.

"You've been caught, PK." Spittle splashed against my neck as Hulk leaned over my back, his seat right behind mine. "You'll not go unpunished."

Clenching my jaw, I kept my eyes forward. I knew the consequences of my inaction. But there was only so much of my soul I could sell.

I wondered for the millionth time what could have been. If I'd listened to Eliza—refused to bow all those months before. She would not be at the unlikely mercy of the ravenous Party. I would not be a corpse walking about with a decaying spirit and dwindling hope. There were things worse than hiding, things worse than death. I was living it now as a Jackal, and I could see no way out.

Energy continued to surge through the gathering, the kind that curled darkness over my being and pressed heavily in my chest. It reminded me of the last time I saw my dad. Pressed between two thick sheets of steel until all the life had been squeezed out of him. This was my pressing, a different kind of murder. One which I had submitted to.

"We who know the path to restoration have the obligation to keep it clear."

I focused on Charlotte Sanger, who managed the crowd with captivating skill. No wonder it was rumored that she was the real power behind Kasen Asend. Behind the Party as a whole. She fed the energy when needed, restored order without an appearance of effort, and captivated all with her persuasion.

Her charisma reminded me of my dad. In a horrible, twisted sort of way.

"We will fight for the direction we know is best," Sanger boasted. "When necessary, we will purge what is poisoning our progress. For the greater good, we march forward. Will you march?"

The voice of the people rose, casting a thick

roar into the air. Up to heaven. *Try to defy us.*

Sanger's voice lifted, her cadence more demanding. "Will you do what is necessary?"

"Yes," the crowd responded again.

The corners of her mouth lifted in a satisfied smirk. "Then stand."

All who had been seated, which were not many, rose. Hands tapped the ink on their necks, then hearts, and stretched forward again. A fist from behind grabbed my elbow and yanked it forward.

Hulk seethed into my ear, "Do not make a mockery of us here."

My heart squeezed with a jerky rhythm, and my hand, shaking, stayed outstretched. How much more would God forgive me?

"We are only as strong as you are willing to become," the stateswoman continued. "And what we become will be by our hands."

The chant needed no more encouragement. "By our hands, by our hands, by our hands."

Memories crashed, bruising my heart. The first rally I'd gone to after the football game. The smoke of the bonfire. The smell of drugs. The sound of angry rebellion.

And Eliza's warning about all of it. *The Party has swept the nation... We won't find safety—not if we're going to be unsealed.*

I'd asked her if that was an *if*. She'd said it wasn't for her. She'd meant it. And she'd also known my answer, even if neither of us had been willing to admit it back then.

Nauseous from the practice playing out before me and heartsick from the memories, I dropped my hand to my side and turned my gaze away from the woman leading this frenzy. Scanning the faces of the crowd, I saw sameness. The same determination. Manipulated conviction. Loyalty bought with promises and paid for with unthinkable acts.

One face stood out. Horror, not agreement, engraved her expression. Unbought. Unconvinced. I wanted desperately to grab hold of relief that I'd found a soul who had not been enslaved.

I couldn't though, because I knew her. She should not have been there in the first place.

twelve

Braxton

The LiteRail swayed with a gentle rhythm as we traveled back. The silence seemed a black contrast to the energy and shouting that had happened in the arena. Then again, after a feeding frenzy came exhaustion. Slumped in the seats around me, the Jackals and a few of the girls from the Pride slept.

I did not.

Her face stubbornly burned in my mind. For a moment, when I'd caught that familiar profile, the soft, almond-toned skin and thick, wavy dark hair, my heart lurched. *Eliza.* Her name swirled in my mind as hope raced through my veins. But that moment only lasted a blink. The girl I'd seen was not Eliza, but I knew her almost as well. It didn't make sense. She was supposed to have been gone. Safe at the Refuge.

But that girl at the rally was Hannah. The certainty of it throbbed through my core. I had not only failed to keep the girl I loved safe, but somehow her little sister had slipped through the protection of the forest and had landed in the mess of the Pride.

I'm sorry, Eliza, Evan. I don't know what happened...

The thoughts scrawled through my mind as if I could mentally write the Knights a note and they would know I was crumbling beneath the guilt. I shut my eyes as the sentences faded, pretending sleep could crowd out the anxiety that filled me, and fighting the moisture that lined my lids.

God, can you fix all that I've broken?

"Luther."

I wanted to ignore the commanding voice penetrating my misery.

"Luther, I promise you want to talk to me rather than Hulk." The seat beside me filled with the presence of a man close to my size. Without looking, I knew it was Stevens.

I folded my arms, refusing to open my eyes. "I don't want to talk to anyone right now."

"Fine," Jed said, his voice nearly husky and yet foreboding. "The Locker it is. Straight away tonight, after we get back."

I clenched my jaw, suppressing a sigh. The strips of flesh that had been ripped raw only a week before had barely begun to heal.

Maybe this time they'd kill me.

* * *

Hannah

I made sure I didn't sit in the Jackals car, despite the urging of some of the other girls. "You'll want to know who's who before you go to the Commons," Analise had said. I didn't ask why that would be, but I didn't have any doubt that it was true.

Dropping into the seat nearest the back of the railcar, I shrugged. "I'm good here."

Analise frowned, her eyebrows dipping with either concern or disapproval. I wasn't sure.

"You won't be able to avoid it forever," she said.

"I'm not avoiding anything." I tipped my head back, resting it against the seat. "I'm tired. Not up for socializing. But please, go ahead. I don't need a babysitter."

That scowl darkened, and she shook her head. "Not babysitting, but whatever, Hannah. You make things hard if you want to."

These secretive hints...I felt them, but I couldn't understand them. Why would a group like the Pride or the Jackals need to be so...obtuse? Just an overblown orphanage gone boot camp.

We will only be as strong as you're willing to become. Our motivational address echoed in my mind. What did she mean, exactly?

"Are you asleep?" Skye's not-so-quiet hiss interrupted my thoughts.

"Not now. Thanks for that."

"Good. We need to talk." She dropped onto the seat next to mine.

I opened my eyes and tipped my head to look at her. "Thought you were hanging with the boys."

"Shut up and listen." Skye's dark eyes held danger. "I can't keep shielding you, so you'd better step up."

"Shielding me?" That knuckle beating on my first day qualified as shielding me?

"You'd better start thinking and stop reacting. That crap you pulled today—"

"What crap?"

"Not saluting?"

"I had no idea what was going on. I'm still new at this, remember?"

Her lips pressed into a line, and she eyed me

with a look that had some kind of meaning I couldn't read. "Fall in line, Hannah. Or you won't be able to do what is necessary when the time comes."

"I don't know what that means."

She shifted, her body rigid and her face focused on the scenery flashing outside our windows. I followed her gaze, puzzling in the silence. Stands of trees, nearly naked by the frosting of late winter, flashed by in a blur, occasionally interrupted by the silver splotch of a pond or a yellow-green hue of a tired field. The countryside was largely unpopulated now, and as a house would blip by every once in a while, I wondered if anyone still occupied it. Likely not. The relocation mandate had shifted many lives, growing towns like Glennbrooke and nearly popping major cities, like the state center, with the inflation of people.

Another mysterious move of the Party. To better provide—that was what they'd said. Ration points were more easily reached that way, and the outlawing of most private vehicles made centralization necessary. Still, something about it seemed un-American. It felt...imposing. Or maybe gripping. Like a shift of control, a loss of autonomy.

"You are not here by mistake, Hannah." Skye's

low voice beckoned me back to our present reality. "I feel it. Even if your reasons for joining aren't the real reasons you're actually here, none of it is by mistake." She set her unwavering gaze back on me, and I was forced to look at her again. "Don't let us down."

My mouth opened, but before I could utter my shock, Skye looked away, rose, and walked down the aisle of the car until the doors opened and she passed into the next one.

The skin on my arms and neck prickled, and my insides rolled as if...as if she'd just spoken prophecy over me. Clenching my fists, I pushed that thought and those feelings away. That wasn't possible. Skye was a Party loyal. And people of the Party believed only one thing: everything was only ever done by our hands.

Destiny had nothing to do with anything.

* * *

Braxton

I spoke to no one once the LiteRail stopped at Glennbrooke station. Life seemed to reinfuse the members of the Jackals and the Pride, but I remained silent. I scanned each face among those surging around me.

There, two cars back, I found her. Hannah walked behind Skye, her mouth pressed shut and her expression void. The Pride must be equally effective as the Den when it came to stripping souls. She looked indifferent and well focused.

If you want to gain a nation, take captive its youth.

The Party knew exactly what they were doing. And if Hannah was any proof, they'd done it well.

As a cold sense of loss settled heavy in my chest, I forced my gaze away from Hannah and focused on nothing. Within minutes we'd be back at the Den, and I'd be in the dark, blood-smattered space of the Locker, facing another round with Hulk. A moment, I was sure, he was looking forward to.

Hate oozed from his pores, unparalleled by any person I'd ever known. What was his story? Why did he keep such a tight grip on anger?

Not sure I cared much, except for the fact that his hate made him strong. And I was about to wear it on my flesh.

Anxiety gripped me, causing my muscles to quiver, but as I walked toward the Den, I kept a stoic mask in place.

Once in the Locker, I waited. Alone. Every lash from the last time rose up in my memory, and my skin burned as the anticipation for round two settled heavy in the terrifying space. The waiting was part of the punishment. The mental beating before the physical one. I fought against the anxiety, losing the battle as the sharp bits at the end of the claw, locked in a tempered glass case across from me, gleamed an evil threat. Dizziness overcame my resolve, and I tipped my head backward. In the dark places of my imagination, I felt the bite of those pieces.

God, please...

There I went again. Praying when I had no right to do so.

I am with you.

Swallowing, I brought my head forward, wondering if I'd imagined the words pressed into my heart.

I'm afraid.

I will be with you.

Surely that hadn't been my imagination.

The door squeaked open before I could examine it further, and a uniformed Jackal stepped into the small space.

Stevens. Not Hulk.

"Luther. You know why you're here." His voice sounded grave, like death had followed him into the room.

"Sir." I licked my lips. "I didn't give honor to the Party."

"Do you regret that?"

Quivering, I raised my look to meet his eyes. Silence spoke my answer. Stevens held my gaze, the dark look in his eyes shifting. One dip of his head acknowledged my insubordination. As he stepped forward, he slipped a hand into the inner pocket of his uniform jacket. I filled my lungs, bracing myself for the strike with whatever weapon he'd concealed near his breast.

A small book emerged from the lapel as he drew his hand out. With one final step closer, Stevens was mere inches from me, and his head drew closer still.

"I think that you'll want this," he whispered as he pushed the book to my chest.

Dazed, I slowly lowered my face to see what he'd given me. My breath caught as recognition flooded my mind.

"Don't say it out loud," Stevens hissed.

As my heart rate picked up, so did my breathing. "Did you steal this from his dead body?"

"We don't have time for those kinds of details. But I want you to have it. Use it."

"I don't understand," I snapped, fear and rage colliding to create a blinding storm. "You defected first—told everyone else that they should too."

Stevens put a hand over my mouth. "Quietly.

Or you'll get us both killed."

After a moment of me staring at him, I nodded. Once his hand slipped away, I continued in a harsh whisper. "I saw what you did at that rally, what you sent with your son. You burned the Bible! Threw the Word of God into the flames. Why are you giving it to me now?"

Jed's mouth twitched, and his Adam's apple bobbed. "I have discovered that grace is bigger than I had imagined." He stopped to swallow again. "And my bad decisions do not have to be my legacy." Drawing a breath, he stared at me with an undercurrent of meaning. "The One who redeems my soul can redeem my life. Is it not so?"

He was asking me? An invisible hand reached into my chest and squeezed. Replays of the last year—of my dad, Eliza, Miranda, and Tristan—blipped through my mind in a collage of pain and resolution. Eliza's final whisper still resonated through every part of my being, stirring my soul and making me hope desperately that she was right.

You're stronger than you know.

I knew I was weak, that I failed where she succeeded. Emotion flooded my sinuses. I looked back to Jed. "Do you believe that?"

"Believe what?"

"That God can redeem my life? After...Eliza? My dad? Now Tristan... Can He make all the bad stuff that I did make sense?"

"Tristan was not your fault." Stevens pushed a hand through his thinning hair. "And I know we're still alive. We're still here. There has to be a reason for it. What I've seen makes me sick. It's wrong. I didn't understand before, but now I know." He met my eyes again and held a long look. "What we choose to do with what we know, that's what matters from this moment forward."

I looked from him to my father's small Bible.

"Guard it," he whispered. "Read it, and keep it safe. You'll know what to do when the time is right."

He walked away, giving me space to process. My jaw quivered, and a single tear escaped before I could blink it back. The Party had a huge shadow. If God was bigger—and He had me here for a reason—He'd have to prove it, because I was insignificant in it all. I swallowed and nodded, tucking the book into the back of my pants.

"Remove your shirt." Steven's quiet voice held sincere regret. "We have to make this look real." The sound of keys jingled against the concrete walls, raising the hairs on my neck.

So it's still to be...

I looked back at him. In his right hand he gripped the claw whip. He blinked several times, and his jaw jumped. I breathed in long and deep, closing my eyes as I stripped to the waist. With both palms braced against the blood-stained wall, I nodded. "Do it."

The first hit ripped across my left shoulder. My eyes flew open, and the little bit of light in the room seemed unnaturally bright and evil. I yelled as the burning pain ripped through the muscles where the claw shredded my flesh. The second blow landed on my side, atop my ribs. I feel to my knees. Unsure how many straps would make this "look real," I squeezed my eyes shut and readied for the next lash.

My mind shifted and focused on Eliza. Her dark eyes, deep with an uncommon understanding and a kindness I'd yet to see matched. Her soft hair, falling in waves against her shoulders. The feel of her mouth against mine...

What was she enduring? I let my imagination stumble over the possibilities as Commander Stevens dealt out his obligatory discipline. I don't remember if I hollered against the pain again. Actually, after the third strike, I didn't feel the pain. My body sort of went numb. Or perhaps he only gave me three lashes.

But my mind? My heart? I imagined Eliza's

suffering in the space between consciousness and darkness.

Death seemed like it would be a kind friend to us both.

* * *

Hannah

A full day of sweat after physical combat training completely removed my unease about Skye's "prophecy." She'd fought like a warrior princess, often singling me out as her favorite target. Her words were meant as a threat, not to inspire. And the girl could make good on her bark.

I'd taken more than one hard fall in the field against her joust, and every muscle in my backside let me know about its displeasure. Jogging back to the Pride took every ounce of my self-discipline as my body rebelled against the motion. Aching, my lungs also protested, and by the time we stopped in front of our housing, I needed that inhaler Quinn had produced as our cover.

Analise stopped beside me, drenched in sweat and mud, a purple bruise marking her left cheek where she'd caught the side blow of another girl in their set. Her sides heaved as she worked to control her breathing, and she looked me up and down.

"Use the inhaler," she said.

"Skye will see it as weakness. She'll attack me again tomorrow."

"Not if you're dead because you can't breathe." Analise slapped the back of my shoulder. "Just use it."

I glanced around, looking for either Skye or Commander Knott. Neither seemed concerned with my actions at the moment, so I produced the inhaler from the waistband of my uniform. Two long puffs and several more deep breaths, and I felt my lungs open again. The world came back into focus, the colors going back to their normal hue and not the overexposed brightness that my oxygen-starved brain had been registering.

"Better, yeah?" Analise, whose breathing had calmed to almost normal, gripped her sides and stretched backward.

"Yes." I slipped the sign of weakness back into the waistband of my pants. "Why do we do this?"

"What?"

"This training. It's medieval. What's the purpose?"

"Vision. Purpose. Excellence."

I huffed at her, knowing that mantra well enough. "This daily beating doesn't seem to have any purpose to me. We have a military. What exactly are we supposed to be?"

"Security at home," Analise said, a thread of pride in her voice. "Military is for offshore insurance. We are the keepers at home."

"Keepers of what?"

Analise scowled. "Of the ideal. Of the Party's purpose."

"And that requires medieval military practice?"

"The rebellious are still out there. They wish to undo all that we've done. We will be the ones holding the line secure. Keeping them from destroying all that we've become. Didn't you pay attention at the rally yesterday?"

Yeah, I'd paid attention, but none of it made sense. I knew what they called "the Rebellion." Though I didn't understand all of it, a sensation nagged that my conclusion about Braxton's dad—about my own father—had been miscalculated. The Party was hiding something, and it felt darker with every passing day I spent in the Pride. While I was with Quinn, I'd been convinced of the Party's goodness—of their right to direct the country and our people. But now?

Fear.

A vision of fire, red and orange and menacing against a black night, flashed through my mind.

Our home burned to the ground that night. We nearly lost my mom, and she'd never really recovered from the damage to her lungs. The Party claimed it was a protest—done on purpose by the Uncloaked. My father and Braxton's. Somehow in my starving, angry condition by the creek all those months ago, I swallowed that claim, made it my belief. Now...

Fear. Nothing in this was right. What had I done?

"Clean up. Commons tonight." The call came from Commander Knott, and I felt her full focus on me.

Meeting her eyes, I nodded.

She wasn't satisfied. She approached me with a leer tipping her mouth. "You'll not be excused this time, Hannah."

"I didn't ask to be," I said.

A little scoff escaped her closed lips. "He's gone now. He can't keep you from fully engaging in our world."

"What?"

"Oh? Did you not know? Didn't they tell you they were going?"

"Who?"

"Stateswoman Charlotte Sanger and her delicious son, Quinn. They left. Right after the rally, they went on to DC." She molded a mocking pout. "Surely you knew?"

Even as a fierce rise of possessive jealousy locked in my gut—*delicious? Eyes to yourself, woman*—a cry curled inside my stomach. *He left me.* I pressed it down, forcing stone to my face. "No. I didn't know. Why would they tell me?"

That mocking laugh sounded from her chest again. "I do have eyes, Hannah. Perhaps he realized he could do so much better."

My heart cracked. *He promised that he wouldn't leave me.*

I sealed away the thoughts, locking them in a place where they could not touch my broken heart and make the ache hurt more.

My shoulders stiff, I lifted my chin and met her jeering eyes. "I don't know what you mean. Quinn is nothing to me, and I am not afraid to become all that you are."

One corner of her mouth tipped upward, making her face look almost evil. "Good. That is why you are here."

t h i r t e e n

Braxton

A deep throb of unholy music pulsed into every part of my body and mind. The smells of stimulants curling throughout the room made me lightheaded and scattered my thoughts. The darkness pierced only by false and jarring lights jolted through my vision like lightning.

The moment was a sick contrast to what the Commons had once been. This former place of worship. Perhaps not former. Now, however, the worship was not of the holy God.

My body still ached. The places of ripped flesh on my shoulders and back still burned. Only two days had gone by, but exhaustion had set into my mind. I saw no point to any of this. Jed Stevens had tried to offer me hope, sneaking my father's Bible to me. It was only as a reminder that I was a sellout. And now this...I scanned the dim scene of depravity...this was my life.

The girls from the Pride trickled around the tables. They didn't flirt like they would have back in high school—with giggles, sassy smiles, clever banter. An unnatural age replaced the innocence. They approached the Jackals with sultry boldness, animallike challenge, and an undefined chill.

No emotion. Connection was unnecessary. No, connection was dangerous. This was the evolution of man. To become all that we could be, we would tear off the limitations of the heart. Love. Family. Even friendship. Nothing that would interfere with loyalty.

I wondered if anyone else saw this. And with those thoughts, the actions of the Party and the role of the Jackals became clear. Those who would not willingly separate their attachment were being ripped apart.

That was why they went after the children.

That was why Stevens was now alone. His own family torn apart in the name of Party loyalty.

I scanned the faces around me, shrouded in the shadows where we hid. Eyes cold. Kept distant. Focused on self. They had taught us how to remain detached. They meant to satisfy our fleshly desires while starving our human hearts. And they were succeeding.

As I passed over the emotionless faces, one drew my full attention. Hannah. Hannah was there. I hadn't imagined her at the rally or in the station. She was there as a part of the Pride, and her expression matched the other girls'.

Alone at a table, she carefully watched the scene. If she was as appalled as I had been my first time, her stony face did not show it. Then again, the Purge girls were no longer a part of this, so perhaps this was more acceptable in her view. I waited as she continued to search the crowd, and I knew the exact moment her eyes found me. She paused, and a flicker of recognition passed over her face before she looked away. The hand that had been resting on the table fisted, and then she pushed to her feet and walked away.

Fierceness rose in my chest, and I left my corner. Determined but unrushed, I followed her until she reached the brick wall at the back side of the room. She turned, still expressionless, and lifted a defiant chin to meet my gaze.

The little girl I'd known was gone. I cringed to think what had removed the innocence from her fierce eyes. Several heartbeats passed in our heated stare, and then I slipped my jacket from my arms, my skin and muscles screaming against the movement.

Her shoulders stiffened as I draped the jacket around her. "What are you doing?" she asked, her voice harsh.

"Making sure no one else touches you." I stepped closer, gripping her elbows.

She moved back until the wall prevented any more retreat. I followed, not allowing her to open the space between us.

"Is this how this works here?" she hissed. "You're claiming me?"

"Only for the moment." I leaned down to whisper near her ear. "And you can push me away any time. You're not a Purge girl, after all. Aren't you lucky?"

She jerked her face away, her stare wild and angry as she looked up to me.

"You don't know what that is, do you?" I asked.

Her angry silence answered.

"Be thankful. Although, it's possible that your sister became one..." My stomach rolled at my words.

"Whose fault was that?"

Silence rang hard between us, and then she tried to push me away. I gripped her arm tighter.

"Don't," I hissed, my mouth near her ear

again. "You don't know what you're getting into. Neither did I. And you're right—Eliza was my fault. I can't do anything to help her. I have to live with that. But right now, you're here, and I *can* do something about that."

I felt her tremble under my grip. Slowly, my fingers uncurled, and I moved so that I could see her eyes.

"This is restitution then? You'll protect me because you failed to protect her?" Her words cut hard, but her expression softened.

I couldn't look at her anymore. So much like Eliza in the physical department, and way too much like me in the action realm. Lifting my attention, I let my eyes focus on the grout lines running in between the bricks behind her. Somewhere in the hard stillness between us, Hannah sighed, and I felt her relax against me.

"Do you know where she is?" Her whisper drifted as she nuzzled against my chest. Clearly Hannah understood this charade.

Again, I felt sick knowing she played this role so well.

"No." I forced my arms to wrap her close, hating that this was the only way I could think to keep her from the others.

She stayed still against me, her head leaning, as if she'd found refuge. The thought made me feel a little better in the midst of this awkwardness.

"Now what?" she whispered.

"I don't know. For now, I'll take you out of here, keep you safe for the night. But tomorrow, you have to go back to the Pride."

Her chin lifted, and I looked down. Defiance reignited in her expression. "And that's a bad thing?"

"You like being a part of the Pride?"

"Perhaps you've misunderstood, Braxton. The Pride is where I belong."

I stepped back, dropping my arms and reaching for one of her hands. With a tug, not a very gentle one, I brought her to my side and led her through the stage curtains. As we passed from the stale hot air of the Commons into the crispness of the night, I leaned down and muttered, "Perhaps the misunderstanding is not mine."

She didn't break stride with me, but she stiffened. It occurred to me that Hannah Knight could be the end of whatever I was doing with the Jackals.

* * *

Hannah

Hiding again.

I was sick to death of hiding, and of these men

in my world who thought I couldn't handle the life in front of me. As Braxton pushed through the heavy rusted door of the factory, I ripped my hand from his grip. The creak of the old hinges echoed through the dark vaulted space as the door clanged shut. Braxton whirled back to face me, his large hand gripping my elbow.

"Knock it off." I jerked away from him again. "I don't need your protection."

He stepped forward. Clearly his eyesight had adjusted to the dim light faster than mine.

"You don't know what you need," he said, once again reclaiming his hold on my arm. "I swear, Hannah. You are about as blind as..."

He let the insult hang.

"You?" I snorted, stumbling against the uneven floor as he led me to the metal stairs.

"Yeah. That's about right." He stopped, turning to face me as he towered over my head.

An intentional pose, meant to intimidate.

"Does that make you feel better, kid? I did a lot of stupid, so I can't judge you, right?"

Pretty much, yeah. Although it sounded childish coming from him, with that condescending tone he'd mastered.

"You'd do well to figure out the difference between judgment and caution." The preacher's son in him seemed to step forward for the first time ever. "And the honest desire to protect.

Which is where I'm coming from."

My fists doubled at my sides, and I lifted my chin, unwilling to bow to his air of superiority. "You're coming from guilt, and that's about it, Braxton Luther. Don't try to paint your attempts as noble when really they're driven by your own stupidity."

Both of his hands grabbed my shoulders, and his hold sank deep. "That's exactly what I'm telling you, foolish girl. *I. Was. Stupid.* Now here I am, stuck in a nightmare I couldn't imagine." Heat rippled from his voice. "Why won't you listen? Why are you here? I told you to run. I told you it was awful, and instead of going with your parents someplace safe, you joined the Pride? What are you trying to prove?"

"That I'm not my sister!" With both palms against his chest, I pushed. Though he stumbled back, he didn't let go, and for two steps, we danced a clumsy set in the darkness of our argument. My eyes finally adjusted to the lack of light enough to make out his face. His wide, dark eyes. The pain etched in his expression.

Slowly his fingers loosened, though he didn't remove his hold. "No one expects you to be Eliza."

"Of course they don't." I spat the words, all the ugliness I thought I'd stuffed away surfacing like a green branch on black water. "Because I can't be that good. That perfect."

Silence followed the echo of my outburst, and I bit my trembling lip. All the months that had gone by, and I hadn't moved past it yet. She still held my freedom captive.

It's not her hand that holds you...

I brushed my mother's voice away, growing angrier by the memory. She always took my sister's side. Always found her right and me wrong.

"Hannah..." My name fluttered from Braxton's breath, a tag of sympathy that both coddled my bruised spirit and needled my inflated pride.

Sniffing, I went rigid again. "Don't." I gripped his hands and flung them from my shoulders. "I don't want your lectures or your pity."

"You won't have either."

Tipping my head to the side, I raised an eyebrow, challenging his statement.

"How could I lecture you?" One palm cupped the side of my head, and he released a long, sorry breath before he whispered, "It's like looking into a mirror."

A look of total humility crossed his face, and his shoulders drooped.

I'd never expected to see him broken like that. Nor could I have imagined how close his reaction came to breaking me. Because really, I was terrified. Nothing of the Pride, or the Jackals, or the Party for that matter, made sense anymore. The further into it I got, the murkier it all became. And just like Braxton, I'd run into the mess by my own decisions.

I was stuck too.

fourteen

Braxton

A firm grip on the back of my neck jarred me from blackness. Sucking air through my nose, I jolted upward, grabbing the hand that had trespassed.

A male voice whispered as the arm invading my space fell away. "Easy, Luther. It's me."

The shadows within the factory remained thick and dark, and as far as I knew, Hannah and I had been the only ones within the metal relic's belly.

Scrambling to my feet, my attention zipped to the doorway on my right. Closed. I let the air seep from my lungs as relief nudged a bit of my edginess. Hannah should still be in there. Alone. Safe. I turned back to the intruder, still unsure who had woken me from a sleep I shouldn't have been in in the first place.

"What are you doing here?"

"I brought your things. You need to go."

It wasn't Hulk, which wasn't surprising. He would have smashed my jaw until I was awake, not shaken my neck.

"Stevens?"

"Yes."

"Have I been reassigned?"

He paused, and I squinted against the shadows to see him look away. "Yes. I've made new arrangements for you. You're not safe here. Not with Hulk."

Puzzle pieces locked into place, creating a hopeful picture. "Tristan..."

"You'll find him where you are going."

I couldn't stop the air from rushing out of my lungs. "Why didn't you tell me?"

"You know that answer."

Because it wasn't safe. Stevens was putting his neck on the line. Again—for me? I should have been grateful, but...

"I can't go."

"You're gonna have to. I can't undo this."

"Hannah—"

"She's made her own choices."

"That's not good enough. I can't leave her here."

"Son, you don't have a choice."

I surged forward. With both hands on his arms, I pushed him against the back wall. "Don't call me son. And I've heard that long enough. I have a choice, and I'm not leaving her."

* * *

Hannah

"Get up."

The boot tapping my thigh wasn't exactly gentle. Stiff from a night on a cold, hard floor, I jerked my leg away from the intruder and lifted my face. "Such a gentleman. I don't know what my sister saw in you..."

Lies. More lies from my twisted-up heart.

"Yeah. I don't know either," he said.

My stiff shoulders sagged. I didn't mean to jab at a wound. Should have known better, because I knew he felt responsible.

I pushed up to a sitting position. "What happened that night?"

Though the room was hardly light—the weak morning sun didn't penetrate much through the rust-littered steel building—I could see him turn his face away, looking toward the floor.

"We don't have time." His voice bit, but unmistakable remorse snaked through his tone. "Look. I've been reassigned, and I'm supposed to be on the seven a.m. rail west. Get what you need. We're going."

"Where?"

He stepped toward the door, which was not far from my feet. I thought he'd toss an answer back to me, but when he left the threshold and his footsteps continued down the catwalk toward the stairway, I scrambled to my feet. Ignoring the cramped muscles in my back, I jogged after him.

"Where are we going?"

"You have to go back to the Pride." He jostled down the stairway, and I tailed him.

"And you?"

"I told you. I've been reassigned."

Halfway across the broken concrete floor, Braxton stopped and turned an about-face. My momentum didn't switch as fast as his, and I smashed into the front buttons of his jacket, fully colliding with his chest.

He wasn't a boy anymore. Muscles, hard and tense, met my face and then my palm as I pushed away from him, righting myself. His build was every bit man and similar enough to Quinn's that my heart squeezed with ache.

He left me. And now Braxton was too.

Braxton gripped my elbow with one hand, steadying me as I righted my clumsiness. Not something I would have wanted Skye to see. I glanced around, probing the dim corners for witnesses. Though none made themselves known, I scowled at the man whose hand still held my arm, and ripped away from his touch.

He leveled me with a raised-eyebrow stare. "It's not the easy way of life you thought it'd be, is it?"

Though heat flooded my face, I returned his even look. "I don't know what you mean."

"You know exactly what I mean." He crossed his arms, his focus unwavering. "I saw you at the rally."

"Nothing is ever what you think it is from the outside. But I have a home—better than sleeping in a dark hole in the ground, starving."

"Is it?"

I couldn't hold his stare, though sliding my attention from him to the door behind him was certainly a giveaway. "I didn't judge your choices. Don't judge mine."

"You totally judged, Hannah Knight—and you were right. I'm a sellout, and the price was more than I ever imagined. This isn't a game where you get to play with whoever you want however you want and it'll all turn out fine. This is real—

what you saw last night was mild compared to what has been."

I tipped a sassy, disbelieving look at him, even though doubt and fear swirled in my gut. "You always were dramatic."

Anger lit his eyes as he took a step toward me, his solid frame hovering over my smaller build, intimidating me. "Where do you think Tristan and I found Miranda? How do you think she got to Glennbrooke, naked, starving, and her head shaved? You think she chose all of that?"

A hint of nausea rolled through my stomach as last night's Commons experience flashed through my mind. The policy of anything goes had throbbed through the room, and I'd been thankful for Braxton's protection, even if I'd been annoyed that I needed it.

How had Miranda ended up there? She hadn't been sealed, which meant she wasn't part of the Pride, and she'd said that Eliza had cut out her electronic tag. I didn't know what that meant, other than the fact that Miranda had a two-inch incision on the back of her shoulder that Dad had to stitch.

My silence, and the fact that I stood paralyzed, must have given my lack of understanding away.

"Imagine the worst, Hannah, and you might be close." Braxton swallowed, and his expression pinched tight. The battle was clear on his face; he was desperate to erase images in his mind that would not budge.

Don't go to the Commons...

Quinn had been adamant. How had he known?

A shiver shuddered over my body. Braxton didn't miss it. "You have to decide. Which side are you on?"

"I don't want a side," I hissed. "I want a life." *A place where I belonged.*

"That's not among your choices right now."

Why was he doing this now? What was the urgency in his voice—his stance—all about? "What are you trying to tell me?"

"I'll find a way out for you, if that's what you want. But it has to be what you want. The risk is high."

Out. Yes, I wanted out of the Pride. Truth: they terrified me. But my heart...

Quinn.

If I followed Braxton, whatever his plan might be, I'd never see Quinn again. Something cracked in my chest, flooding my veins with liquid ice.

He left me.

But maybe he didn't have a choice. Like me. Really, I didn't have a choice. The world made my decisions for me. All I could do was make the best of it.

"I'm staying," I said, somehow making my voice sound firm and confident.

Braxton examined me for two more breaths. I wasn't sure if I read more disappointment or fear in his eyes.

* * *

Braxton

Grab courage and stand. Don't quit.

Somewhere in the place between awake and asleep, I heard her voice. Soft, like she'd whispered in my ear. My arms and chest ached as I longed to feel her there, pulled tight against me.

I need you, Liza. I can't do this, and I've let you down again.

Though aware I was on the LiteRail and alone, I felt her there. I closed my hand, as if to grip her small, delicate, invisible fingers that distinctly curved into mine.

Please, God, let her be okay. Let me find her...

Forcing my eyes open, I felt them burn. Reality sank fully back into my awareness as I scanned the darkened world beyond the window of my transport. I ached for Eliza. But she wasn't my mission anymore, and I was allowing the longing of my heart to distract me. She'd be disappointed in that.

Stand. That was what she'd said in my dream. I didn't know what my role would be now, but I understood a little more about this massive game I'd become a part of. Jed Stevens had a purpose in sending me to the Vacant Plains. Just like he had in sending Tristan. Courage sprouted in that tiny bit of soil. If Jed, who had sold out first, found a way to undercut the Party, then maybe all was not hopeless. Maybe a sellout could find redemption.

Except, there was Hannah. I offered to find a way out for her. She didn't want me to, and she'd refused to tell me why. Stubborn girl. If she wasn't with me, I couldn't protect her and at the same time do what Eliza had asked me to to—to save our people. Realistically, I probably couldn't even do one of the two.

Trust me.

That time it was not Eliza's voice. It wasn't a voice at all. Only an impression, as clear as the ringing of our school bell at lunchtime, but silent all the same.

Trust God. The failure of all my failures.

I lifted my eyes toward the star-smattered sky as I realized that truth. Everything—every failure of my life, from resenting my father and brothers to joining the Den—could be traced back to one root failure.

I hadn't trusted God.

I couldn't see His hand in my life, so I didn't trust what I could not trace. But He was asking me now to trust Him. In the darkness, the uncertainty of a future that seemed ripped apart in the most ugly and unfixable ways, God wanted my faith.

Would I give it?

A story from my childhood intruded in my mind, one that had been told in every Sunday school classroom since Jesus ascended into heaven. Three men, an arrogant king, a large statue, and a raging-hot fire...

Our God is able to deliver us, but even if He doesn't, we will not bow.

They believed God could. Didn't know if He would. But either way, they trusted Him. I thought that was the most crazy and courageous story I'd ever heard. In that moment, remembering the details, I still thought that— those men were astonishingly bold. What made them so?

They believed. They trusted. Their bone-deep faith put on flesh and walked through the fire. God met them there. Delivered. And changed the heart of a king—of a nation.

Now it was my turn. As the railcar slowed, the whooshing of air falling to a lower octave, a slow cadence, I firmed up my resolve. I'd told Hannah I was a sellout, and I was. But I didn't have to stay that way. Not if I chose to trust.

Not if I chose to stand.

* * *

Hannah

The transport back to the Pride was waiting as I crossed the parking lot. Glancing at the Den, a little tremble quaked in my chest. We'd basically grown up in there, Eliza, Braxton, and me. Back when it was the church Braxton's father had led. Back when life still made sense, at least a little bit. I felt empty as I boarded the transport, and the void inside made me want to curl up and cry.

But I was with the Pride, and we didn't cry.

From the inside out, I stiffed my posture, hardened my heart, shoved away the emotion toying with my tears. I hadn't lost Braxton. Not the way I'd lost Eliza. I'd chosen a different path, just like I had when I'd decided to leave the forest. My life was my own, and I would direct it.

Except it wasn't going the way I'd wanted. I'd wanted to run with Braxton, and I heard a small, demanding voice in my head calling me an idiot for staying.

Fear. The voice was fear, and I didn't decide my life because of fear.

Yes, I did. I didn't leave because I was afraid I'd never see Quinn again.

I dropped into my seat and tipped my head against the tempered glass window to my right, squeezing my eyes shut and muffling the voices arguing in my mind. I was too tired for it. Too wrung out.

"Wild night, huh?" Analise slipped into the seat beside me.

I didn't look at her as I muttered, "Something like that."

"None of the other Pride girls have ever slipped into Luther's coat." Sultry suggestions lay in her voice.

My stomach lurched. Not long ago I would have clamped onto that insinuation and painted it with hope and a sense of victory over my sister. What a twisted girl I'd been, wanting what had belonged to her. As if I had a right to her life. What was wrong with me?

"Glad to hear he's still picky," I said.

Analise snorted. "Not so much. He usually went for a Purge girl. Guess now that they've been banned..."

A Purge girl? *Imagine the worst...*

What had Braxton been doing with those girls? Who were they anyway?

"Up, Lise." Skye's sharp voice sliced through

my wondering. "You're in my spot."

And the morning just kept getting brighter. What did she want now? I'd kept away from her at the Commons—on purpose. What could she possibly find wrong this time?

Still keeping my eyes shut, I felt Analise rise and leave, and the space beside me filled with a stronger, stiffer presence.

I waited. The transport surged forward, and my head slipped back against the padded bench. Still waited.

Nothing. Just her commanding presence that made me defensive.

My muscles coiled, and I couldn't take her silent threats anymore. "What?" I sat up, stabbing her with a look of irritation.

Her black eyebrows rose, and she silently took stock of our surroundings. Gauging for something, though I couldn't know what. Checking for ears that should not be listening?

"How do you know him?"

"Know who?"

Her cold, hard stare demanded an answer, not another question.

"We grew up together. He and my sister..."

Understanding filled her eyes, though her face gave nothing else away. "You're the one..."

"Excuse me?"

She looked away, lifting her chin and settling

her attention on something beyond the seats in front of us. We pulled up to the Pride before she spoke again, and she waited until the transport emptied before she moved, her stubborn presence blocking my path. When the other girls were gone, Skye met my eyes with a stern, demanding gaze.

"You must decide. Figure out who you are, and then don't let anyone shake that identity."

"What?"

"I mean it. Who you are will determine what you do. And what you do will affect us all. You have to decide." She held eye contact for one more breath and then stood, leaving me as if what she'd said both made sense and hadn't been cryptic.

I didn't understand. But I knew I was terrified.

f i f t e e n

Braxton

I'd never seen anything so vast, so empty, and so intimidating. The land spread wide and long, interrupted by nothing. No trees. No hills. Only wide grass-covered dirt that bowed to the constant wind.

The Vacant Plains.

I stepped off the railcar alone, my eyes sore from searching for something to break up the brown monotony. Only the meeting of land and sky at the distant horizon offered relief. Who would ever want to live there?

The LiteRail pulled away, exposing the view on the other side of the station. Waiting on a dust-covered road bearing the faint marks of an old paved highway, a car sat, puffing black exhaust into the hazy air.

Dark blue, with rust peppering the wheel wells, the vehicle struck me as off. It was the old-fashioned kind—the kind that had been outlawed in my father's younger days. Even more odd, the boy who climbed from the driver's seat wore the same uniform I did. Government issued. He was a Jackal driving an illegal car.

"Get in." The boy reached for the back of the vehicle and tugged. The back popped up, and he tossed a hand toward the opening. "I assume you can manage your own junk. Toss it in and let's go. We have a long drive."

I stood watching while he walked to the driver's side and slid back into the car. With a glance, first right and then left and then behind me, I checked for other options. Nothing. Absolutely nothing.

A horn blared, shattering the whooshing sound of the wind with an intrusive demand.

The boy leaned over the passenger's seat and shouted through the open window. "No one else is coming, fool. Get in or get left. I'm not waiting any longer."

Getting left didn't sound good. Who knew

when the LiteRail would come back through, and there was nothing out there for shelter, food, or hope. I stepped forward, tossed my shouldered duffel into the back, shut the door, and moved to slide onto the passenger's seat.

The other Jackal didn't say a word. He shifted the car into drive and wasted no time gaining speed on the abandoned road. I glanced at him, trying hard not to make my curiosity obvious as I built up a hard wall around my rising fear. Jed had sent me here. Must have had a reason.

Unless I'd misunderstood.

"Where are we going?" I said, keeping my voice stiff.

"Reformation Camp."

Icy liquid swept through my body. *No. Oh, dear God, I can't—I haven't done what I was supposed to do yet.*

"Must be some kind of soldier, boy," he said after a moment. "Only the toughest Jackals get assigned here."

My pulse returned, throbbing, and I examined the guy. His skin was darker than mine, the dark-almond color of Eliza's, and his dark hair stubble hinted the same Hispanic heritage Jayla Knight had claimed. He had a hard jaw, which remained set in a firm, unwavering frown as he stared forward.

"Well?" With a slow turn of his head, he

challenged me with one look, his brown eyes chilling and dark.

"Well what?"

Again, with slow, intentional movements, he refocused on the road ahead. "What did you do to earn this right?"

"That's my business, not yours."

His Adam's apple did one slow bob, but other than that, he maintained a motionless blank stare. I fought away the gooseflesh that threatened to prickle the skin on my arm.

"How about you?" I dared to ask, because I didn't want him to sense my alarm.

Once more his face turned toward me, and the first hint of a grin tipped his mouth. It was more chilling than his frown. "You don't want to know."

A sick feeling settled in my stomach, a sure sign that he was right. I didn't want to know. "Fine. How about a name at least?"

"Henson."

Last or first name? I didn't ask. Didn't care that much.

"And you're Luther." Henson's mouth tipped, as if he knew something.

Maybe he did. In that moment, I didn't want to know that either. I turned my attention to my right, focusing on the enormous space flashing by my window.

The land continued to sweep by, unchanged. Uninteresting and yet mesmerizing in its unyielding sameness. Every now and again, a rise would emerge, as if trying to rebel from the flat nothing, and then it would fall, unsuccessful in its attempt at uniqueness. The solid plane would claim it again, and that was that.

The view continued for over an hour, and then we turned north onto another abandoned road artery. After thirty minutes, the landscape lost its mighty grip on nothing and fell into a deep ravine. Corpses of trees, now completely lifeless and weathered gray against the sand-colored grass and pale-blue sky, gathered at the deepest point of impression. Dead limbs littered the basin, where water should have flowed. Two dwellings pocked the earth, one on each side of the road and staggered from each other.

As we approached them, I searched their faces, looking for life. There was only death. One roof sagged, the neglected shingles torn at the lowest dip. The other house boasted no windows, and the front door stood half open, tilted at a broken angle.

"What happened here?" I asked, my voice tight from lack of use over this long, silent journey.

"The Plains aren't inhabitable, remember?" Henson said.

"Where did the people go?" And more to the point, why were we there if it wasn't safe to stay? Not a question I was willing to bet Henson would answer.

"Who knows?" Henson said, as if he didn't care. "To a distribution point somewhere. A city."

As the car climbed the rise in front of us, I scanned the Plains more carefully. What I'd seen as lifeless probably hadn't been. Not all along. I strained my eyes to see past the view immediately available from the road. They were out there. Old farmhouses. Homes. Abandoned, probably by force. Distribution points. Vehicle restrictions. Illegal fuels. All seemed harmless back home—progressive even, if I remembered the little I'd paid attention to over the years when I didn't really care. But here...

The laws had stripped the land of people. People of their homes. How did you live so far away from anyone or anything when you could no longer own a vehicle? When rations replaced salary? When you couldn't produce what you knew how to produce because it didn't fall into your Career Track?

Progress. What had we done?

"I wouldn't worry about it," Henson said, his right brow lifted in a challenge. "Majority. That's what we do. We take care of the majority. I'm sure they moved to a city and found that life is better that way. Or, they didn't and found out other things."

"Just never imagined a place like this."

"Well, who would? Why would anyone want to live here anyway? Especially after the explosion."

I filed through my memories, trying to place his reference. The only one that surfaced was of a brief blip I'd seen on the television back when we still had a home. Dad and Mom and both been upset about it. I hadn't given a rip.

It seemed to matter quite a bit now.

"Wasn't it chemical?"

Henson shrugged. "That's the story."

I couldn't resist the question. "Then why are we here?"

Again he eyed me, his eyebrows cocked in challenge. "It's the job. Do it, keep your questions to yourself, and don't worry about the rest."

Sure, no problem. That was basically how I'd lived my life up until the year before. Live and let live, and don't worry about the other stuff.

"What is the job?"

"Security." Henson chuckled, as if it were a joke. "But mostly, we play cards. Kick it. If you get really bored, there's always the camp girls..."

Bile burned the back of my throat. I looked

away, hoping to hide the wince I couldn't stop.

"Don't worry about it. Party doesn't care what we do out here. As long as the perimeter is maintained, we're fine. Doesn't take much to manage that. It's all done by satellite anyway."

Miranda flashed through my mind. She'd explained a little bit about it—how that chip we dug out of her shoulder was like an electric dog collar. Only deadly. Approach the border, get a little zap. Keep going, the pulses came harder. Ignore that, the electric pulse became a jolt, striking the heart and dropping the prisoner.

She said some chose to run into the border. Suicide. At the time, I couldn't grasp why they would—Reformation Camp wasn't supposed to be torture. The ignorance of my youth...

I curled a fist and worked to bury my disgust. This was my chance to look for Eliza. That must have been why Stevens sent me. And Tristan? Stevens said my friend would be here too. There was something big at play.

"How's that work?" I asked, keeping my voice detached.

"What? The perimeter?"

"Right."

He snorted another laugh. "Like that kind of information just hangs around." In the beat of silence, I saw his jaw flex. "Look. This is an easy gig. But if you don't keep to those simple rules, you'll find yourself with a tag buried in your shoulder and a shaved head, just like the rest of them. And trust me—you don't want to be one of them."

Do the job. Keep my questions to myself. Sounded like the kink in the Party's armor lay somewhere in the Vacant Plains.

Jed had sent me to exploit it.

* * *

Hannah

Three weeks. In three weeks' time, I'd visited the Commons twice, didn't hear from Quinn once, and couldn't make out what happened to Braxton.

But I saw stuff.

A shiver snaked down my body as I leaned back against the transport seat. The phrase *anything goes* had taken on a new meaning—a vile, nauseating sensation that gripped me inside and out as I replayed the night.

Psychotic came to mind. The way most everyone left their sense of dignity to satiate every imaginable human craving. Indulgence was the order of the Commons. Eating—more like gorging—until the food came back up in putrid sludge, only to wipe the mouth, turn around, and stuff more down. Drinking—alcohol flooded the room like we were fish and fermented drink was the ocean. And drugs...I couldn't name what had been passed, and I didn't take any of it.

But I saw.

Dignified girls stripped, giggling as if baring their nakedness really did thrill their souls rather than rob their dignity. Boys I'd grown up with, whom I'd known to be nice and decent, took what only selfish, evil men take, and felt nothing but visceral pleasure in doing so.

Most of them wouldn't even remember it all come dawn. But I did.

Only one reason lay behind the fact that, aside from Hulk's leering gaze, none of the other Jackals had approached me either of the times that I'd been there when Braxton had been absent. He'd claimed me. Somehow marked me as *do not touch*.

As much as that made my trembling heart relieved, it also made me angry. Who did he think he was? I was my own person, could stand on my own two feet. I wasn't Eliza, had never been in need of his protection. Just like Skye, who handled herself with so much authority that the boys didn't lift a finger near her, I could manage myself.

In the six weeks I'd been with the Pride, I'd proven myself. Every drill, every combat, I came out the victor. There was only one who could maintain her rank over me. And Skye seemed somehow fine with my rising strength. Only when I challenged her directly, which my bruised and swollen fingers reminded me that I had done so only two days before, did she stare at me with that pinched, absolutely fearless and condescending expression in her deadly calm eyes. Even then, something else lurked in that cool look.

Admiration?

My chest puffed a little as I rested my head against the back of the seat. Perhaps that was what had been in Skye's eyes. And I'd earned it. She wouldn't be singling me out anytime soon. She wouldn't risk her unquestionable leadership among the Pride by messing with me. I had found my place. All on my own. Didn't need Braxton or Eliza.

Or Quinn.

My billowing sense of self deflated with that thought. Quinn was gone. He'd really left me. Without a word. A care.

Those tender looks, all the gentle touches. The kisses. Meant nothing to him. It meant nothing to me then. I'd found my strength. Training beat the weakness out of my body. Surely my heart wouldn't be much different.

I didn't need Quinn Sanger any more than I needed Braxton Luther, and realizing that I didn't could only make me stronger. I shut my eyes and allowed a little grin to tug on the corners of my mouth. I didn't need the distractions they offered at the Commons. I'd found my own source of pleasure, and it didn't need to leave me degraded, confused, or bound to a system.

I was the writer of my own story, and I would plot my own course.

A presence filled the space beside me again. I didn't need to look to know it was Skye.

"You're not one of them," she whispered.

I didn't move. Didn't allow her the power of thinking she commanded a response from me. "Don't know what you mean."

"Yes you do."

Despite my self-assured resistance to her throaty implication, I opened my eyes and looked at her. "Are you one of them?"

She stared. That same look. The one she would hold steady when we faced off on the mat, our grips firm on the poles, our intent made clear to each other and to everyone around us. *I will not back down.* That was what our locked gazes said. What her hard stare said now.

"You're coming with me," Skye said, the command leaving no room for question.

I ignored the closed tone of her voice. "Where?"

"Assignment. We leave as soon as we get back. Take everything. Tell no one." Skye rose to walk away. I gripped her arm before she could.

"What if I say no?"

From her standing position, she glared at me over her shoulder. "Then you have made your choice, and I am not responsible." With a subtle move, she jerked her arm from my grasp and walked away.

At least this time I could make my choice. Not that I wouldn't have anyway. But it was nice to have someone acknowledge it.

* * *

Braxton

Shutting my eyes didn't help. The image of Reformation Camp had been permanently tattooed into my mind.

That first day, Henson had driven the illegal car up to what looked like an old airport. A large hangar loomed in the center, its steel structure like a silver bubble in the middle of the brown plain. Smaller steel buildings surrounded it, each looking like a relic from two generations past, at least.

"What is this?" I asked.

"RFC." Henson tossed his answer back to me as he opened the trunk. "You don't want to go into the big hangar, but you can do just about anything else." He lifted my bag and threw it at my chest. "Remember, our only real responsibility is to watch the perimeter, and that's not a big deal. If they run, the jolt will drop 'em within fifty yards of the line."

He grinned, and it made me shudder.

"If you feel like target practice, you can go ahead and shoot, but either way, they'll go down. There's no escaping RFC."

Burying the impulse to plow my fist into his wicked face, I scanned the land. Dust swirled in the wind, creating a brownish haze against the silver sheen of the buildings. Nothing else was worth attention. No barbed-wire fence. No movement. Nothing.

"Where are they?"

"The prisoners?"

That was the first time ever I'd heard someone besides me call those who'd been sent to Reformation Camp a name that accurately stated what they were. Prisoners. I nodded as my jaw jumped.

"Field work." Henson stepped away from the

desolate scene and moved toward a transport waiting about fifty yards away. "They won't be in until sundown."

"All of them?"

"Except for the quarantined." He nodded toward the largest hangar. "Which is why you don't want to go in there."

"Quarantined? What do they—"

"What'd I tell you about questions?" He had stopped just outside of the bus, his hand resting on the side of the metal. "Just know that you don't want it, so stay away. Everything else is easy, Luther. Just fall in line, and you'll be fine."

That'd been a couple weeks ago, but that first entry into RFC had burned into my mind. Fall in line. That was what Hulk had told me to do way back before being sealed was even a thing. Fall in line. Or else.

Or else... Reformation Camp. Or else death.

Thing of it was, falling in line hadn't helped anything. It'd only made me a sellout.

But I'd have to be careful at Reformation Camp, even if I'd left Hulk behind. So I faked it. With a mask of severe detachment, I worked beside Henson in a Nest—a guard tower on the southeast perimeter of the camp. From there I could see the Party's prisoners at a distance. Thin, weak, hunched-over people would drizzle out of the smaller steel structures in the morning, sit in the dirt, and, with their fingers, scoop bean mush out of large pots scattered throughout their yard. A small amount of tin cups would be passed among the hundreds of skeleton people littering the dusty space. Water, I assumed. When the cup was empty, the holder would go back to the well, dip the cup in the bucket, and return to the next thirsty, malnourished soul in line. Silence reigned over the crowd, unnatural, deathly. Heartbreaking.

And yet they stayed. In their unyielding silence, they shouted their defiance to the Party. All one needed to do was walk over to the surrender station, take the oath, receive the seal, and they'd be sent back to society, released from this prison of dirt, little food, and nothing else. But they didn't. For over two weeks I watched from the Nest as they began every morning the same way, worked every day in the fields doing what modern machinery could do in a fraction of the time, and ended every day with the unchanging bean mush and community water cup.

They did not yield.

Their resilient courage beckoned to me. No more selling out. No more bowing. Courage stood. Courage did what was right, even if the cost was everything. Courage looked like my father, like Eliza, like the many below my perch who everyday resolved to live what they believed, whether in comfort or in agony.

I was still alive. I could still grab hold of courage, still live up to the name I'd been given. Because I remembered the quote Eliza had left me with... *To go against one's conscience was neither right nor safe.*

Commotion below stole my attention away from the stirring of defiance in my mind.

"Carson, no!"

I couldn't identify the woman yelling, but her cry carried the shrill of a terrified mother. Suddenly a boy, a year or two younger than me, broke away from the sepia-toned scene we affectionately called slop time. One backward glance was all the boy gave, and then he sprinted away. He leaned forward as he charged toward the boundary line, and the Nests stationed every hundred yards erupted with jeers.

"Run, little rebel!"

"See how far you make it, you ungrateful vermin."

"Come on, roach. Run!"

Laughter, evil and hair raising, accompanied their calls, the sound coming to me as though from the vile Beast from hell himself. I wanted to cover my ears, to huddle on the ground in a fetal position as I pictured the faces belonging to the people who had hid in the dugout all those months ago. Images of kids running from the infernos that had once been their homes, until the Jackals had lit firebombs to destroy them, blended with those of the people I loved who had been taken.

How had we come to this?

A shout, a cry of enormous pain, sliced through the ugly calls of my fellow guards, and the boy dropped to his knees.

"Found the jolt line, did you?" Henson shouted and then chuckled sadistically. "Keep going, smart guy. You're almost there."

Though unwilling, I looked at the kid, who now rolled in agony on the ground as electricity pulsed through his body.

"Come back," I whispered.

Henson slugged my shoulder. "Soft spot, huh?" He snickered. "Well, he can't come back. He's tased, and now he's stuck. He'll sit there and fry slowly, like a bug caught in boiling syrup."

Wide-eyed, I stared at Henson. This did not bother him one bit.

"He should have run faster." The devil smiled, eyes on his helpless victim, watching like a spider who'd caught a small butterfly in his sticky web. "Maybe he would have reached the kill zone before the jolt dropped him. Guess he gets to die slowly instead."

My head whirled as thoughts chased emotions. Anger and helplessness wound around the need to do something. Now. Without blowing my cover, my purpose.

"What did you say you did to earn this post?"

Henson's grin faded, and his eyes pinched. "I didn't."

"Right."

"Why?"

"Bet you didn't do anything. They keep the useful leaders in the Dens."

As the kid's soul-piecing screams continued on the ground, I prayed Henson would take the bait without turning it on me.

"Did you just hint that I'm useless?"

"Are you?" I asked.

Henson's face hardened.

I smirked. "Prove it."

"Prove what?"

"You're trained. That you are the killer you claim to be."

He folded his arms over his chest and took a ready-fight stance. "You want me to drop you?"

"No." I mirrored his arm-folded position and indicated the writhing kid with a nod of my head. "Him. From right here. One shot."

Henson rolled his eyes as his shoulders relaxed. "Right, Luther."

God, please have mercy. I couldn't look at the dying boy again, though his mother's cries singed my heart.

"Just like I thought." I said, maintaining a baiting tone. "All talk."

A hard scowl replaced Henson's smirk, and in one breath he went from glaring at me to aiming his automatic weapon. In the next heartbeat, the shot ripped through the air, and the boy's body stopped twitching. He rolled to his back, arms spread, and his lifeless face tipped toward the sky.

Go in peace. The thought turned to prayer, and I hoped God had a special welcome for the tortured faithful.

Tears burned under the rims of my eyelids.

s i x t e e n

Hannah

The water had tasted funny that night. That was all I could remember.

When I forced my eyes open, lifting my dizzy head, I knew I wasn't where I should have been. The hard, cold slab beneath me wasn't my bunk, and I had the distinct feeling of movement. That could have been vertigo.

I fought through it, forcing my numb muscles to flex, my wobbly limbs to move. With a groan I couldn't swallow, I pushed up on my elbow.

"Just stay put."

Skye's commanding voice hissed through the foggy darkness of my reality.

"What did you do?"

"I told you that you were coming. It wasn't optional."

"I told you I didn't want to," I snapped, working to make my words unslurred. "You said it was my choice."

She didn't respond.

I pushed up on my hip.

"Sit. Back." Her low voice held warning.

I swayed, wanting to defy her but unable to find the balance or strength to do so. "You kidnapped me."

"You'll thank me later. Just sit back. You won't be able to sit up without puking, so you might as well stay where you are."

I didn't try to fight my way up anymore, but I didn't lay back either. "Where are we going?"

"The Vacant Plains."

Shutting my eyes, I focused on the movement I sensed as I'd woken. Not a transport bus. The LiteRail. Skye wasn't lying.

"Nobody goes there. They're forbidden—hazardous."

Skye shifted in the darkness, her presence seeming to relax. "For some."

"For some? The news said the explosion made them uninhabitable."

A soft snort punctuated the silence, but then

Skye said nothing.

Secrets seemed to breed among the Pride—perhaps among the Party. The growing sense of doubt about the Sangers, about the system, about our nation, began snaking through me again. We lived in the Pride almost as savage mercenaries. Where Charlotte had spoken of compassion, the strength of kindness, we'd been fed anger, power, and a deep sense of *destroy or be destroyed*. These ideas weren't compatible. And yet the Party funded the Pride and the Den, sent thousands of teenagers into the system, encouraged them to stay. It didn't make sense.

"What is it you know that you're not telling me?" I spoke into the tight silence, unsure if she'd answer. Unsure about everything.

"I know where I stand. I know where you should stand." Skye leaned closer, the warmth of her body hovering over me. "I guess we'll see what you're really made of soon enough. I hope..."

She pulled away, and I heard her settling back against the bench across from mine.

"You hope what?" I asked.

"I hope Luther isn't wrong. I hope we didn't risk everything for someone who can't see the truth—or isn't strong enough to do something with it."

Braxton? Skye had some conspiracy going

with *him*? A surge of hot rage washed over me. Braxton Luther was behind this—my kidnapping. I'd made myself clear to him. I didn't want his protection or his interference. I didn't need him.

"Your silence is telling," Skye hissed, her voice tight again. "It isn't reassuring. But know this, Knight. If this fails, everything is lost. And that means more than you think. Figure it out before we get to the camp. You can't stand on the fence once we're there. You'll get everyone killed, including yourself, and then you'll have nothing left to prove."

My mind zeroed in on the word *camp*. I knew of only one reference that could mean, and I didn't want to think about it. Fear chilled the molten anger, and I tried to push the whispered rumors about the Party's dirty little secret away. They couldn't be true. Just wasn't possible. No one was that evil, that sick. No one. They were wrong—my dad, Mr. Luther, Braxton, and now, apparently, Skye. Darkness like that couldn't be real—especially when I'd lived in the kindness of high-ranking officials.

They'd see. The truth would be exposed, and Skye, along with Braxton, would see how stupid they'd been. The rebels within the Reformation Camp would be fine, living in a resort-like place, fed and warm and cared for until they could see that the Party truly meant them no harm. Until the threat of their rebellion could be neutralized. And then they'd be free to join the rest of society, fully supportive of the Party's Reform.

So this "assignment" was a good thing, even if I hadn't agreed to it. Finally, we'd all see the truth.

* * *

Braxton

I knew the screams were only in my mind as I lay in my bunk. I let them bleed into my reality though, saturating my consciousness as sleep stayed locked away.

Could have been Eliza. Maybe, at some point, it had been. I hoped, if she had given up, ran for the freedom of death, as the boy yesterday had done, that she'd made it to the kill zone before she dropped.

Or that one of the guards had taken pity.

The image of the boy filled my vision behind my eyelids. We'd left him there.

"The birds and the dogs will pick him clean," a guard had told me when I asked in the mess hall that night. "Not our problem. Unless you want to drag his dead body to the Purge?"

And then I knew what the constant spew of

black smoke was at the west end of the RFC. Should have known from the start.

Another boy had turned to Henson as we scraped our full plates with forks. "Feel a surge of pity there, killer?"

Henson grinned that same evil smile he'd turned on me up in the Nest. "Nope. Just took a bet. One shot." He smirked at me. "I won."

The guard who'd asked him laughed and stuffed a piece of chocolate cake into his mouth. Not bothering to swallow first, he spoke again. "Watch out. They'll think you're soft, and you'll get stuck in the kitchen."

"Naw." Henson jammed a forkful of roast into his mouth. "They know better. And they wouldn't lose a sniper right now anyway. Not when the grid is compromised."

Chocolate cake boy scowled, eyeing me.

"Chillax," Henson said, glancing my way. "They don't send us questionables. Luther's fine."

Energy tingled in every cell of my body. The chink in the armor had just revealed itself. If I could unscramble what they'd been talking about...

"How about it, Luther?"

"What?" I forced my attention to the kid now working on his second slice of baked sugar.

"Tonight. We'll head into town."

I forced an interested expression. "Yeah? What's there?"

"Lots." Henson jabbed my arm. "Everything the people left behind."

"Isn't it toxic beyond the camp?"

Both boys laughed. "You think if it was as toxic as they'd billed we'd still be alive and eating beef raised on the very land they'd claimed was foul?"

I looked from one face to the other. Both quirked their eyebrows, as if I'd been stupid. Apparently, I had been. Right along with the rest of the country that bought that elaborate lie. Shouldn't have surprised me.

"Everyone left within twenty-four hours, taking only what they could fit into the boxes the Party had distributed," Henson said, his eyes bright with greed. "Full stores, houses still ripe with treasure, lay empty, just waiting for us to save them."

"Ah, so we're salvage masters." I tried to match his enthusiastic energy.

"Yep. Only one cost."

My stomach clenched, and the supper I'd managed to put down soured. As evil as I'd seen, I didn't want to take a stab at the price.

"Aren't you going to ask?" Henson said.

I drew a breath, desperately grasping at a veil of indifference. "Okay. What?"

Chocolate cake guy's grin grew. "There's a liquor store, fully stocked—well mostly." He stopped to laugh at an apparently inside joke. "Whatever we put in front of you, you drink. Got it?"

Alcohol? Of all the atrocities they could require of me, they wanted me to drink? Probably wasn't that simple. But maybe I could unravel it or figure a way out of it by the time we got to the ghost town. Either way, I was going. As with most things since I'd taken the seal, I didn't have a choice.

"Whatever, man." I shrugged.

First cake eater laughed, and then Henson, and the latter snarled an arm around my neck. "I knew you'd be game." He squeezed and shook me a little, like I was suddenly his little brother. "It'll be fun."

Yeah, fun. Strange how different that idea could be from person to person. In the meantime, I had some things to figure. Like how I was going to avoid getting drunk—or worse— with these guys, and what exactly they meant when they said the grid was down. That second piece was vital, which meant I absolutely had to figure out the first.

* * *

Hannah

Nothing could have prepared me to see my father again. Emotions rumbled within my soul, shifting, surging, making me feel vulnerable. Afraid.

Weak.

Honestly, a big part of me believed he was dead, and it shamed me to realize there had been a tiny bit of relief in that idea. Because if he was dead, maybe he couldn't be ashamed of my choices. He wouldn't resent me for defying him.

But there he was, very much alive, and the look he narrowed on me wasn't shame.

I felt my bottom lip tremble as my hardened heart began to melt under his warm gaze.

"Daddy," I whispered.

He stepped forward, and I didn't need any more invitation. His arms waited to surround me as I surged into his chest.

Here? Skye had brought me here—to my father? How had she known?

Arms that were stronger than they had been at the cellar, yet not what they were when I was a child, held me secure, and I heard him whisper "Thank you, Jesus" as he gathered the hair I'd bound into a ponytail.

I pulled away, looked into his eyes, still searching for condemnation. There was none.

"I thought I'd never see you again," he said,

one hand still resting at the back of my head.

I couldn't voice what'd I'd thought. Blinking back the tears I refused to set free, I glanced around the village-like community. Tents, teepees, a few sore-looking buildings peppered the area that rested in the protection of gently rising hills.

"This is Reformation Camp?" I asked, my attention wandering to Skye.

"No, sweetheart," my father answered as he stepped beside me, an arm draping over my shoulders. "This is the Refuge. You are safe here."

Confusion and resentment swirled inside me. I'd been safe where I was with the Pride. They were still delusional about everything, and I didn't want to be a part of it. And Skye...

"You're a traitor," I hissed, scowling at the girl who'd brought me.

"A Cloaked," she said, not a trace of shame in it. "And we need you."

I glared at her for a breath and then turned a look on my father. "I'm not a part of this."

"Hannah—"

"No." I stepped away, letting his arm drop away from me and to his side. "You're wrong about everything. I don't know what you want from me, but I'm not a rebel."

"You're not one of them," Skye said, her tone commanding.

"What do you know?"

"I know what I've seen in your eyes—the horror you feel when you see the dirty secrets we keep, how appalled you were at the rally. You're not one of them, and you're only holding on to this fairy tale about the goodness of the Party—a fairy tale you *know* to be untrue, because of Quinn."

"Quinn?" My father looked to me and then Skye.

Skye didn't answer him, and we all knew I wasn't going to either. Silence pushed us apart as we stood in angry confrontation.

"I told you that you had to decide—" Skye spoke low and dark.

I shook my head and cut her off with a slice of my hand through the air between us. "I told you I didn't want to come."

A flicker of fear passed through her eyes. The first I'd ever seen in her.

"I'm not part of this." I stepped into her space. "Take me back and leave me be. I don't want to be in whatever this is."

"You can't go back," Skye said.

I glared at her, and then with the strength I'd gained from the Pride, I shoved her to the ground. Skye landed on her backside, sprawled on the dirt like a helpless girl. I gripped the feeling of power, of control, that move ignited.

"You can't make me stay."

* * *

Braxton

The vacantness of the wide-open plains gave way to a fragment of human presence. Or what once had been inhabitation. The town looked like it could have held a few thousand, with perhaps more people occupying the outlying areas. As we approached the crest of the small, nearly imperceptible hill on which the community had been built, an unexpected view opened beyond.

Massive propellers littered the land, protruding into the sky. I'd seen this view scattered along the way when the LiteRail had entered the region of the Vacant Plains. Wind farms. They powered the cities on the fringe of this region, their energy collection clean. Looking at the seemingly unending scene of white tubes supporting propellers that glided through the air punctured by their height, I suddenly wondered what the people who'd lived in this little town had thought.

Probably it hadn't mattered.

"Nice view, eh?" The voice that spoke from

behind was one I hadn't expected to hear again. Ever.

I drew a steady breath and turned slowly, knowing I shouldn't give away our familiarity. I met Tristan's green eyes, holding a mask of distance in my expression. "It's interesting."

He nodded and then stepped around me, heading toward the boarded store where we'd parked our illegal vehicle.

"Well, Luther. Now you know what a real-live ghost town looks like." Henson squeezed my shoulder with a firm grip. "What do you think?"

I shrugged. "Don't know. Am I supposed to care?"

He laughed, smacked my back, and pushed me toward a smaller shop, which was also boarded up, down the cracked and heaving sidewalk. "Nope. Only that it's ours now, and we can do whatever we want."

Joining him as he walked, I arched an eyebrow and cast him a side glance. "What is it we want to do?"

Henson stopped at a door. The boards had been ripped out with a crowbar, and the glass had been shattered, which meant it was old and hadn't been replaced with the standard treated glass I'd known all my life. He reached through the hole, flipped the doorknob from the inside, and then held the entry open while I passed.

"Drink," he said, his voice lower and darker than I'd heard before. "Tonight, we drink. Because we can. No one cares."

I glanced at him but resisted the urge to study his face. He wouldn't allow me to anyway. Suddenly his back was turned, and he strode toward the shelves still heavy with every kind of alcohol one could imagine. Not even glancing at a label, he gripped the narrow neck of the largest bottle in front of him, marched to the desk where a cash register should have been, and smashed the top against the counter. The glass shattered, giving him splintered access to the liquid within. Without any apparent concern for shards lingering on the opening, he gripped a glass that had been waiting on the counter, poured the clear liquid until it rimmed the top of the shot glass, and lifted it to his mouth. He inhaled, his eyes sliding shut, and paused for a moment before he nailed a look on me.

"To not caring," Henson muttered, holding the glass up in a small salute. The moment his lips met liquid, his eyes shut again, and he threw his head back.

I watched him, stepping slowly his direction, as the four other boys—Tristan among them—reached for a shot as well. A boy with skin whiter than mine ripped the open bottle from Henson's grasp and poured his own portion before passing the bottle to the next willing hand. Around they went, the toast echoing from each mouth.

"To not caring."

Tristan filled his shot, raised his glass, and said the words. I wondered if I was the only one among us that could hear the lie in his voice.

Probably. Because I knew him. He did care.

Then again, there was a lie in every one of those toasts. I could see it. The way their jaws clenched. The way they couldn't meet the eyes of the others. The way they were more eager for the next shot than they had been for the first.

"You're up, Luther," Henson barked at me, but he didn't look my way. He was too busy pouring his second round.

I stepped forward, my gaze connecting with Tristan's. He snagged a free glass and poured, and I noticed the bottle he gripped wasn't the same one that Henson had broken into.

"Drink up," Tristan said in a low voice. "That was the deal."

I held his glance, remembering the time he'd drugged me so that I'd go to the Commons. Unease filled my stomach. I never could read him. But I knew where he stood, so I had to trust that he had a plan.

I took the glass and lifted it to my mouth. Henson's hand curled around my wrist before I could down whatever was in it.

"Say it." His voice seethed, as if I'd insulted him.

Turning my head, I caught the fire in his eyes. Fury. Hate.

Guilt.

I lifted the shot in his direction and kept my voice even. "To not caring." Down the hatch. The warm liquid was thick and sweet. My stomach curled inward, and I glanced at Tristan. His stoic mask gave nothing away, and I was certain I'd feel dizzy before the next round.

But I didn't see guilt in his eyes. Which meant that even if he'd just given me a shot of persuasion, I'd have to trust him.

I implanted that thought in the front of my mind, even as the fuzzy fade of a blackout began to creep into my consciousness.

Trust him.

By the third round, I knew I'd be out within minutes.

seventeen

Braxton

I was paralyzed, and I knew exactly why. My brain began firing reason before my body could shake the numbness and lack of coordination.

"Just sit tight, Luther."

Tristan spoke from a distance I could both hear and feel. But then again, he could have been right next to me. I couldn't discern much in the way of reality.

"Persuasion?" I mumbled, hoping I aimed my scowl in his direction.

"You know the drill."

He seemed closer.

A spot on my shoulder warmed as the tingles

shot through my arm, chasing the numbness away. I tried to push away the heat, certain it was there because Tristan's grip was on my arm.

"Easy, buddy. Just give it another minute or two."

I thrust my hand at the spot again, even as his touch became clearer to my senses. Yes, that was his hand. For some reason, he felt he needed to keep me steady.

"Why?" I spat out the word. This guy...couldn't he just tell me what was going on? Did he have to resort to drugging me every time?

"Didn't want you drunk with the rest of them. I need you to see what I'm about to show you."

"And there's a difference between this and drunk?"

"Stop whining, li'l Luther." He shook me, and then his hand moved to my elbow, and he tugged me to an upright position. "I knocked you out just long enough for the others to drink themselves stupid. They'll be wrestling with a beast of a hangover long after you've regained your senses. Just breathe deep. You're almost there."

I blinked, and my vision began to clear. Objects that had been too fuzzy to discern realigned, and the dim light of what I assumed was the gray of early dawn broke through the darkness of my mind.

We were moving. I felt it more than saw it, but every now and then a lone skeleton of a tree blipped by the window I had been leaning against.

"Are we back in the vehicle?"

"Yes."

On my left, Tristan stared ahead, his hands gripping the steering wheel.

"What about the others? Won't they get suspicious when we're gone and so is the truck?"

"I stole this one from a parking lot. They won't know the difference, nor will they care when they get back to the camp and we're already there."

"That's where we're going?"

"Eventually. We have a stop to make first."

"Is this where you reveal your dark self and I die?"

Tristan snorted a laugh. "You were always afraid of me, weren't you?"

My lips pressed together, I looked back out the window.

"Even back when life was normal, you were afraid."

"I wasn't afraid." I'd stood up to Hulk, hadn't I? Continued to play football with guys who outweighed me by an average of fifty pounds.

"You were something. Even if you didn't want

to admit it then, maybe you should face it now."

I clenched my teeth and inhaled, the reality of what was around me becoming sharper with every clean breath. But even as irritation pricked along the back of my neck, I didn't give in to the anger that lurked just behind it. Tristan had proven himself. Time and again. And truthfully, we were the same. Different in build and looks and experience, but with this—we were the same. He'd been afraid too—and I had a feeling he'd already admitted it to himself.

"I didn't know who I was." I spoke low, still facing the window on my right. "So yeah, I guess I was afraid—but it wasn't of you. I was afraid I'd never measure up. And I guess I proved to everyone that I couldn't."

The air between us rested in silence for a minute, allowing me to absorb my own confession. Did I know who I was then, sitting in that truck, heading to something unknown, followed by something awful? I knew I wasn't a loyal citizen. I knew I regretted taking the seal. I knew I'd failed Eliza in the worst possible way, and even if I ever found her, she might not ever forgive me.

But I also knew she saw greatness in me. That was the part I gripped. What if that was my real self?

I wanted, almost more than to see her again, to truly become the guy that she saw. Because then, if I didn't find her, if she was really gone, at least her hope would be validated, and that would mean something of her beautiful heart lived on.

Tristan's tight voice broke through the silence. "I was afraid everything I worked for would be stripped away."

The pause before he spoke again felt like that moment before you leap into something you were pretty sure was going to be a disaster.

"Bet you didn't know I grew up in the poor part of Glennbrooke, did you?"

Tristan Melzner? No. I didn't know that. He'd been in Career Track at school—which wasn't part of regular public enrollment. Take away the tuition, even getting into Career Track wasn't cheap. The testing fees eliminated over half of all possible students before they could even write their names down. Not to mention the required travel to the state center where the exam was given.

"How did you swing it?"

"My mom did laundry. Mended clothing. Made ready-to-bake meals. Scrubbed toilets. Whatever she could to get me into the program. She and my dad remembered the days before the Bloody Faith Conflict, when things like public education were useful, when hard work truly could overcome obstacles. She said it didn't have to be different now. If the obstacle was money, she'd figure out a way around it. They wanted us—Aniah and me—to have a chance to regain the life that they'd lost. When the Party took over, demanding our allegiance or more of our dreams would be stripped, fear began to settle. Then when Hulk..."

His speech broke, leaving his story open and raw, like that jagged edge on the bottleneck Henson had shattered the night before.

"Aniah." I filled in where he left off. "When he threatened Aniah, fear took over."

Light began to chase away the gray covering of dawn, and as the sun spilled a yellow glow over the Vacant Plains, I glanced back at Tristan. His jaw jumped, and emotion—regret and pain—passed over his expression. His Adam's apple dipped, and then he looked back at me.

"We can't be afraid anymore. I know who I am now—and I'm willing to bet you've figured out who you are too. Where we're going—what I'm going to show you—demands that we both move past the fear." The car slowed and came to a stop. His knuckles paled around the wheel. "So I need to know, Braxton. Do you know who you are?"

"I'm here, and I'm ready." I nodded, glancing

over the empty land. "I've been a sellout and a coward. But not anymore. I will stand, even if I have to stand alone."

"Good news, Luther. You won't have to stand alone." Tristan shifted back into drive, and the vehicle moved forward again. "But you're going to need every scrap of courage you can gather. We've entered the Umbrella of the Refuge—the government can't track us right now. And there's a plan coming together."

"A plan?" I leaned forward, shifting so I could face him better. "What kind of plan?"

"To release the captives. And tell the truth." Tristan glanced at me, his eyebrows raised in both challenge and hope. "It's time the American people knew—saw for themselves—what we know and see. We're going to tear the veil."

My pulse climbed. Tearing the veil of the Party's lies...that could change everything. But that was a big gamble, because trying could cost us everything. Failing could cast the country into thicker blackness. Which meant the cost was worth it—and we couldn't fail.

Ahead, the land began to change. Flat plains rose up. Trees, green even against the winter chill, dotted the camel-colored hills and contrasted sharply with the skeletons of deciduous trees already in their winter slumber. The road bent in an S curve and took us into the folds of the rounded hills, and we entered into the shadows cast by the rise. Though the sunlight was blocked and the landscape felt unfamiliar, a sense of safety drifted over me.

"This is part of the Refuge? The one Evan was taking the group to?"

"It is." Tristan guided the truck around another curve.

"Did they make it?"

"Yes. Evan is here."

"And Jayla?"

"Jayla made it, but she isn't well. Pneumonia again."

"Do they have supplies, something to take care of her?"

"Limited. And Evan has given her what he can. But she has been weak ever since the fire. It doesn't look good."

That bad news weighed down the rise of hope I felt building. All was not well, even if they were safe—for the moment—from the Party.

"What's the plan?" I asked, not wanting to focus on the negative.

"It's not mine to tell. Jude, when you meet him, will tell you what you need to know, what you'll need to do."

"Wait. I have an assignment already?"

Tristan set a look of challenge on me again.

"You said you were in."

"How did this Jude guy know I would be?"

As he faced the road again, Tristan's jaw locked. "This is bigger than you're imagining right now, Luther, and it's been set in motion long before you left Glennbrooke. In fact, it's the reason you're here."

The reason I was there—in the Vacant Plains—was because I'd been reassigned. Jed Stevens had sent—

Oh.

It was like the tumblers on a lock suddenly clicked into place, and I understood.

"Jed is part of this?"

"Yes."

I thought back to the night Tristan disappeared. "He sent you away before Hulk could accuse you."

"Right again," he said. "And I was able to find what they needed me to find."

A thrill surged through my veins. This was real. This was happening. "Which is?"

"The gap in the RFC security system. If we can release the captives, the rest of the plan can move forward."

"Then why haven't you done it?"

Tristan glanced at me, his look meaningful. "We can't without you."

"Me? Why me? I mean nothing to anyone."

"No. You mean quite a lot to Hannah Knight. And she has become the key to our success."

Hope plummeted, landing somewhere under the treads of my boots. I couldn't see how Hannah would be a part of any of this, but if what Tristan was saying was true, I'd already failed.

Hannah Knight was with the Pride. And that was where she'd chosen to stay.

* * *

Hannah

"We can't afford to send you back, Hannah."

In the semidarkness of a windowless room, I glared at the man—what was left of a man—strapped to the chair, his mechanized voice causing the hairs on the back of my neck to rise.

I inhaled, the dank smell of earth fueling my anger. I didn't want this life again. "I didn't ask to come."

"I'm aware of that. But we took a chance, and now you're here. We can't send you back."

"You can't keep me either."

The man's head, which leaned awkwardly against a padded board jutting up from his chair, shifted ever so slightly in a nod. "No, I cannot. But should you leave, you'll be on your own in the Vacant Plains. We cannot offer assistance."

"I don't need your help." I spat my declaration,

but as soon as the words dropped from my mouth, I knew that wasn't true. I had no idea where I was, and from what I could see, there was nothing beyond this village, this Refuge.

"Hannah..." His deep voice trailed off, and though I expected anger to drift in his expression, it was not there. Instead, my name from his mouth and the look in his eyes seemed to wrap me in warmth—an invitation, a calling that reached deep inside of me for reasons I couldn't understand.

I fought against the temptation to soften. "No. Come morning, I'm gone. You'll have to find someone else to do whatever it was you thought I would do."

He studied me, sadness in his careful examination.

The silent rebuke shook me all the way through.

eighteen

Braxton

The Refuge didn't look like much. A small village at best, centered around a large barn, originally intended for horses or cattle or other agriculture-related things. Deeper in the valley, a relic farmhouse, probably dating back to the early-nineteen hundreds, and a peppering of other buildings, the largest made of metal, were scattered throughout the wide opening between the rolling hills. Between the buildings were makeshift shelters—tents in the style of Native Americans. In the distance, behind the house and barn, a bluff peeked between two humps of land.

I scanned the valley, grasping at that sense of security that had seeped into me when we'd first entered the hill region. Trees, both evergreen and skeletal deciduous varieties, climbed the gentle slopes that enveloped the hidden community. I traced the hillside up to where the rise brushed the sky overhead. Not mountains— I remembered the mountains of the Pacific Northwest from my childhood. Those were imposing, white-capped, and often the peaks were lost to the clouds that drifted high above the fertile valleys. These hills were not so grand, but they were soft and comforting just the same. In their folds, the Refuge was protected from wind and exposure, and it was easy to imagine the hills cradling this little community of outcasts, like a pair of gentle hands scooping up a handful of terrified newborn chicks.

Tipping my head back, I let my inspection travel the length of freshly hued blue sky, given new vibrancy by the continuing rise of the sun. Staring into the unsearchable depth of sky, I wondered what the Umbrella was, how it protected the people, and how far it stretched to keep them out of the government's eye.

"Jude's waiting." Tristan bumped my shoulder, having decided, apparently, that I'd inspected the Refuge long enough. "Let's go. We've got to get back before midmorning.

Before the other boys make it back from the ghost town."

Always on a mission. But now, this mission mattered. I wanted to be a part of it. Nodding, I fell into step behind him, and he led the way through the sprinkling of tents to a metal building that I hadn't seen from the truck. Tucked behind the bulge of a hill, I found, as we rounded the corner, that it was actually built into the rise, its roof disappearing beneath the skirt of dirt and roots.

I paused at the metal door, which Tristan had tugged open, searching the inside. Darkness stared back at me, its blackness the opposite of inviting. A flashback of the hose factory oozed through my mind, and I remembered the cold brush of fear I felt the first day I'd gone into the bowels of that building in search of my father. A shiver traced down my spine as the memory played out.

"It's fine. They just don't have enough electricity to run all of the lights. There will be light where we're going."

Light. That seemed to be what we were in search of. The reason we sought Jude. The hope of tearing the veil. We would break the darkness with light. Because darkness hid what we did not want to see, but light would bring truth to the darkness, chasing away the fear.

Or it would simply show us what we didn't know we needed to be afraid of.

Another shiver rippled down my back. *Courage. Grip courage. Be the man Eliza believed you to be.*

Tristan stepped forward, and I found the will to follow him in. After five steps, he paused, and not seeing his delay, I ran into the side of his bulky shoulder. Before I could step back, the white light of an LED bulb crowded away the darkness, and I could see. Hard-packed dirt under my feet. Steel beams supporting the metal sheeting and roof.

Tristan walked, his path illuminated. "This building goes deep into the hill. It was where he originally set up his equipment. He maintains the Umbrella from a room in the back."

"What exactly does the Umbrella do?"

The long, narrow hall continued, and Tristan led me through it. "It blocks the satellites and any other technology that can be operated overhead. Somehow Jude rigged an image—a hologram or something—so that all the government sees is the emptiness of the Vacant Plains. He's blocked their vision of this place for years—since the Bloody Faith Conflict. They've forgotten that these hills even exist."

We reached another metal door, this one with

both a doorknob and a deadbolt lock. The hairs prickled along my neck as I remembered opening another metal door within a steel building. I tried pushing away the memory, but the pain needled in my heart.

I thought I'd rescued my dad that day. He'd died anyway. If he'd known about this place, would he have—

"Look—Jude isn't like anyone you've met before. He looks...different. Talks different."

Turning to face Tristan, I was both thankful for his distraction and curious as to why he would think I needed warned.

"Remember you said you were in, okay?"

"Okay..."

Tristan barely waited for me to agree. He knocked on the windowless steel in front of us, the three raps sounding suspiciously like the clicking pattern Eliza and I used in the forest.

"Is that—"

Tristan flashed me a grin. "See, you've been useful for longer than you thought."

So it was. Pirates. Thinking about Jude snatching my wordless "code" teased a small grin to the corners of my mouth. I liked being useful there.

The door clicked and then opened, and a deep, computerized voice filled the vaulted space of the large room we'd just entered.

"Welcome, Mr. Luther."

Tristan stopped in front of me, and I stepped around him, searching for the source of the unnatural speech. A man—maybe fiftyish—sat in a wheeled chair. *Man* was generous; he seemed to be half a man. The space where his legs should have filled the chair was empty. His torso was misshapen, bent where it should have been straight, so that he sat at a strange angle, his head requiring support in order to stay upright. Only one arm extended from his body, and he kept that covered with a long black sleeve and a matching glove. His face...

Did not look human. Scars covered what should have been his cheeks, chin, forehead, and nose. Rippled flesh that looked like it had been melted and re-formed. He shifted, pressing his neck—his vocal cords—to a spot on his head support.

"I am human—I promise." That mechanical voice spoke again. "And though my shell is not pretty, my brain works just fine."

I fought against the urge to stare at the abnormalness of his body and face and found his eyes beneath the browless pucker of stretched flesh.

Yes. Human indeed. Kind, deep intelligence met my gaze, and he seemed to measure my humanity as I measured his.

"What happened to you?"

My mother would have given me that scolding, I-raised-you-better-than-that look for asking. Still with the mismanaged tongue. Guess growing up some didn't change everything.

Jude's eyes glimmered a hint of a smile, communicating that he wasn't offended by my blunt rudeness. "A story for another day. Today has only room for what we need to prepare. It is time to lift the strangle of power. Are you in?"

I finally let my eyes roam away from his face, taking in the vault where he worked and kept himself hidden. A row of five screens sat on the table in the center of the room, a miniature com station like those on sophisticated ships I'd seen in movies. The faces of the screens were tipped downward, kept at an angle that allowed Jude to see easily, but I could not make out the grainy images and letters on each. Wires, braided and multicolored—blue, red, green, white, and brown—ran across the floor and rose like a vine up the opposite wall until they finally disappeared through the darkness of the ceiling.

"You did all this?" I asked.

"I imagined it," Jude said. "My father built it."

"Why?"

"Another story not meant for this day." Jude's

eyes shifted away from me toward Tristan.

"You have assurance?"

"I do. He's in."

With an almost imperceptible nod, Jude accepted Tristan's word, and that was that. I was in. Whatever this was, I was now a part of it.

Or, judging by that knock, I'd been a part of it longer than I'd been a part of the Party. There was an odd sense of rightness and comfort about that.

"This will be short and sweet." With the movement of one finger, Jude directed the mechanical workings of his wheelchair, moving himself to the dock of screens in the middle of the room. "You and Tristan will plant these blockers on the watchtowers back at the camp."

I glanced to Tristan to gauge his reaction. By the unflinching mask settled there, I guessed he'd already known this.

"Why didn't Tristan do this himself?"

"We weren't ready yet. Not all the pieces were in place."

"And they are now?"

"Nearly. But I do have something for you, Mr. Luther. An assignment only you can complete." Jude's eyes moved back to Tristan, and then his head gave a slight tip again, this time to the door where we'd entered.

Tristan nodded, moving to go to the door, and

then paused. "They both made it?"

"Indeed. Though one not as willing as we'd hoped."

"I warned you about that."

Jude's mouth stretched, and the thin skin looked painful under the demands of his small grin. "We have Luther now. She'll understand."

My heart stuttered and then surged. *Eliza. Oh, let it please be...*

Tristan moved back to the door and disappeared into the hall again. Moments later, footfalls scuffled in from the darkness beyond, and then Tristan reemerged, followed by two girls.

I couldn't fight the plummet of my heart. Though familiar, neither face belonged to the girl I loved.

But both wore the uniform of the Pride.

"Braxton Luther." The shorter of the two stepped forward, her thick dark hair bound back at the base of her head, and her eyes snapping with furry. Looking nothing like her gentle sister.

"Hello, Hannah." I spoke in monotone, desperate to cover my deep disappointment and total shock. "I'm glad you're safe."

"I was safe back home," she snapped, flashing a glare at Skye, who stood by her side. "I told you

I didn't want to come with you."

"I didn't do this, Hannah."

"Right. And it's not your fault Eliza is gone either."

Heat flooded my body, followed by an ache so strong I wanted to curl up in a dark corner and cry. Because that arrow was right on point. Setting my jaw, I looked away from her angry face, catching the glance that passed between Jude and Tristan.

Neither of them saw this coming. If they'd figured I'd have influence over Hannah, they had badly miscalculated. And whatever they had planned clearly required her cooperation.

Which meant my role in whatever this was, was sliding rapidly toward failure.

nineteen

Hannah

I'd kill him.

I'd known every second since Skye had tricked me, taking me away from my only chance to ever see Quinn again, that Braxton had been behind the whole plan.

Now, proof stood in front of me, devilishly disguising his part in my unwilling participation in this with a mask of shock at seeing me. I didn't buy it.

"Wipe the fake surprise off your face, Luther." Folding my arms over my chest, I stepped forward, my muscles tight, ready for a fight. "I know you were in this."

"What?" He almost snarled as his eyebrows came to a *V*. "I didn't know you were here. I didn't even know here existed." Eying me, his expression eased. "But I'm glad. I had nothing to do with any of this, but I'm glad to see you're safe. Eliza will—"

"Eliza's dead." I moved forward again. "And I'm not interested in swimming in her wake. Tell them to send me back."

Braxton's face flooded with a deep shade of red. Anger or shame, I wasn't sure which, but I didn't care either. Everyone in this room deserved to know what he was—a fake. Sellout. Poser. And once they realized that, they'd ditch whatever stupid plan he had cooking and let me go back.

"Mr. Luther is telling the truth." The man in the chair spoke as he wheeled toward the place Braxton and I were facing off. "As Skye has already explained to you. We are not in the business of lying around here. Quite the opposite, in fact."

I didn't look at him—I couldn't. I'd never seen anyone like him, so misformed and damaged, and having him speak to me in that unhuman voice sparked my nerves. Plus, I couldn't remove that sense of calling and purpose that our conversation the night before had beckoned, no matter how strange this man was.

Eliza would have been moved with pity or compassion or whatever she called it, treated Jude with utmost respect—starting by looking at him as though he were, in fact, human—and then she would have listened.

Yet another example—I was not my sister. And at that moment, I didn't care one speck of dirt that I didn't measure up to her by half. I'd found where I belonged, and though it wasn't with the Pride, it definitely wasn't in this hole in the ground either.

I'd lived enough in a dirt pit of the earth to last me a lifetime. That was the reason I'd left the cellar in the first place. I belonged with Quinn, and I'd fight my way back.

"I don't care what this is. I don't want in." I scowled at Braxton. "Send me back."

"Hannah, be reason—"

"No." I felt my voice grind hard in my throat. "I've been stuck here long enough. Every day I'm gone is a possible day that Quinn comes back, and I might miss him. I'm not losing him for you or for anyone else."

Braxton drew back, his face turning quizzical. "Quinn?"

Snap. Too much information. Braxton's attention slid off of me, landed on a spot over my shoulder, and held.

Skye spoke from behind me. "Sanger. Quinn Sanger."

Recognition sparked in his eyes, and one eyebrow dug into his forehead. "How do you know Quinn Sanger?"

As I turned so that I could see both Braxton and Skye, as well as Tristan, who stood beside Skye, my attention bounced from Braxton to her and back again. "What does that matter? How do you know him?"

"I don't." His voice bit hard. "Just *of* him." He stalked toward me and didn't stop when he stepped into my space.

His intrusion was unexpected, and I drew away on instinct, stepping backward until I bumped into the cold hard-packed dirt of the wall behind me. The impact jolted and triggered the training I'd been in for the past few weeks. I drew up straight. Though my forehead barely reached his chin, I frowned right back at him.

"Don't think I'm afraid of you."

He didn't move, though his jaw jumped. "I expect an answer."

"You're not gonna get one," I said, matching his low tone.

"She stayed with them." Skye's voice interrupted the tense argument sparking between us. "Before she joined the Pride."

"Stayed?" Braxton's brown eyes seemed

almost black as he stared hard at me. "For how long?"

I pressed my lips tight, refusing to flinch, though my stomach got warm and queasy. I didn't know what he thought he knew about the Sangers, but clearly he didn't think highly of them, and I knew exactly what he would think if he found out that I'd—

"Three months."

I'd kill Skye too. Right after Braxton.

His nostrils flared, and rage took a wild flight through his dark eyes. "You lived with him?"

"Let me go. You know nothing about him— and you don't know anything about what—"

Suddenly two iron hands gripped my upper arms, and I was pinned against the wall. "You lived with a man—with *Quinn Sanger*—instead of going to safety with your parents?"

"Luther—"

I took advantage of the distraction Tristan provided, kicking my boot into Braxton's shin and shoving my shoulder deep into his chest when he folded in pain.

"I told you to let go, Braxton." When his grip loosened, I ripped my right arm away and threw a fist toward his face.

His caught the punch before I could land it, twisted my arm backward, turning me in the process, and pushed me back into the wall. I inhaled fiercely, the smell of cold earth and roots filling my nose as the grainy surface of the wall pressed into my cheek.

"Stay out of gripping range when you take on someone bigger, Hannah." Braxton's hot breath tapped my ear as he bit out the words near my face. "Didn't they teach you that in the Pride?"

"Get off, Luther!" I wiggled against the earth at my face, trying to force his heavy body away.

Braxton leaned in harder. "You just don't learn, do you? I told you to stay in the forest. You ignored me and went into town. I told you to keep away from the Pride. Next thing I know, you're wearing their uniform. Clearly you didn't pay attention during your combat training, or you'd know to use your emotions to your benefit, not allow them to give your enemy the upper hand."

His grip tightened, firing a stream of pain through my fingers and up my arm, and then suddenly I was free, and he stepped away. My heart throbbed with seething rage, and I turned to dig a hot stare into his eyes.

"Don't ever—"

"Or what?"

Words evaporated from my mind. Because he was right. If he'd wanted to hurt me, I'd been pinned helpless because I reacted with stupidity.

"We done, children?" Skye stepped toward the growing distance between us.

I turned my glare on her. She simply raised an eyebrow as if to say, *Don't do anything else dumb.*

"Why is she here?" Braxton's gaze didn't leave my face, nor did the scorn lift from his voice.

Maybe it was just heat, not scorn. But it felt like scorn.

"You don't think I can do anything, do you?"

"I don't know why you're a part of this. I don't know why you didn't come here with your parents, rather than getting involved in something this ugly. And I still don't understand what the heck you were doing with *Charlotte Sanger's* son."

"Enough." The computerized voice undercut our reigniting fight. "She has become an asset. One we need—more than you can imagine. If she agrees."

I turned a fierce look to the lump of flesh in the chair. "To what?"

"To go back to Quinn. To show him the truth."

Inhaling, I drew back as if cold water had just splashed my face. He'd send me back to Quinn? Why hadn't Skye said that in the first place?

"No." Slashing the air with his hand, Braxton stepped in the space between me and Jude. "She had no business being with him in the first place."

"It is necessary."

The hair on my head began to prickle as I sensed a trap. I didn't mind being the bait, but luring Quinn into whatever they were scheming wasn't okay with me. "Why? What are you planning?"

"To tear the veil. Tell the truth. And I need you—and Quinn Sanger—to do it."

"What truth?"

"The people need to see the darkness that the Party is hiding. We need to show them what things are really happening."

My eyebrows drew in tight, and I stared at the eyes peering at me from the stretched skin of his face. He didn't flinch, but I wasn't playing whatever game he had planned.

"I don't know what you're talking about. The Uncloaked—*you*—have been feeding me fearful lies since the election almost three years ago. You're spreading hate where there shouldn't be, and I'm not going to be your pawn."

Tristan moved, stepping to Braxton's side. "Hannah, what you think you know isn't the truth." Looking to the floor, he paused and then refocused on me. "We all bought it. But—"

Shaking my head, I stepped forward, interrupting his attempt at manipulation. "I've lived in their home. They're not the monsters you clearly think they are. And all the gloom and doom I heard about in the forest? None of it was true."

"Why do you think we're all here?" This time Skye moved in, impatience punctuating her voice. "All the combat training? The Commons? Nothing of it made you feel...sick?"

"She didn't see the worst of the Commons." Braxton shook his head, folding his arms. "She's stubborn—maybe more than any of us. She's not going to listen. The only way to make her believe is to show her."

The three Cloaked traitors fell silent, and the air in the room felt tight. Slowly, the man in the wheelchair bobbed his head, even while resting it at that weird angle.

"This is so. I can see it." He moved his hand against the armrest, and the chair moved toward me. "This makes things complicated. But it is still doable." With only his eyes, he shifted his attention from me to Tristan. "You will take her back with you. Make sure she sees before you plant the coins. Make sure she sees it all."

Tristan shook his head. "She's not approved. I can't get her in."

"Skye is. We'll make it work." Jude lifted his head, his eyes connecting with each of the three across from me in some grave message. "We have to."

When that serious look met my eyes, I felt the tug of his desperation. Even in the layers of anger and resentment I kept over my conscience, I felt it.

But I still didn't want to be a part of this. Not if it meant betraying Quinn. It'd take the gates of hell opening under my feet to change my mind.

* * *

Braxton

I knew that stubborn jut of her jaw. Eliza did it too. Except when Eliza did it, I knew in my gut that I should listen. With Hannah...well, it just made me mad.

And guilty. Because with Hannah, it was like looking into a mirror, seeing myself three years before, being stupidly stubborn about things I refused to comprehend.

But she was about to comprehend. Like lightning firing dead center on a tree, Hannah was about to get jolted into reality, and I felt awful about that. Seeing what was really happening behind the carefully monitored news stories and the prettily arranged faces of "compassion" and "hope" of the Party—of which Charlotte and Quinn Sanger were often front and center—seeing the darkness behind the mask still turned hot nausea in my stomach. I didn't want Hannah to see it firsthand, which was why I'd protected her at the Commons.

I couldn't protect her at the RFC. Her soul would be exposed to the worst of humanity, the blackness of the most depraved hearts. It would feel like fire consuming her from the inside out, like suffocating in a cloud of heavy black smoke, and like being held, facedown, in a pool of thick ink. Everything would hurt, and the worst was that those things could not be unseen. Unknown. Not ever.

The thrust of darkness would forever leave a pitted mark on my soul. And now Hannah's. We were about to push her into a lifetime of nightmarish memories.

Thirty minutes after we left the shelter of the hills and the road straightened to arrow-like uniformity, Tristan directed the truck toward the relic of a hangar where World War II aircraft had once upon another unhappy time been kept on this vast inland sea of dirt and wind. Three other hangars, all smaller, were behind that large one, but they were a part of the prisoners' camp and not currently our destination. Guards assigned to RFC stayed in this larger shelter. Bunks lined one long side of the dirt-packed floor within, and the other side was littered with tables set up for cards, eating, and whatever anyone else did with their limited spare time. I didn't know what that would be. I spent mine with my eyes shut, desperately trying to scrub my mind of the images I looked upon every day from the Nest where I'd been assigned. And begging God for forgiveness.

Tristan set the parking brake and turned the key to kill the engine, but neither of us made a move to get out of the truck. Stuck between us, Hannah cut a glare at me and then him.

"Well, show me already," she said, her tone biting.

Above her head, I connected with Tristan's eyes. Yeah, same. Neither of us really wanted for her to see.

"Look, Hannah," I said, reaching for her hand.

She ripped it away. "Don't act all sweet, Luther. I know where I stand with you—where I've always stood. Just get this over with. And then send me home, because I'm not changing my mind. I'm not helping you."

Tristan tipped forward, leaning toward her. "You don't get this now, Knight, but you're blind. Right now, we just need to know you're with us on this part. If you rat us out..."

"I'm not going to."

"But you have to remember—"

"I'm Skye, not Hannah. I was sent here on guard rotation. It's an honor only given to the most brutal of the Pride and Den." She stopped, twisted her mouth, and gave me a dumb look. "Which sounds like a load of crap right off the bat. Why would they send you here if that were true?"

Stevens, that was why. But she didn't need to know the details. Right now this was risky enough. If Hannah turned on us, our lives were gone. But we could be replaced. Jed was in a unique and powerful position, and we needed him there.

"One thing at a time," I answered. "Just don't screw up, okay, Knight?"

Her silent glare said *you're one to talk,* which singed guilt deep down.

Tristan popped his door open, and I followed his lead, letting Hannah out before I shut the door. The three of us strode toward the side entry of the hangar, and as we neared, the group of boys we'd gone to town with the night before streamed out.

Henson stepped in front of the group, folding his arms like a scolding parent. "Where have you been?"

Tristan met his posture with a mirrored version of his own. "Picking up a transfer. Like we'd been told."

"Who told you?"

The well-built linebacker I remembered from high school stepped forward, dwarfing the pompous Henson, who struggled against his instinct to wilt. A flash of Tristan towering over Kipper Elliot back in econ class pushed a surge of resentment in my chest.

He was trying to protect his sister...

For a moment I shut my eyes, purposely replacing that memory with the one of him protecting Miranda, confessing to me what had happened to Aniah. The image eased the surge of anger, but didn't dry it up.

None of us were getting through this without scars. Deep, ugly, painful pits of regret. And somehow we were going to have to find a way to forgive. Each other. Every one of us.

I was pretty sure I needed it most.

twenty

Hannah

Skye. I'm Skye today.

I kept my chin held up and my expression blank as I watched Tristan intimidate whoever this other boy was.

"Transfer?" The shorter guy tried to disguise the crack in his voice with an exaggerated frown and a rough clearing of his throat. "I knew nothing about this. And a girl? Why would they send us another girl? They don't do well here."

Tristan leaned forward, forcing the mouthy guy to nearly cower. "You were drunk, so who knows what you remember or don't remember. I've got my orders, and I don't report to you, so get out of my way."

Who did we report to? At the moment, it didn't matter. I had to prove myself. I stepped between Tristan and Braxton, careful to keep my posture tight and to stay just out of reach, like Braxton had reminded me to.

"What do you mean another girl?"

Little Man set his glare on me. "I mean just what I said. There's a reason you only see boys here."

"Yeah, what's that?"

"Girls can't stomach the job."

I flicked an eyebrow. "Clearly you've never heard of me."

Tristan and Braxton stood mannequin still on either side of me while Little Man eyed them before returning his attention to me. "Fine. We'll see, killer. And actually, Melzner, you do report to me today. Commander Azah is off site. So that means I give the shift assignments." A smirk carved his mouth as he looked at each one of us. "You two are up in the Nests. Killer here can suit up. Quarantine duty for you, tough girl."

Neither boy at my side moved. Little Man held one last smug look on us and then pivoted to march away, his little crew of uniformed followers trailing close behind.

"Nice, Hannah," Braxton muttered.

"Skye. Here, I'm Skye."

"Fine. Skye. You've just landed yourself the worst possible job. Not to mention, Henson now hates you. So congratulations on that."

"It might be okay, Luther." Tristan turned to face us both. "It might be helpful. She can get a few coins into the Quarantine. And she'll be able to tell us what we're dealing with in there."

"Wait. You don't know what's in there?" Dread tugged hard in my stomach.

"All we know is that when they say suit up, they're talking about hazmat suits. The full deal." Braxton paused, and a muscle on his jaw jumped. "And sometimes the guards that go in don't come back out."

"Why?"

"They get infected."

"With what?"

"Whatever is quarantined in there. As of right now, there isn't a cure." Again, Braxton stopped, but his look said more than his words.

I'd pretty much written my own death sentence.

Tristan looked around the area, checking for others before he moved toward me. His hand rested on my shoulder and then squeezed. "Just be careful, and get back out, okay? We need you, so do what you need to do to stay safe." He grazed the area with another inspection and then moved to take my hand with his free one. Something round and cool pressed into my palm. "Find places that won't be noticed. In blankets. On the ground, covered with dirt. Somewhere that won't be suspicious, even if they're found."

Without another word, Tristan dropped both hands and stepped away, leaving me with Braxton. I fingered the coins, which felt like quarters—which would be strange, as we used currency on our All-In-One, but maybe out here in the middle of nowhere, I could spin a story if I needed to.

I felt Braxton's gaze pinned on me and pushed away the small ball of warmth in my chest his notice provoked.

"What?" I snapped, lifting my chin so that I could meet his stare directly.

"Be careful."

"You already said that."

"Hannah, I'm not sure you know this..." He closed the space between us by half a step. "But I do care about you. You do matter. I get mad at you because I'm worried. And because I know what you're thinking—you're too much like me."

A year before I would have melted into a puddle right there on that naked, cold plain. But now? I wasn't that idiotic girl with a stupid crush anymore. "You don't know anything about what I think, Braxton. And don't lie to me. I was nothing more than Eliza's weird little sister to you. Don't make this something it's not."

He scowled. "I'm not making it more than it is. Yeah, you're Eliza's sister, and I worry about you. Is that so bad?"

I bit the inside of my cheek. The expected resentment at his reference to Eliza didn't burn. Why had I expected it to? Maybe all this time, I'd been looking for something that simply wasn't mine to have. Braxton loved my sister. That hadn't changed even without her around. What if, all those months ago, I'd been happy for them instead of jealous of her?

A crack of gunfire ripped through the air, jolting me out of my wondering and making me jump. Beside me, I felt Braxton tense and watched his face as he surveyed the area. When he looked back at me, apparently satisfied that we weren't in any danger, his eyes had darkened. Not with anger, but with sorrow.

He knew what happened. I wanted to ask, but I wasn't sure I really wanted to know. Chances were I was going to find out in the near future anyway. That strong fist of dread curled inside me again, warning that there was a very real possibility that Tristan and Braxton and Skye had been right. Whatever I was about to see was awful, and I should have listened to them.

* * *

I'd had nightmares that were nicer.

Now I was doomed to have nightmares that looked just like this. For the rest of my life. And I'd never be able to tell myself that it was just a dream, because it wasn't.

Sweat trickled down my back and beaded on my legs and arms. Inside the hazmat suit, my body heat was trapped, cloaking me in a prison of my own horror. Every breath I took was a fight against panic, and more often than not, I swallowed back bile.

The walk across the camp outside had been surreal. The smells of wood fire, filthy bodies, and human waste had grown thick and pungent as we neared the larger of the three hangars on the prisoner side. In the distance, beyond the large hangar they were calling the Quarantine, a fist of charcoal smoke rose deep into the blue sky, leaving its dark imprint in my imagination. My gut told me what that place was, but I refused to accept that unimaginable idea as truth.

I wondered out loud why the people stayed when there wasn't a barrier to keep them in. The boy who had challenged Tristan—Henson was his name—released a vile sort of laugh from his snarled lips.

"Oh, there's a fence," he said. "And it doesn't fail."

He nodded toward the eastern "border" of the camp, where two towers sat parallel, one to the north and one to the south. On the ground, sprawled out unnaturally, was a body.

I remember the gunshot from earlier. "What if one sneaks out and you don't see them?"

"We only shoot out of pity. Or boredom. Otherwise the electricity gets 'em. It takes longer and is a whole lot noisier. But it gets the job done. They know it too. They only run to die."

Inside my chest, I had felt my soul shrink into a curled-up ball of terror, like it had at the rally. I had wanted to hide. To crawl into a dark hole and cry.

That was hours before I'd even put the suit on. Now, inside the Quarantine, surrounded with intense suffering and hopelessness, I knew hiding wouldn't be enough. This was inescapable.

Men, women, boys, girls. All ages, skin colors. The disease was indiscriminate. Tiny bumps, about the size of mosquito bites, covered their faces, their necks, their arms. Some were infected with such a thick coating that their closed eyes were puffy, riddled with the small bumps. Many had scratched them open, and puss oozed thick and bloody yellow over their skin. Near the front of the room lay the milder cases—probably those who hadn't progressed as far yet. The infected bodies became worse as I walked toward the back, some of them entirely covered with the painful sores. Children cried inconsolably, and some of the adults muffled their own sobs, filling the steel vault with the haunted choir of the suffering, the dying, and the tortured.

"What is it?" I asked the boy who'd been assigned Quarantine duty with me.

"Don't know," he said. "Just know that I don't want it. Don't let them touch you. And no matter how hot you get, don't take the suit off. Don't expose even just a little skin."

I didn't want to look at their faces while I passed out small tins of water, carefully keeping my distance as I placed the cups on the dirt beside them. But I couldn't help looking. As if their misery demanded that I see. Some of the eyes that stared at me through the swelling pocks of their eyelids were vacant, as if they really didn't see me at all. Some silently begged me for mercy. Some burned into me their unrelenting pain.

"Please," one woman rasped. She was near the middle of the room, and she didn't turn to me when she spoke. "I can't see, and I'm so thirsty. Please help me drink."

My hands shook as I considered the gravity of her request. *Don't let them touch you...* I'd have to touch her if I were to help. I didn't want to get sick. This plague, whatever it was, was beyond awful, and I couldn't stomach looking at it, let alone thinking about getting sick with it myself.

"Please..." she begged again.

"It's okay, Alda." The whispered voice spoke from a few places down. I followed the sound and saw a girl about my size roll to her side and push herself up into a crawling position. Every movement looked like agony as she picked her way over sick bodies and dirt, making her way to the blind woman. "It's okay," the girl gasped again. "I'll help you."

My throat swelled, and the burn of bile filled my chest again. This time from shame. Shaking so bad that the water sloshed over the edge of the cup, I reached to hand the girl a drink for the woman. She didn't look at me, but I studied her.

Her head had been shaved like the other prisoners. I didn't know why. The bumps covered her scalp and neck, and her labored breathing said that she felt just as awful as anyone lying sick on that cold dirt floor. But she lifted the blind woman's head, bringing the tin cup to her lips with a gentle touch.

I knew a girl with that kind of heart. Her goodness made me feel black in comparison, much as this girl's actions did right then.

"She drank it all," the girl whispered to me. "Please, can she have more?"

"I...I'm not suppos..." I couldn't finish, and the plastic screen separating me from them fogged over.

"She can have mine. Please?" She looked up at me, and in the dimness of the room, I made out the color of her eyes.

Brown. Just like mine.

The world shattered around me, and the violent tremble that overtook me sent all of the water cups crashing to the floor. I couldn't breathe. The only thought I could make out was a silent scream to heaven.

NO!

I saw what I'd become. Reflected right there, in my sister's eyes.

twenty-one

Braxton

"Another boring day at the RFC." Ashton, my partner for the day, stepped off his route on the opposite side of our twelve-by-twelve-foot landing.

I kept my voice neutral. "Yeah. The life."

"Ever miss the Den?"

Not even a little bit, though I wished with nearly every thought that I wasn't at the RFC either. I shrugged. "One job's as good as another, I guess."

Ashton glanced at me. "At least there were people there. Girls. Although..." He looked across the wasteland below us, an ugly mask of lust slathering his face. Quickly, however, the look contorted into disgust. "Wish they didn't shave their heads. They're so ugly."

My chest clamped like a fist of iron. I was sure every girl down there wished the Party hadn't stripped her of every last shred of dignity and identity too. And ugly? How could this guy live with himself?

"Why do you think they're so stubborn?"

Apparently, my partner was chatty. *Because they know who they are and who they're not willing to become.* Again I shrugged, forcing the words of defense to stay safely on my tongue.

The Nests gave me a full view of the camp—the aimless wandering of those we were guarding. Dirty, hungry, cold, and tired, they moved about the grounds slowly, shoulders slumped. Their thin clothes hung off the sharp angles of their bony shoulders and gaunt hips, their faces shallow, lips cracked, eyes dull and cast toward the ground. Unless they were assigned field work, every day was just another day lived without purpose or hope. Given just enough to survive, the only hint of flavor in their bland existence was the astringent fear that kept them locked where they were. Exactly as the Party designed, with the ever carrot-on-a-stick dangling in their sorry lives—a small shelter in the corner of the camp, built with modern-style and conveniences, such as warm water and toilets, and branded with the taunting invitation.

Yield and be saved.

It looked like a satanic twist on true salvation, only rather than turning to God, this required denying Him entirely.

Check a box...get on with your life.

Looking over the desperate, ugly scene, I wondered how I truly believed that ignorant idea. Yet I knew for certain, so many did just that: believed they could go with whatever and all would be fine.

This was not fine, and I had the responsibility to show it.

The chill of metal, round and small, seeped into my skin beneath the material of my gloves. These coins—nine in total between Tristan, Hannah, and me—were going to tear the veil. But we had to plant them first. Somewhere not suspicious but strategic. I didn't understand it all—Jude's brilliance certainly must have passed my full potential by the time he was five years old—but somehow these little replica relics of twentieth-century America were going to set the captives free.

If I did what I was supposed to. And if Tristan and Hannah did as well.

Tristan wasn't even a question. Failure didn't

run in his veins. Hannah and me...

I needed to focus on me, because worrying about Hannah twisted my bowels into uncomfortable knots. Careful to keep a stern, hard expression on my face, I surveyed the dirt and people below me, moving over the boards of my perch with purpose.

Ashton pivoted opposite of me, and I found my first opportunity. While his back was still turned, I slipped one coin from between my glove and wrist and knelt on the open platform close to the corner. The four posts that held up our watch point had been secured with heavy bolts drilled into the thick two-by-eight timber slabs at a forty-five-degree angle and sunk beneath the surface of the pilot hole. That left a coin-sized circle imprinted in the post. Perfect for Jude's coins. After sneaking a glance over my shoulder, I pressed his quarter-replica into the hole, securing it there with my thumb.

"What's wrong?"

Footfalls approached my back, and I fought the rise of panic.

I shrugged, looked back at him, and then looked down toward the ground below as if studying. "How far a drop is that, do you think?"

"Thirty feet. Or so. Who cares?"

"Just wondering why they didn't put rails on the Nests. You know, for safety."

Ashton snorted. "Scared, Luther?"

I rose to my full height, which took me above his head by three inches. "Only when it's windy. And I was just wondering anyway. Seems like this assignment—it's a last stop."

His eyebrows drew in deep, carving a wrinkled V into his head. "Don't know what you're talking about."

He turned away, and I moved the opposite direction. But after two steps, I felt his presence lunging toward me.

"Watch out!" he shouted, gripping my shoulders and pushing me toward the deck's edge.

My heart lodged in my neck as my pulse throbbed hard through my veins. With one swift kick, I cleared his feet from beneath him, and he landed on his backside. He didn't even draw in another breath before I had his back pinned to the flat timbers beneath us.

For a wild, death-chilled moment, his eyes met mine and held. Then he rolled his head to the side and laughed. "You are jumpy, Luther. Henson was right. You've got to loosen up. The Party will take care of us."

I didn't loosen the grip I held on his shoulders as I leaned in close. "Don't ever do that again." I waited until he looked back at my face, and then lifted him so his head came off the deck. "Ever," I seethed, and then released my hold.

Ashton scrambled to his feet, and I continued to glare at him. I wondered if he questioned what he'd just said. That the Party would take care of him. Actually, I hoped he'd just realized how stupid that idea was. With one quick shove, I could have thrown him off the Nest, and likely he would have died.

Nobody in the Party would have cared.

* * *

Hannah

I could still feel death. It crawled over every cell of my skin, like the scratchy legs of grasshoppers clinging where they didn't belong, refusing to let go. It seeped into my chest, unraveling the resentment I kept there for strength.

It lingered in the image of my sister's eyes.

My stomach lurched, and I could not fight the upward thrust as it emptied onto the dirt at my feet. Alone in the dimming light of early evening, I lost everything that was in my tummy as I leaned against the cold metal of the building where we were to sleep. No one would come near me right now, as I had just come from the Quarantine and was considered a risk. At least they wouldn't see me crack.

When everything emptied and the dry heaves stopped, I kicked at the dirt, burying the vomit. Unfortunately, I could neither expel the images now branded in my mind, as I had my food, nor bury what I had seen. It was there, ever before my vision, silently accusing me. With both palms flat against the building, I leaned into the shame.

This was what the Party did. This was their work. And I...

I fingered the spot where I knew the ink had been tattooed onto my skin. I was one of them. But I hadn't known.

Quinn. What did he know? He couldn't be a part of this. Could he?

Hot rage seared through my body. If Quinn knew this...

He didn't. He just couldn't.

But he'd insisted I stay away from the Den. Knew there were things there that he didn't want me involved with. How much did he know about that? And did he know about this too?

"You okay?"

Startled, I jerked away from the building. The light had nearly snuffed out beneath the western horizon, and the boy coming toward me was merely a shadow in the gray. Tall, built like his father, the legendary football preacher, Braxton couldn't hide his identity even in the falling darkness.

He seemed to know that now. Owned it. When once he would have kept to the shadows, he now walked into the open cloak of night, as if daring it to take him down. His father's son. Where had he found this resolve, this strength to become what he never believed he could be? What, it had seemed, he had never wanted?

"Hannah." His large hand covered my shoulder, and without hesitation, he turned me into his chest. "Are you okay?"

I understood this hold now, the touch of sincere concern and offered friendship. Brotherly kindness. He'd been this way the whole time. He loved my sister, and I'd resented that. Maybe hated it. But all the while, he cared about me too. I mattered to him—not the same way Eliza had, but somehow I realized that it was the way it should have been.

Anxiety accompanied that small release of a past grudge, and I pushed away from him. "I haven't been cleared yet. You should stay away."

One stubborn hand stayed on my shoulder, and I felt him study me. "If you're sick, it's too late for me now." He shrugged. "I guess we'll hope for the best."

I looked to the ground, aware that I probably

smelled awful—of the sweat that had been trapped in my hazmat suit all day, and of human waste, which had saturated the suffocating air in the Quarantine. And now, of puke.

"Want to walk?" He nudged me toward the opposite direction of the building.

I did. I wanted to walk away and keep walking until everything I'd witnessed disappeared from sight. From memory. From existence. Walk until a new life spread under my feet and before my vision—the kind of life that was good and light and beautiful.

"Will the others be suspicious?" I asked as I stepped beside him, and we paced away from where the others gathered.

"They'll talk." His voice was flat and dark.

I understood. They'd say ugly things that would never be true. And laugh. And think that it was all normal and perfectly right. But they wouldn't suspect what this really was.

The muffled scuffs of our footfalls against the thin, short dry grass and dusty earth accompanied the silence between us as we wandered away from the camp. Nothing else. The sounds of nature—the fluttering of bats, the hoots of an owl, the call of a coyote—none of it filled the chilly air. It was as if the earth and all of nature with it also held still in silent terror, wondering if the sun would come up again tomorrow.

Perhaps hoping it wouldn't.

Braxton stopped when we came to a small dip in the earth, and with a long sigh, he folded his legs and sat down. "You didn't answer me."

I sat beside him, the cold of the earth seeping through my Pride-issued pants. Still, I couldn't find an answer.

He snapped the head of a blade of grass nearby, his movements rustling against the quiet. "What's in there? In the Quarantine?"

A shiver gripped my whole body, and I swallowed, trying to make room in my throat for air. "Death," I said, my voice ragged and hoarse.

Braxton grew still beside me. Waiting.

"I've never seen anything so..." I swallowed again. "Horrifying."

"What is it?"

"I don't know. Some kind of disease, but I don't know what. They're covered with small sores—like bug bites, only rounder and puffier. Some even have them on their eyes. One woman was blind. The sicker they were, the more completely covered their bodies were with those...pox."

"How many were in there?"

I shut my eyes and unwillingly focused on the burned-in image of that awful sight within the

Quarantine. How many? They lay side by side on the floor, shoulder to shoulder, in four rows stretching all the way back to the end of the large hangar.

"Hannah?"

"Hundreds. Three, maybe four hundred. All lined up for their turn at agony and death."

I felt him shudder at my side. "Do any survive, do you think?"

There hadn't been a shred of evidence that those who entered the Quarantine would ever come out alive. Hot liquid singed my eyes as I looked in the direction of that awful billow of black smoke on the west side of the camp. It never dwindled, spewing its dark mark against the wide-open sky, and with it, the smell of burning. Flesh. That was the dreadful stench that had drifted to me when we first arrived. Burnt flesh. Incineration of the sick—the victims of the Party's viral death.

I squeezed my eyes shut, and two tears trailed parallel strips down my cheeks as I tucked my nose into my shoulder.

"No." Braxton answered his own question. "I've never seen anyone come out of there."

My bottom lip trembled as I pictured Eliza again. Her shaved, pox-riddled head and face. The pain in her eyes. Her kindness to others in spite of it. A sob stole over me before I could grip control over it. Braxton's arm came around me again.

"I'm sorry," he said, his voice barely heard even in the unnatural stillness surrounding us.

But he didn't understand. Not entirely. And I didn't want to tell him.

Another silent cry rattled through me. His other arm wrapped around me, and he pulled me into a tight hug.

How could I tell him?

How could I not?

With both palms flat against his Jackal coat, I pushed away and searched for my voice.

"Brax—" My throat closed again, cutting off the rest of his name. With the heels of my palms, I smeared the tears away from my eyes and then squeezed them shut again.

Eliza's haunting face remained burned into my mind. I cleared my throat and forced my strained voice to work.

"She's there."

I felt him stiffen beside me. "What?"

I drew in another staggering breath and made the words lift from my throat. "Liza. I saw Eliza in the Quarantine."

The last brush of warmth from the hand he'd kept on my shoulder fell away, and I waited to hear him breathe.

He didn't—not for several moments. And then I heard his stuttering draw of air as he grappled with what I'd just said.

Some moments cut so deep you'd think your soul had been separated from your body, and the pain was unspeakable.

Braxton folded against his knees, and the shadows of his hands covered his head.

For him, this nightmare simply had no end. And mine...though I had fought against it, denied it, my nightmare was really just beginning.

Still, I didn't know what to think about Quinn.

twenty-two

Braxton

"How do I land Quarantine duty?"

Achy and stiff from a night spent folded up out on the cold open plain under the black mournful sky, I had to force my unwilling muscles into a jog to catch up with Tristan just as the sun peeked over the east horizon. I'd known he'd be up. Alone. He did that—got up before everyone else and wandered off by himself every morning. I didn't know why or what he did. No one seemed to care much, as long as he wielded the automatic weapon we'd been issued.

Tristan met me with a look of guarded suspicion. "You don't want that job."

"Eliza's in there." With a hand to his shoulder, I stopped him, forcing him to turn to face me. "I have to see her."

A heavy look of sorrow passed through his already burdened eyes. After a moment of held breath, he sighed, his shoulders slumping as he looked to the ground. "I'm sorry."

"Don't do that." I shoved him upright with a surge of charged determination. "Don't you dare give up. She's not dead, and Jude will know what to do. I just need to see her."

"No one has survived whatever is in there, Braxton."

"So what? No one had escaped from the fate of the Purge until you got Miranda free." I stepped closer, lowering my voice to almost a threat. "And she wouldn't have made it out alive if it wasn't for Eliza. Don't you dare quit on her now. We owe her."

Tristan's lips rolled inward, and he slowly brought his eyes up to meet mine again. After yet another doubtful pause, he dipped a single nod.

"I'll talk to Henson," he said. "Tell him you were out all night and need a lesson in order or something."

My heart still throbbed in my chest, the surge of adrenaline not yet done with my pulse. But I couldn't speak—my lips felt wobbly, and my eyes burned.

I didn't want to see her the way Hannah had described. But I knew for certain I didn't have a choice.

* * *

My breath came with such a rapid demand that the mask on my hazmat suit fogged.

"Easy, Luther." The boy helping me check the suit for gaps spoke as he continued his last once-over inspection before I walked into the Quarantine. "Just keep your distance from them. As long as they can't reach you, touch you, your suit should stay in place, and you'll be fine."

I inhaled, long and deep, fighting to slow the demand for air. "What's in there?" I asked, checking my gloves. "What do they have?"

"Don't know for sure. All I know is that the world isn't ready for it, and we've got to keep it contained here." He checked the seam where my pants and my boots met and then reached for an overshoe bootie. "They keep hoping one will survive."

"They?"

"Yeah. They. Whoever's in charge. They."

It struck me as massively ignorant and straight-up stupid that we worked for some unnamed person. The Party? The government—

which was basically one and the same now? Someone else, an individual? Who managed Reformation Camps?

I redirected my thoughts to a question that might have an answer. "Why do they hope one of them will survive?"

The boy finished securing the overshoes and stood. He scowled at me, like Tristan would have because I was asking too many questions. "Don't know. Don't care that much either. Just do what you're told—got it? They can have water, and when the bread rations come, I'll deliver them to the back door. Distribute them however you see fit." He began to walk away.

"Wait." I reached a hand toward him. "What about medications? Do we give them anything?"

Again he frowned, this time with a look that said I was an idiot. "To prisoners? Rebels? No. We don't waste what belongs to citizens on worms."

Contempt contorted his face as he looked me over one last time, and then he marched away.

How had it come to this? How did people take on such a cold, hardhearted view of human life? Worms? They were people in there. Dying. And how did the Party or whoever "they" were expect to gain a survivor if they didn't at least try to take care of the sick?

If I'd only understood the hard ideology of the

Party when I'd been sixteen. I'd missed it—had been blinded or distracted by the things that made life easy and comfortable, by my selfish ambitions and pride and anger. Funny, though, in all of my me-centeredness, I'd never really understood who I was, and relationally, who the Party was. It was easier to just go along with the tide. I didn't have to think about my own identity or worry about who I was following either. Because if I had, there would have been conflict. Maybe that was all intentional—the me not thinking about identity or worrying about anything but what would make my life easy. A veil of distraction, of comfort, made for pretty good hiding for evil.

And here they hid. Out of the sight of most citizens, isolated by miles and miles of empty land.

But that was going to change.

First though, I had to find Eliza.

Blowing out another hot breath that sent a wave of fog over my mask, I stepped to the doorway and pulled on the heavy steel entry. It didn't give easily, and as I slipped through the space wide enough for me and my suit, darkness once again consumed the light. I stood motionless while the door behind me creaked shut, and with the click of the latch, the natural light fled. It took about five blinks before my eyes adjusted, and I was able to take in the scene within the Quarantine.

Bodies lay on the ground—on old pads probably from high school gyms that had long since been closed in the small towns dotting the surrounding plains. The pads weren't of much use—thin, torn, and covered with pale dirt. The sick lay shoulder to shoulder without room to roll over, let alone to really stretch out. The smell of human waste and sweaty, sick bodies saturated the air so thickly that I began to cough against the offense reaching my lungs. Heads, in various stages of baldness, shaved as a means to both humiliate and to strip identity, glistened with feverish sweat, and tiny raised bumps littered their scalps. The pox, white and scaly, some of them open and bleeding a red-yellow puss, also covered their faces, necks, and arms.

My stomach rolled hard, and a wave of nausea kicked me backward. I leaned against the door that had just shut behind me, choking against the bile that built in my throat. Who could survive this? Would anyone want to?

"Water..." A faint rasp drifted from a spot on the floor ten feet in front of me. "Please. Please, may I have some water?"

I snapped out of my horrified stupor and looked around the edges of the building. The little bit of fragmented light illuminating the large room came from the wall on my left. Three folding tables, the kind found in the basement of an old church, sat against the wall, with several large thermoses set at the front edge, with battery-operated lanterns—which looked like holdovers from World War II and probably had been, given our location—set up between them.

At least there was that.

After pushing away from the door, I moved to where tin cups sat on one end of a table, and I filled one. In the semidarkness, I could make out the depth of water in the cup, but not much more. I grabbed another, filled it as well, and turned back to the place where the plea had come.

"Who wanted a drink?" I scanned the tangled web of legs and arms, looking for someone to sit up, or at least a hand to raise.

I saw nothing but the minuscule rise and fall of chests taking in shallow breaths and wheezing out toxic air. Finding the narrow aisle created between one row of feet and another, I continued walking toward where I thought the voice had come.

"Water?" I said, my voice oddly muffled because of my mask. "Would anyone like water?"

A chorus of low moans came as reply. Everyone wanted water. They just couldn't ask.

Or sit up to drink it. I stopped at the body whose feet were nearest mine and leaned down, reaching as much as I dared toward the ill person. I couldn't tell, in the darkness, and with the gaunt forms of most of the people, if it was a man or a woman.

"Here," I said, holding out the cup. "Take it. Drink."

A hand lifted from the ground but fell short of my offering.

I leaned farther. "Here."

Again, the hand tried. Again, it failed. The body it belonged to was simply too weak, too sick. I looked around, struck again by the near-death stillness of the room, by the shallow wheeze of labored breathing, the low moans of pain.

How could they drink if we didn't touch them? How could they get well if we didn't help? No wonder no one had survived.

Careful to check my position so I didn't land on a sick person, I knelt on one knee and bent to lift the head of the one who could not reach. The face winced—I must have brushed one or many of the painful sores, but the lips parted in expectation and drank when I tipped the cup. The body in my hold trembled, and the filtered light lit the path of a tear as it rolled across the swollen and pox-littered cheek.

"Thank you."

The words barely touched my ears.

I sank my teeth into my bottom lip until the quivering there stopped. "How long since you've had a drink?"

Again the body shook as the person I held fought for another breath. "Three days."

My hand trembled as again I tipped the cup to the lips. Incredibly sick and three days without water.

"We are the sickest." The voice came a bit stronger with a hint of feminine undertones. "Spend more time with the others. They might have a chance."

I studied this dying woman. Likely she would not last through the night. Around her, the others were the same. Covered with pox, lips swollen and cracked from dehydration and fever.

"Someone over here called for water," I answered, laying her gently back to the floor. "Who called for water?"

For a moment, only the raspy sound of hard-fought breaths answered. Then, "Here. Me."

One row up and three bodies over, I saw the slightest fluttering of fingers on what had probably been a wide chest once upon a time. Careful again not to step on anyone scattered in the path, I picked my way to the man who had spoken and knelt at his side. When I lifted his head, he looked into my eyes instead of the cup in my hand.

"You are him," he whispered.

I froze, wondering if the man saw me at all or if he was in some other place. "Here." I lifted the cup to his lips. "Drink."

The man did, his eyes never leaving my masked face. "He promised to send such a one."

I frowned because I was certain he saw me. He was clearly talking to me, not some image his fevered brain had produced. "Me?"

"Yes. He promised to send the hands of compassion."

Alarm and shame drained through me because I could see he wasn't crazed, but I knew I wasn't what he said. Hoping he wouldn't speak again, I replaced the cup at his lips.

He drank and then shut his eyes. But his voice, though faint and raspy, sounded again. "The burden is heavy, but you will not bear it alone."

Carefully I laid him back to the mat, and he went willingly, his eyes still closed. But before I could rise, his soft, forced words caught me again.

"You are your father's son, sent for such a time as this. Help will come."

Every muscle in my neck and back stiffened as I listened to his final pronouncement. His words sounded like the mutterings of a crazy dying man. But though this man was certainly dying, I was equally sure he was not crazy.

I had that feeling again—the one I'd had almost three years before when Eliza had spoken of hardships to come. The sense that something prophetic had just been spoken.

This time, though I was still terrified, I chose to listen.

* * *

Hannah

I found Braxton near the wash station where he'd found me the night before. The glaze over his eyes, the sullen draw of his mouth...all of it tugged my rent soul.

He'd found Eliza, for sure. And he'd seen the rest of hell on earth kept in that dark container of almost death. No doubt he wished with everything inside of himself that he could wash off that ink we'd branded into our necks, never claim the name of the Party, associate with them, or even have heard of them.

I knew. Because that was what I wanted.

Sizzling pain ricocheted in my stomach as my attention drifted from his beaten profile to the billow of black-gray smoke to the west. I'd guessed what that was but had hoped I'd been wrong.

That day I had been proven correct. The incinerator. And here we stood, inhaling the tainted air, hints of wood and ash and an acrid undertone of burned flesh.

By our hands.

I remembered once reading in classic literature of a woman who could not wash the stain of blood from her hands. Lady Macbeth. One of the cruelest women in all of story, she would stop at nothing until power had been in her grip. And then...total insanity.

Here I stood, witnessing Shakespeare's morbid character come to life. The stain of blood that Neptune's great ocean could not wash from Macbeth's hands was on mine as well. And Quinn's...

Tears, angry, burning drops of rage, stung my eyes, and I turned away from the smudged horizon, looking back at Braxton.

"Eliza—"

"Is still alive." His voice caught, cracked, and then dropped. "For the moment." He looked across the prairie—away from our bunker, and decidedly not at the furnace to our left. "How could anyone..."

Indeed. How could they? We?

Ignorance? Yes.

Apathy? Likely.

Just like I'd known what that smoke on the other side of the camp really was, but I didn't want to know. No one really wanted to know. We wanted our comfortable lives. To succeed. To be happy. The cost...well, if you didn't know the cost, then you didn't have to care.

Then again, maybe it wasn't all our fault. The evil we'd conceded to had been hidden. Veiled.

It's time to tear the veil.

Jude's words. Spoken to me, about me. Now he had me. And I knew exactly why he wanted me.

"We'll go to Jude. He'll know what to do."

Slowly, as if life was drizzling back into his body, one small drop at a time, soaking into the scorched landscape of who he was, Braxton shifted his gaze back to me.

"Do you think he knows what's killing them? In the Quarantine?"

I shivered, praying, maybe truly for the first time in my life, that he did. What hope did we have beyond that? "Jude sent us here on purpose—he has a plan for all of this. We have to hope he can figure out what's killing them too."

Braxton squatted, as if standing took more strength than he had, and with both hands he gripped the back of his hair. "And if he doesn't?"

"Just do the next thing, Luther. That's what she would want."

"She wanted me to do the *right* thing." His voice wavered, dark, broken emotion shaking his body in the dusk of evening.

My lips quivered, and I couldn't look at him when I said, "Tear the veil."

He shifted beside me, and I could feel the question in his penetrating stare, though I still couldn't look him in the eyes.

"You know that might mean..."

"I know," I said, my voice harsh even as a whisper.

I would confront Quinn. The truth would be ripped from the cloaked darkness. And I would see what exactly that was.

I wasn't sure I was ready for it.

But it was the *right* thing. Even if it might rip my heart apart too.

twenty-three

Braxton

Apparently, town visits were something like clockwork. Predictably patterned, so Tristan was able to pull off the same "drinking" stunt he'd done several days before. Once the others were safely snockered, he snuck Hannah and me out, and we went back to the safety of the Refuge.

"Did you plant all of the coins?" Jude asked, though it didn't seem as if he really meant it as a question. Somehow this disfigured man in the chair, living in the semidarkness of this dugout laboratory he'd created, commanded all of our respect, attention, and complete compliance.

It struck me how similar those traits were to

what the Party leaders demanded, and yet this seemed different. Good. Right. Leadership was a gift, I guessed, but those who possessed it got to choose how to use it.

Jude was using his to free the captives. Maybe for that reason alone, we were willing to lay everything on the line to do it with him.

"The weakness in their grid can be manipulated, but it has to be timed just right. Hannah will need to go DC..."

My brain caught up to the plan Jude was outlining as his eyes flickered toward Eliza's little sister. The girl I was supposed to protect because I'd failed the girl I had wanted to protect.

Hannah back to DC? To get to Quinn. I'd understood that, hadn't I? Surely I had. But standing there, realizing as if for the first time what was really at stake, and what would most likely happen to Hannah, a surge of rebellious stubbornness streaked through.

"Wait. Hannah doesn't have to go." I stepped forward and in front of her. "It doesn't have to go down like that. I can get to him. She can send a message on the same video you spliced of the camp."

Though in his chair, with his head supported by the padding jutting up from behind his neck, it seemed that Jude denied me with a single, authority-laced scowl.

"You know that won't work," Jude said.

"I know she can't go."

"Braxton." Hannah spoke from behind me, her voice soft but sharp.

"No." I stepped backward, reaching a hand behind me until I found her arm. "She's not doing this. Come up with another plan."

"She's our only way in." Tristan turned to face me, his move putting us eye to eye. "You know that. We all understood that."

"Quinn will listen to me, Braxton," Hannah said softly.

With a quick spin, I faced her, heat suddenly flooding my chest. "He isn't what you want him to be, Hannah. And either way, you'll be ruined. I'm not letting you do this."

She lifted her chin and met my eyes, a move that made her look exactly like her sister. Except, Eliza wasn't stupid.

"You don't have a choice," Hannah said.

Jude's voice broke the taught argument flaring between us. "This is what must happen, young Luther. Your protection of her is admirable, but in this you must yield. Allow her to make the same sacrifices that you are willing to make. Allow Hannah to take the opportunity at redemption as well."

"Redemption?" I turned my face to look at

him. "This is death, not redemption. You know exactly what—"

"I know the risks, and so does she. I also know the possibilities."

A chill of silence fell on all of us, though I continued to glare at Jude. I'd understood all of this just days ago, but now...

She's not strong enough. She can't do this.

Was it that I didn't trust Quinn—which I had no reason to—or that I didn't trust her?

I needed air. To think. I looked back at Jude one more time, and he seemed to give me permission, though again, I didn't know how. The calm, wise look in his gaze? His steady, unchallenging silence? I wasn't sure what, but somehow I knew he was saying *Go. Work it through.*

Without looking at the others, I moved away from the group and through the darkness of the compound until sunlight spilled across my path. Rather than heading toward the village, which was what the refugees had generously come to call the few outbuildings and tents spread across the flat part of the small canyon, I turned right and began stepping up the grass-covered incline.

I stalked the rise until I reached the top of the hill under which Jude's hideaway had been dug. The vast emptiness of the Vacant Plains seemed almost an assault on my eyes as I stared across the horizon. I'd lived with thick forests my whole life. I'd never seen the wide span of earth like this, and it felt too big.

I followed the snaking trail of the river splitting the land in front of me, it's flat, meandering path striking me as an ironic symbol of peace in this country ravaged by power.

Ravaged. No one was to be left untouched by the desolation of power—and I suspected the worse was still to come. Shutting my eyes, my mind, as usual, settled on Eliza. *Please stay alive.* It was a selfish hope. To live through the camps—and whatever was killing those in the Quarantine—was to survive hell on earth. Why would I want that for Eliza? But Miranda had survived, and somehow her strength had become more. Her compassion, her ability to sacrifice, to love, to give, all of it had become greater. God used the hell in her life to bring some healing and purpose to mine.

Why would He do that? Could He do that with Eliza too? Or would she be ruined by the scars?

The dry grass rustled behind me, and I turned, my body tight in the trained defense mode life as a Jackal had taught me. She was coming. That girl never knew when to back down—or what fights she should really take on.

This one wasn't one of them. She couldn't go. How could I tell Eliza that I'd let her sister walk into a death trap, knowing exactly what it was?

Hannah motioned with a halfhearted wave of her hand as she approached. I watched as she walked the last few yards toward me, her stride and posture now that of a trained warrior. The Pride. The Den. They trained us well. Power punctuated our every move, driving fear into the intended target. Who would stand against them?

Me. Jude. Tristan. Miranda.

Hannah? She'd been just like me—a sellout. Stubborn, foolish, and blind. But now that she'd seen the truth, what would she do with it? Because of Quinn, her heart was completely messed up. She didn't seem to have an identity without him, which meant her identity had been pressed into the Party's.

With one smooth motion, she came down to the ground beside me. "I'm going with you."

"No, you're not."

"Shut up and listen." She turned her face to me. Determination glowed in her eyes. "I'm going to DC, and you're not going to argue."

"Oh. Ohh...kay, sure." I grunted. "Not happening, so get it out of your head."

She scowled, but her hand gripped my arm as

if she were begging me to understand. "I have to, Braxton. I have to confront him."

Confront him? Yeah, she'd confront him all right, and in all her emotional stability, either she'd be undone by his persuasive power, or she'd lose all sensibility in a fit of rage and get herself killed. But telling her that? Futile effort. Which was exactly why I couldn't let her be a part of this mission—not like this.

"No," I said.

"I need to know—" She cut off and didn't finish.

Needed to know if he actually loved her.

"You want to know if it was *real?*" I hung air quotes with my fingers and laughed. "Right. Do you really think a guy who would condone the things that happen in Reformation Camp is capable of love? What will you do, Hannah?" I leaned a bit closer, a plan to prove my point snowballing in my mind. "You think if you show Quinn what you've seen, he'll be surprised? Wake up, little girl. He's one of *them.*"

Her face crumpled into an ugly blend of anger and pain. "You don't know him."

"What, like you?" I snorted. "Yeah, I'm not sleeping with him, if that's what you mean."

She jumped to her feet, and I followed, folding my arms over my chest. Like a fiddle...I almost had her. "Did you even bother to find out who he was before you fell into his bed? Or were you so desperate to be held that you didn't care whose arms you filled?"

"Shut up! He's not like them, and it wasn't like that. We never... He didn't know—he couldn't have known." Tears glazed over her livid eyes, but she didn't let them fall.

"There's no way you can believe that." I inched closer. "Not a chance that Quinn doesn't know about it. Why did he keep you away from the Den, Hannah? Why do you think he didn't want you in the Commons?" I didn't wait for her to answer because I knew that she wouldn't. One more push should do it... "He knows it all. Every last disgusting, brutal detail. He was using you, and you were so desperate you were willing to pretend it was real."

Got her. Her jaw set hard, and then she lunged.

Trained or not, I could take her down without breaking a sweat. Especially when she was like this. I caught her by the shoulders, and with a quick swipe of my foot, I took her feet out from under her. Though I kept my hold on her, she still hit the ground with a thud, sending up a low cloud of pale dirt.

"This is why I can't let you go," I hissed, leaning into her face. "Not if this is how you handle things. If you go in to confront him running on nothing but emotion, you're not going to come out alive."

"Like you've never done anything stupid before."

"Common knowledge, but not a good excuse, Hannah, so quit using it." I shook my head. "The difference is I'm not content to stay stupid. You seem to like it there."

She pushed at me, and I caught her hands, pinning them to the ground. "See. You're not thinking, are you? Use your brain, Hannah. They taught you better in the Pride. Don't go for my hands when you know I'm stronger than you. Start thinking."

Her eyes still blazed, but the fog of passion cleared. I watched as she started to process—to remember what they'd taught her, and I wondered where she would calculate my weakest spot to be.

Please don't go below the belt.

I shifted, anticipating *that* move. With my attention distracted, and my movement tilting toward her, she arched her back, and then her head flew forward.

Pain screamed into my brain as my nose cracked against her skull. The metallic taste of blood filled the back of my mouth at the same moment the thick, warm ooze began to flood my nostrils.

Nicely done, Hannah.

Except she wasn't done. I let loose of her hands to cover my nose, and as I moved away, her elbow came flying into my periphery. If I'd been paying attention, I could have blocked it with my own elbow, but I wasn't. Next thing I knew, she'd hit me in the jugular.

I rocked back and tried to inhale. Failure. Panic tried to take over my thinking. *Air. Air now!*

My body gasped, but my lungs seemed to have collapsed. I rolled to my back, and blood drained into my throat, causing a spasm of coughs. Hannah pulled me up to a sitting position, and I sprayed out a stream of red mucus. Finally, I could breathe again.

"Better," I sputtered.

She rubbed the center of her forehead where she'd cracked it against my nose. "Just keep breathing, you stupid punk."

"No." I coughed again and then looked at her. "I meant that was better. Think with your head, and you'll be fine."

"Thanks." She tossed some dirt at me. "Jerk."

I chuckled as I stripped my shirt off and wadded it up. Pressing it to my nose, I looked back at her.

"Sorry." I meant it. Heartache wasn't a

stranger to me, and though hers was different, I knew how much she hurt.

Her eyes lost the last shred of heat and went vacant. The chasm of pain did that. I'd seen it in Miranda's eyes and in the eyes of those who dared to look at me in the camp. The man in the Quarantine. The mother who sobbed across the invisible electric-charged line for her dead son.

Hannah's heart would never be the same.

She stared at the river beyond the rise, and her lips quivered. "I love him," she whispered.

"I know." I swallowed, wondering if Eliza had had this kind of conversation with her dad after I left. "You don't have to go back. I can do it without you."

She looked back to me. "I have to go." Her tears finally spilled. "He's good. I know he is." Again, she stopped, her quiet cries taking her voice. "But if he knows, then I'll hate him, and I'm afraid of how much that will hurt."

Betrayed by love. Pain like that...I didn't know the words. Suddenly the night before Eliza's capture replayed—the meeting, the bottle of persuasion...the reason she'd been caught. My stomach rocked. Looking at Hannah's broken trust, I felt like I was looking at Eliza.

I wondered again how she could ever forgive me.

* * *

Hannah

He'd provoked me on purpose.

Sometimes I thought I hated that guy. When I wasn't crushing on him—which I wasn't, because that was so over. And when I didn't let myself dwell on the fact that for all the stupid stuff he'd pulled in the past, Braxton really had become someone I completely respected.

Sellout to superhero. By way of the Den. Who could have seen that coming?

Not me. Eliza, though...probably. She never looked at someone without seeing past the moment into hope. Part of her saintliness that had made me crazy.

I glanced back at Braxton as we cut a trail back down the hill where he'd retreated. Blood had smeared over the dark shadow of whiskers under the nutmeg tones of his upper lip. A satisfied grin tickled my mouth, and I didn't try to fight it. Such a punk.

But I'd remember the lesson.

Think. Don't lead with my emotions. Use them to my advantage.

I had to remember. Had to keep control. Because facing Quinn—either way, whether he'd known about all the demonic stuff the Party was doing out here or not—facing him as a traitor was going to take all the courage and control I had.

I probably needed to thank Braxton for the setup just now. Which meant I didn't hate him. Maybe I even hoped I could be like him.

twenty-four

Braxton

"You have to be clear on this, Luther."

I sat across from Jude, my face hard and my back straight. I still didn't want Hannah in on it. Obviously, I didn't get a vote.

"I'm clear," I said.

"No, I mean *you won't fail* kind of clear. Whether Hannah is able to convince the Sanger boy to broadcast this video or not, it has to get onto the airwaves. There's not any room for that to *not* happen. We have to have Charlotte and her snake in Washington watching that video."

Snag on that. I still wasn't sure about the connection between Charlotte Sanger and

President Kasen Asend, although there certainly was one, and I really didn't understand why Jude seemed to rank her over him, which seemed backward. But that wasn't the mystery of the moment.

"Why do they need to see it? I doubt it'll be a surprise to either Charlotte or Kasen to see what's going on out here."

Jude inhaled, his warm, intelligent eyes intense with determination. "Sleight of hand, Luther. Sleight of hand."

I waited.

Jude simply stared.

"That's it?" I said, feeling more like the dumb kid back at Glennbrooke High than the man Jude had selected for this covert op. The one that couldn't fail. He'd rattled my confidence, and I bit my bottom lip.

"That's it," Jude answered, a satisfied gleam in his eyes. "Sometimes knowledge needs broken into pieces. If you keep it whole, you might unintentionally place the key in enemy's hands."

I drew back. "Are you saying you don't trust me?" I really shouldn't have been offended. Of the two of us sitting there, I was the one who'd been inked.

"I wouldn't send you with Hannah to DC if I didn't trust you. Now..." With a movement of his right index finger, he began rolling backward and toward the row of lockers he kept lined against the far wall. "I need you to trust me."

I stood and followed him as he rolled to the last locker on the left.

He stopped, wiggled his head until he looked up at me, and then locked gazes with mine. "Can you?"

"Trust you?"

His silence seemed to say yes.

"I do." It was true. Nearly more than anyone else I'd met, I trusted this quirky, genius guy strapped in a chair. Maybe like Frodo trusted Gandalf, understanding that the older, wiser man knew things that the hobbit just couldn't know and that the wizard had been sent as help.

For such a time as this...

"You'll trust me in regards to Hannah?"

I swallowed, holding on to that fledgling vine of trust. "Yes."

"And Eliza?"

I felt my eyes grow and my lips part. I hadn't mentioned her. Ever. Not even when we'd told Jude about the black illness ravaging the prisoners in the Quarantine. I'd kept her out of the conversation on purpose, because I didn't want Jude to think that I was only after the longing of my heart. Even if it was a little bit of the truth.

"Yes, Braxton, I know about Eliza Knight. I know what happened. And I know that she's still alive."

"How?" The word came off my lips in a breath of wonder and maybe disbelief.

Jude laughed a little. "Don't faint on me. I'm not a diviner. Evan has spoken to me, and I talked to Hannah about what she saw in the Quarantine. I am smart enough to put it together."

No doubting that.

"I need to know if you will trust me with it all," Jude continued, still watching me. "When the veil is torn, everything else will be set in motion. It must all work together, but I need you in DC, with Hannah. You cannot be here, not even in your mind. You must trust me with this."

Again he paused, and I felt as if the center of all of his plans had suddenly zoomed in on me.

The sellout? The li'l Luther? The disappointment of my father, the failure of my family?

How could Jude trust me with this?

Maybe the more relevant question of that moment was: Clearly he did trust me—how could I *not* trust him?

I nodded.

"Good. Remember, even when everything else is chaos and the darkness is so thick it feels like it's crushing you. Trust me."

His words made me remember those moments with Eliza when she'd say something that seemed prophetic. Inspired. Like they meant something relevant at that moment, for that situation, but also, they meant more.

Like maybe it wasn't just Jude asking me to trust him in the darkness.

Maybe we were all truly trusting that, somehow, though we couldn't see it or even imagine it right then, we were going to see the Light.

* * *

Hannah

I'd understood.

Seriously, I had. When we'd boarded the LiteRail south of the shielded Refuge, I was clear on what we needed to do, how important it was that I not fail.

That had been two days before. But now...

The speed of the railcars had dropped noticeably. We had zipped through the Vacant Plains, beyond the borders of the uninhabitable, and also through the wooded heartland of the Midwest. The route had taken on a more serpentine feel after we'd passed through all that had been familiar to me, and we climbed and descended through the cutting pass carved into the Appalachian Mountains. We'd pressed a bit north again, hardly noticing as we passed over the larger rivers slicing the land of the eastern seaboard. Now the LiteRail slowed, and the decrease in speed triggered a rapid rise in my heart rate.

DC. We'd arrived, and the rail would deliver Braxton, Tristan, and me directly to the National Mall. I'd never been, but I'd heard about it from others. The monuments celebrating the heroes of America's past. The museums containing everything important to our history and progress. The political center stage, for both past and present. Everything important was there.

Including Quinn.

Jude had studied the boy I'd clearly known little about. He knew Quinn's daily routine—the shared breakfast with his mother, Charlotte, of which I had once been a brief participant, and his continued education, though now on a practical front right there on Capitol Hill.

His mysterious relationship to his "uncle" Kasen Asend—who I was now certain was not truly his uncle at all. Charlotte hadn't been married and didn't claim Kasen as her brother. It didn't add up, and Jude wouldn't fill in those details.

"It isn't necessary to know right now, Hannah.

Let it be enough for you to know that there is a tie there, and it may be difficult to sever."

I replayed the long conversation I'd had with Jude. We had just come back from our "surveillance" mission at the camp, and I was still deeply shredded by what I'd witnessed. Jude sent for me, and when I'd arrived in his cave that served as mission central, he was alone at a crude wooden table. Two tin cups and a loaf of crusty bread sat on the rough boards, and he invited me to sit.

Turned inside out and angry at everything I'd seen, I stomped toward the middle of the room, where the table sat, and glared down at the crippled man who'd just torn my world into shreds.

"You could have told me," I spat.

"Would you have believed me?"

My teeth ground together as I clenched my jaw, remembering what Braxton had said before we'd gone to the camp. That I had to see. I wouldn't see things the way they were unless I saw them with my own eyes.

Because of Quinn. And because I was so stubborn.

I blinked as hot emotion swirled into a stormy wind at the thought of the boy I believed I'd loved.

"Hannah." Jude spoke with a hushed and gentle tone. "We don't know that he knows all of this."

How did this man, bound to a chair and seemingly locked inside this dugout, know my thoughts? Know what was going on out there? For a moment I focused on this mysterious man who was catapulting my life into chaos, and yet somehow, in ways I couldn't place exactly, he was calming the storm that had been raging long before I realized the danger around me.

"What do you think he is?" I asked, sincerely wanting to know his opinion.

Jude motioned with a simple flicker of his eyes for me to sit. I did, waiting for his response.

"Even when it looks like evil has taken control, I believe we should hope to see good."

"So you see good in Quinn?"

"What I know of him is still a puzzle. He is deeply connected with Kasen, and his ties make him vulnerable and questionable. But there are other things that make me grip hope."

I watched him, hoping to see something in his expression that would give me a more decisive answer. I knew what I wanted to believe—that Quinn knew nothing, had nothing to do with any of the nightmare I'd witnessed. But I also knew Charlotte was not a woman I trusted. Perhaps she'd taught her son well in the ways of dark and total deception. And there was the unarguable, obvious question I had seen in Braxton's doubtful expression.

How could Quinn not know?

Jude seemed to sense me drowning in the hopelessness of that thought. "It is possible to go blindly along with something you don't truly understand, isn't it?"

His question, made more as a statement than a question, found its intended mark. Me. Braxton. That was exactly what we'd done.

"And that is your reason for hope?"

"Among a few others. Including you, Hannah."

"Me?"

"Did he not protect you? Even from the beginning, before either of you felt what you feel, was he not kind?"

Very kind. He was the final evidence to convince me that my parents and Eliza had been wrong about the Party. That their creed was not rebellion but a battle cry toward something good. Compassion, strength, and rebuilding the dignity of our nation. Things we all wanted.

"Do you think his goodness was sincere?" I asked, my voice wobbly.

"I don't have reason to believe otherwise."

"There are other kindnesses though. Acts done by the Party that would seem to show that really, they are not evil. But the camps..."

"Kindness is not the same thing as gaining social capital."

"What?" I drew back...this was not a normal conversation. Then again, Jude was not a normal person. "What on earth is social capital?"

"Giving or doing something with the intent to gain something for yourself. That's not kindness, Hannah, and people have been confusing the two for far too long. What Quinn offered you—shelter and protection—doesn't seem right now to have gained him anything. And he didn't seem to hope for it to. He was being kind to a stranger who couldn't pay him back. But all the programs and government-paid-for freebies the Party is giving? That's not free, and it's not kind. There's an agenda there—they are buying loyalty. They're also enslaving captives. If you are entirely dependent on something for your welfare, then you are not free, and that is not kindness."

Coming back to the present moment, I lifted my eyes to study the land beyond my window. The sun had barely touched the hood of night at this early hour in the morning, but the lights and movement of the city didn't seem to notice. DC had a life that never really rested, a pulse that ever raced and didn't seem to feel a need for recovery. A throb of panic pushed through my veins, but I wasn't sure if it was because I was about to face what I didn't want to confront, or if it was just my physical reaction trying to match the natural state of the environment.

Panic doesn't serve well. I shut my eyes and focused on that thought. *Control your emotions, Hannah. Use them to your advantage. Do not let someone else use them for his...* I thought it strange that I heard the words in Braxton's voice rather than my own, even though he had said nearly the same thing to me just days before as we'd struggled up on the hill. Strange, because it meant more, had a greater impact on me, when I put them in his voice rather than mine.

Maybe that was significant. All my life I'd only listened to the voice in my head—to myself. But there was strength when I listened to Braxton. And that tussle on the hill proved it. His nose had been broken, and the faint streak of purpley-green hue under his eyes testified to my actions.

The throb still slugged through my veins, but I recaptured it. Panic wouldn't rule me. I would use the adrenaline for fuel.

Beside me, Braxton turned, leaning slightly to speak in a low tone. "Are you ready?"

I nodded, feeling his intense scrutiny. He was looking for weakness—for my emotions to take me captive. I harnessed them tighter, and he seemed satisfied with my discipline.

"You remember where Jude said we'd find him?"

"I remember." I stared straight ahead, not glancing at either the city outside the railcar or at Braxton. "You can't be with me when I talk to him."

"That isn't the deal."

"It doesn't matter, Braxton. It is the way that it will be. I need to do this alone."

"Why?"

"Because I need the truth."

I heard his breath draw into his lungs and then release in a long, controlled exhale. "What will you do with it?"

Finally, I turned to him, meeting his intense gaze. "Whatever I must." I paused, hoping he could feel my determination, that he would believe me. "I won't fail this time, Braxton. I promise."

His look turned gentle, and the line across his mouth softened. "I never thought you were a failure, Hannah."

I hadn't expected that, and as his words sank past my crusted armor and planted into my heart, I was shocked to find how much they affected me. I blinked, clenching my jaw as I struggled to regain emotional control. But as I looked away, focusing on the chair in front of me, my grip on my thoughts and reactions continued to slip. The past replayed in my mind in a way that had me watching like a spectator at a show. All I'd really wanted was to be seen, to be known—and not as Eliza's little sister. I'd been so focused on fighting for an identity for myself, to be *somebody*, that I'd taken the identity of a monster I hadn't understood.

I *had* failed. My family, my sister, whom I did truly love. Braxton. Ultimately, God.

Why had I done this?

"Because you didn't know who you were," Braxton said.

I hadn't realized I'd asked that question out loud. Turning toward him again, I waited for him to say more.

"How can we stand with courage when we don't have an identity, Hannah?" The surge of emotions he battled passed through his eyes. "We thought we had to fight for ourselves, didn't we? You and I, we're the same. We were lost in the weeds of selfishness, determined to have our own way. But now, Hannah, we've been shown something greater."

He was right. I was sure of it, but I still couldn't define it—the thing that we'd been shown. "What?"

"Our identity isn't defined by what we fight

for. We fight for what is right *because* of who we are. We lost that—or maybe we just didn't understand it before. We took on an identity that wasn't really our own. Because it looked easier, it seemed nicer. But it was false, and now we know it. But we also know who we are."

I bit my lip, desperate to grasp this—whatever Braxton had found, whatever gave him this courage. It was profound, and strangely, I knew I'd seen it before. It didn't belong to him alone, which made me hope that it could really be mine as well.

"Who are you then, Braxton Luther?"

Light seemed to touch his face, and he lifted his chin just enough to show a fresh confidence—but not arrogance. A surety in what he was about to say.

"I am my *Father's* son."

His deep, low proclamation penetrated the center of my being. The very thing he'd fought against—being Patrick Luther's son.

No. That wasn't what he meant—not entirely. Understanding glowed warm and inviting as I studied the steadfast conviction in his eyes. A look that was familiar. I'd seen it many times reflected in another pair of brown eyes.

My sister's.

Strangely, as I realized this, the habit of envy didn't consume my heart. Longing, yes. But not envy. If Braxton Luther, the boy who'd first abandoned us to be inked, who'd broken my sister's heart, if he could own this solid identity after all that he'd messed up, then maybe...

"Have you figured it out yet, Hannah?"

I cocked an eyebrow, lifting my gaze back to his. "Who I am?"

The silent lift of his brows prodded me on.

"Hannah Knight. Eliza's little sister." I faltered, a lump swelling in my throat. "And maybe, now I can be like her after all. A true daughter of the King."

For the first time in my life, that was really what I wanted. I wished she were there to show me how to do it.

* * *

Braxton

Something had lit inside her.

Hannah sat next to me wearing the same determined strength I knew well. She looked like Eliza, and I couldn't help but feel proud of her.

And terrified.

I knew what Eliza's convictions had cost. So did Hannah though, and it hadn't been right of me to try to prevent her from doing what she knew needed to be done.

A whoosh of air and the crackle of electrical

currents vibrated the air around us as the momentum of the stopping train rocked us forward and then back. It was time. We stood, three kids dressed as Party loyals among many others. Blending, we followed the nameless faces out of the railcar and onto the landing station.

The humid bite of winter air seeped into my lungs, and I nearly gasped against the sudden icy prickles. The crowd moved off the landing, and we surged with it. As the people dispersed into the thin gray gauze of early morning, Tristan separated from us, on a mission to secure our transportation back to the Refuge. Hannah and I wound our way toward the Political Education Center. According to Jude, who had detailed our tasks, making us repeat every step of the plan until we had it down cold, the PEC had once been a museum of some sort, but the history had been deemed unimportant to Reformed purposes, and the building had been repurposed.

The Party elite went there now—their chosen ones. For full indoctrination. Which would explain why Quinn would be found within those halls.

The white puffs of my breath staggered as I released another quivering breath. "You're sure you want to try alone?"

"It's best," Hannah said. She looked straight

ahead, but her face had paled. She was scared. "He won't trust you."

"You remember the distress code?"

Her lips pressed together, and she nodded. *#failed.* That was the code. Likely, though, if she did fail, she wouldn't have a chance to send it to me using Jude's modified All-In-One, so the plan was pretty much irrelevant. I was fairly sure she and I both understood that.

"You have thirty minutes, and then I'm coming in." I glanced at her to catch her nod, and then I took a sharp left turn. I fought the urge to check over my shoulder, to watch her as she walked with her stiff, confident posture into the moment we'd both been dreading.

God, please keep her safe...

My stride continued down the pathway that fronted the many buildings lining the mall. I'd been there once, as a kid. My older brother Annyon had taken a research position at the Washington VA hospital, not far from where I was walking right then.

Without a conscious effort, my pace quickened. He was still there, last I knew. He still worked as a researcher—virology. My mind sorted through the ghastly images that had been permanently burned into my memory, stopping at the old man who'd spoken to me as I'd lifted the tin cup of water to his lips. And Eliza.

Maybe Annyon would know what was killing them. Maybe he'd know of the cure.

A chill rippled down my spine as I hopped onto a bus on Capitol Street. Mother had cried when she'd found out what Annyon was doing. I'd thought, at the time, she was being emotional and silly. Thought that she'd been upset that he was staying in DC rather than moving closer to home. But—

I pushed away the threatening dark thoughts. If Annyon had answers, I needed them. The rest, at that moment, didn't matter.

Even in the early morning, there was plenty of coming and going on the bus, and I was glad that it wasn't any later in the day. As it was, this was risky, and a small voice in my head reminded me of what Jude had said.

This was a no-fail mission, and I couldn't think about Eliza. I had to leave her back there on the Vacant Plains, in Jude's hands. But this wasn't just about Eliza. There'd been hundreds, maybe thousands of people, prisoners, infected with that death virus. Annyon might hold the answers we needed.

I was still fighting to stifle that quiet but persistent warning to go back, to stay focused, when the bus finally stopped in front of what I remembered to be the campus where Annyon worked. The grounds were gated, and a few well-dressed people scurried past the locked entry on their way to work. I'd come that far. It was worth a try.

Following an older man wearing a dark wool coat, I listened carefully as he spoke to the communication portal on the gate.

"Research department," he said.

"Name?" A computerized response.

"Josiah Hend." He said both names with clarity.

Voice recognition?

I could hope. Dad often mistook Annyon for me and me for him on the phone.

This could go so very wrong. I could blow everything...

And yet I moved forward, stopping in front of the portal.

"Research department." I parroted the man who'd gone ahead of me.

"Name?"

I made sure to match the cadence of the man as I spoke. "Annyon Luther."

Holding my breath, I watched the red blinking light under the speaker pause. Then blink. *Red.* My breath hitched. *Red.* My pulse surged. *Green.* I stifled a sigh of relief, striding through the gate that swung slowly open in front of me.

Now I was in. How would I get out?

I'd figure it out after I found where Annyon worked. Striding as if I actually knew what I was doing, I swept the campus walkways, looking for the man who'd walked in ahead of me. He'd come to a door on the building to my right, and without much of a pause, he opened it and passed through. Which meant, most likely, there wasn't more security ahead. I traced his path to that doorway, held my breath as I reached for the handle, and exhaled when the door opened with ease. Stepping inside, I found a hallway I vaguely remembered visiting as a kid, and with those patchy memories as my guide, I turned right and walked down the corridor.

Virology.

The third door on my left halted my progress, and I stalled for a long breath before I reached for the entry.

God, help...

An odd sensation fell over me as I touched the knob in front of me. A fresh strength, a sense of security that I knew was so much more than the false confidence I'd often fed myself in the past.

Turning the knob, I pushed through the door. A small space with a desk and a lamp separated the entry from the lab consuming the rest of the room. A man, wearing the same kind of hazmat suit I'd worn when I'd gone into the Quarantine, paused his work in the glass-encased lab where he stood. His head lifted. Slowly he turned, and then his eyes met mine.

Though I hadn't seen him since I'd been a boy, I recognized his face.

Annyon looked just like our father.

twenty-five

Hannah

He wasn't hard to find.

With his blond hair gelled into a trendy mess and his crisp white shirt fastened to one button below the collar, Quinn sat alone in the library, just like Jude had predicted. I wondered again at how Jude knew so much. Perhaps someday he would reveal his secrets.

But that day I had a revelation of my own to share.

A jolt of electrical current zipped through my veins, my physical response to seeing him warning me yet again to guard my emotions. Perhaps I would always see him in some light of attraction, though that remained to be seen after the coming discussion.

My fist curled tight around my All-In-One, the message embedded within destined to change at least one of our lives forever. Keeping my head down but my gaze fastened on the boy who'd once called me a frightened bunny hiding in the woods, I strode to the table where he sat, his face intent on whatever it was he studied.

Quinn didn't stir, unaware of my presence, until I slid into a wooden chair beside him. Startled from his deep study, alarm covered his face when he jerked up to look at me. Quickly, though, that look of surprise melted into one of...relief?

"Hannah," he whispered, my name a tender breath from his lips.

My heart warmed. Pleasure oozed through my limbs.

Self-control.

Quinn glanced around, clearly looking for spectators, and then fastened his warm gaze back on me. "I was afraid..."

"You'd never see me again?" I snapped, desperate to keep my attraction and longing for him tamped down. "I wonder why. Couldn't be because you left me."

"I didn't—"

"Have a choice?" I paused, letting my distrust penetrate the silent look we held. "Seems real choices are rare in our world. More so than we ever thought."

His Adam's apple bobbed, and the longing in his eyes faded to confusion. "You left me. That was your choice."

"Did your mother teach you how to manipulate, or does it just come naturally?"

Wide-eyed, he stared.

"Look," I said, refocusing on my task. "That isn't really the reason I'm here."

Still he stared, as confused and thrown off balance as he would have been if I'd taken him down. "It isn't?"

I slid my All-In-One onto the table between us, never taking my focus from him. "There's something in here I need you to explain."

He glanced to the table and then looked to me again. "What?"

It was my turn to look around, searching for an audience. "Not here," I said.

Quinn followed my inspection, nodded his understanding, and then gripped my hand.

I wanted to melt. Instead, I snagged the All-In-One, stiffened my shoulders, and removed my hand from his. When his shoulders sagged, I felt a pang of regret before I could block it away. He didn't question me or make another advance for my hand though. When he stepped away from the table and walked out of the library, I followed.

Silence bound us in a shiver of anguish until he led me through an unmarked door. Darkness swallowed me as I stepped through. A surge of panic overtook my heart when the door clicked shut and I felt him turn to lean over me, his solid hand securing the exit behind me as the lights in the room flickered on. We were in a small closet where electronics and wires and things I couldn't identify had been kept. The only way in or out lay beneath his hand.

Trapped.

I felt myself becoming the frightened bunny again, and before I could stop the reaction, I shrank against the door.

"What's going on, Hannah?" Quinn's fierce whisper felt warm against my face.

My hands began to shake. "I need to know the truth."

His stance changed, and though he still hovered over me, the hand that seemed to be my keeper lifted from the door, his fingertips brushing my face.

"I didn't have a choice, Hannah." He lifted my chin, forcing my eyes to meet his. "I promise I didn't want to leave. I went back to Glennbrooke, to get you out of the Pride, but they said you'd been transferred, and I couldn't find out where they'd moved you."

Oh, how my heart leapt to believe that. But even if it were so, it wasn't what I was there for.

"Tell me why you didn't want me in the Pride."

His shoulders dropped again, and he looked away.

"You knew, didn't you?"

"Knew what?"

"All of it. All of the ugliness, the evil." Though still a whisper, my voice became harsh. Outraged. "Though the rest of our world is ignorant of every black detail, you weren't. You knew!"

"I knew there were things that happened in the Pride and in the Den that I didn't want you to be a part of, yes." Dark and angry, he scowled down at me. "Why does that make you mad?"

"Is this the compassion of the Party? The strength? The dignity?"

"What?"

"The Commons? The Purge? The camps? Is this the beautiful revolution of your people?"

"I don't know—"

My right hand rose, ready to fly against his shaved cheek, but then I remembered. *Don't give him my hands when he's bigger than me.*

Stronger. Don't open a window to weakness.

Instead, I fisted that hand and glared into his eyes. "Don't lie to me, Quinn!"

Dazed, angry, bewildered, he stared at me, both hands pushed into his hair. "I can't lie to you if I don't know what you're talking about."

The cool shape of my All-In-One sank into my left palm, and I lifted it so that he could see the screen. Wordlessly, he watched it, waiting for me to show him. I wondered if this was more of his mother's manipulation or if his confusion was sincere. Determined to see the truth play out in his reaction, I tapped the screen until the video Jude had made bloomed into action, and then I focused on his face while he watched.

And he did watch. His hands lowered, slowly coming to cup the device I still held, the warmth of his palms covering my fingers. The confusion in his eyes slowly morphed to alarm, and then...

Horror.

His grip tightened around my hands, around the video, and the veins on his neck bulged, allowing me to see the surge of his raging pulse. "What is this?"

"Reformation Camp."

Searing heat flashed through his eyes as he moved his attention from the video to me. "Liar."

"*I* am not the liar."

He ripped the All-In-One from my fingers. "This is false. Propaganda. Where did you get it?"

"I *saw* it, Quinn. I was there, assigned to guard them."

"No." He shook his head, but his hands were shaking. Torn. He was fighting to believe what he had been sold. To not believe what he'd just seen. What was the truth. "It's not possible. This is not what we do."

"Really?" I pushed off of the door. Stepped into his space with a renewed boldness. "Then why were you afraid for me? Why didn't you want me to go to the Pride, to go to the Commons?"

"I knew what happened there—" His voice rose to an angry bark, and then his hand pushed through his hair again. "But everyone there had a choice! I just didn't want you to be a part of it."

"They're orphans, Quinn. Do you really think they had a choice? What other options did they have? Sure, the Party says they'll help, they'll meet the needs—but there's always an exchange, isn't there? Always a price to be paid."

"That's not true, Hannah. *You* had a choice—"

"Only because of you. Without you, I didn't. My options were to starve in the woods or join the Pride. Become one of you or die. That's not really a choice, is it?"

"But my mother—" A cloud settled over his expression, as dark and as hurt as ever I'd seen. She couldn't be trusted, and he knew it firsthand. I had not been her first act of betrayal toward him. Something festering, painful, and ugly lay beneath that look. I wondered what else...

"She's one of them," I whispered. "But I think you're not. Are you?"

Our argument froze, and Quinn stared at the screen in his palms. His jaw jumped twice, and he blinked. A sheen covered his eyes when he looked back at me.

"Swear to me, Hannah." His lips trembled. His voice wavered. "Swear to me you actually saw this. That this isn't a recording some guy gave you to scare us. To get to me."

"Why would I throw everything away like that?" I dared another inch closer, until the warmth of his body brushed mine. "Things aren't what the Party claims. They have secrets hidden beneath their facade."

His gaze pinned me again. Measuring. Wavering. I stared back at him, willing him to see the truth. To believe it. Me. Even if it meant he saw my heart breaking.

"How do I know I can trust you?" he whispered.

"Because I just put my life in your hands by bringing you this. Now you get to decide what to do with it. What you'll do with me."

He looked away, to the floor. "I have dreams sometimes. Nightmares..." His eyelids fluttered, and he shook the thoughts away.

I couldn't trace his thoughts, guess what he'd been about to reveal. Holding my breath, willing my heart to slow its storming pace, I waited.

"What do you want me to do?" Earnest vulnerability corded his voice, and he sought my answer with a broken look. "I don't know what else is real, what my mother is about, why I'm here. But I know that I trust you. So tell me, what should I do?"

"Show this to the people. Make them see the truth."

He processed the weight of my request. The cost.

For him it would be everything. Because the video by itself wouldn't have enough meaning. Quinn would have to speak—to put himself behind it. Publicly. To oppose the Party—his mother—in front of everyone.

I'd just laid before him an impossible choice. Because if he joined us, he would likely die.

But at least he would get to choose.

* * *

Braxton

"This is a restricted lab." Annyon scowled at me, the dawn of recognition not yet lighting his expression as he spoke through the intercom.

I buried the sting of him not recognizing his own brother. I guess I was a man now and not the boy he'd last seen five years before. And I had never carried the trademark Luther looks, favoring my mother's side a little, but even that, I lacked a strong family resemblance either way.

But still...

We'd played catch when I was ten. Before he'd gone to the university, following in the athletic footsteps of our father. We'd exchanged Christmas gifts on snowy December mornings through the years, warm and safe in our family's home, with the comfortable and inviting smells of our mother's roasted turkey and dressing hanging in the background.

Another life entirely. One that seemed almost imaginary as I stared at my brother, still hooded and behind the lab glass. A tremor of suspicion rolled through me, and I remembered my mother's anguish at Annyon's decision to take this job.

This *research* in virology.

I stepped into the room, letting the door shut

behind me as I moved to the glass.

"You can't be in here," Annyon said again, a firm bark underlying his voice.

"I need your help."

He paused, raising his eyebrows at the sound of my voice. His study of my face became first intense and then unbelieving.

"What are you—"

"I told you. I need your help."

His mouth held open for another breath, and then he moved to the door that separated the isolated lab from his office. He was careful as he peeled the protective layers of his suit off, and then moved to a sink where he scrubbed from elbows to fingertips for several minutes before he emerged through the door.

"Who let you in here?" he demanded, now scowling again.

"I did. Seems your computerized security can't tell the difference between your voice and mine. Hardly surprising. Father never could either."

Annyon's eyes cast away at the mention of our dad.

"He's dead, you know." I held a careful study of him. "But it looks like you were already aware of that."

No answer.

"Mother was shipped away. I don't know if she

survived. Doubt it."

"Of course she survived," he snapped. "It isn't as if—"

"So you do know. Or at least you think you know."

Silence again.

"Do you know how they killed Dad?"

A patronizing glare filled his expression as Annyon brought his scowl back to me. "He had many chances, Braxton. He chose the path of rebellion. How can you not see that we must maintain justice in order to have a society that thrives?"

"Justice?" I snorted. "Is that what they told you?"

"He set houses on fire."

"He did no such thing. And you should know better than to believe such a wild tale. Our father? A violent rebel? Where is your head, Annyon?"

Annyon stepped forward, heat building in his glare. "Our father was passionate about his beliefs, so passionate it possessed him. You of all people should know how it took him captive. Don't pretend you didn't resent it."

Revelation. I hadn't been the only one.

Shame warmed my face and chest. How greatly I had misunderstood life. My father. My brothers. All I'd ever been able to see was how it affected me. The Braxtonian-centered worldview.

Apparently, I was not the only one who wore that kind of blinder.

I kept my voice measured. "Did they tell you how he died?"

"In the fire."

"No. They murdered him. Right in the middle of town. With a press that crushed his body until he suffocated."

"Don't believe the rebel lies, Braxton."

"I believe my eyes. I stood there and watched him die."

A hard silence settled between us as Annyon looked me over while he processed my story.

"You wear the Jackals uniform."

I felt my life hanging by a slender thread, held precariously in Annyon's distrustful fingers. He was calling me out.

I said nothing.

Annyon took a step closer. "Did you come here just to tell me about our father?"

"No." I reached for the pocket inside my coat, withdrawing my All-In-One. "I told you—I need your help."

I tapped the screen, found the photo app, and slid the pictures until I found what I wanted him to see. Once the image filled the screen, I turned it for him to examine.

"I need to know what this is," I said.

Darkness hooded his eyes as he assessed the sick old man I'd taken a picture of.

"This looks like a research project, Braxton. I hadn't heard you made it into the Med Track."

"I haven't. And it's not research. That man is alive—or he was last week. What does he have?"

Annyon shook his head and laughed. "Someone is messing with you. This picture has to be old. A hundred years, at least. It's probably from a Med textbook."

"*I* took that picture, Annyon. Last. Week. He's one of hundreds. They're all dying of whatever it is you're not telling me."

His eyes lifted from the screen and met mine, the laughter in them fading to a grim stare.

"That's not possible."

"What is it?"

His mouth drew into a tight line.

"You know what it is, so tell me, Annyon. They're dying."

He swallowed, his neck muscles tight, his jaw jumping. My temper flared, and I lunged at him, gripping his button-down shirt in both fists. With the force of every disciplined muscle in my body, I spun him around and backed him into the door.

"Eliza is there—she has it." Control slipped as rage took over. I jerked him forward and then slammed him against the door again. "Tell me what you know!"

He shook beneath my hands, and disbelieving horror crept into his expression. "I don't know how it got out. It's not supposed to be out."

"What?"

He swallowed, the movement of his Adam's apple scraping against my knuckles. "It's smallpox."

I continued to glare at him, not understanding what he was talking about.

"It's been eradicated since the1980s. But—"

"But what?" I stepped back, releasing his shirt and giving him room to move.

His eyes flickered to the lab behind me and then slid shut. I couldn't fathom his reaction.

"If it's been eradicated, then there must be a cure," I said, desperation clinging to my voice. "I need that cure, Annyon."

"There isn't." Finality registered in his words.

"What do you mean there isn't? If they fixed it before then—"

"It's not the same." Again, he looked at the lab. "The strains aren't the same anymore. They've been altered. It's a GMS."

"What is GMS?"

"Genetically modified strain."

My heart stalled. I still didn't understand what he was saying, but I knew defeat—and panic—when I saw it. "How do you know this is GMS smallpox?"

Heat tainted his face, and he looked away. I turned, the import of the lab, of his hazmat suit, the care he took in removing it, in washing...

"You did this..." Rage underscored my whisper, and I felt it build in my body, demanding a release. I lunged at him, again pinning him to the door at his back.

"It wasn't supposed to get out of the lab." With a tortured expression, Annyon turned his face toward me. "I don't know how it got out. I've been looking for the vaccine—the right sequence of proteins that would prevent the virus from attaching to cells. But this modified strain is difficult. It's like it's got a self-destruct mechanism. When we attempt to kill the virus to produce the vaccine, the sequence immediately falls apart and I can't replicate it."

He could have been speaking in Latin for all I understood.

"Why would you be messing with a disease that had been eradicated? Why would you play with Pandora's box like that?"

"To make it safe—manageable."

"Why?" I shouted. "This is biowarfare, isn't it,

Annyon?"

Guilt weighed in his silence.

"The Party," I hissed. "This is their work, and you're part of it. That's what made Mother cry. Why Father was disappointed in you—"

He lifted his head, straightened his shoulders, and pushed my fists away. "They never understood!" he growled. "Never appreciated the things I researched. Called them dangerous. Irresponsible. Never saw the possibilities—"

"What, like this?" I shoved my All-In-One back in his face, anger punctuating my words. "Is this what you envisioned, Annyon? Messing with death, did you see it being unleashed on an entirely defenseless people?"

"I don't even know where they are!" Both of his hands raked through his hair, fisting the top with white knuckles. "I don't know how this happened."

"Well, let me explain it to you, Dr. Frankenstein. These people are in the Reformation Camp. The Quarantine, to be exact. And they were intentionally exposed— probably part of the research you claim to know nothing about. And they're dying. Every last one of them. No one has survived. So congratulations, Dr. Death. You've succeeded."

Annyon's elbows collapsed inward as he physically folded in on himself. "God help..." he mumbled.

The weight. He hadn't measured the costs. Hadn't believed this could happen—not here. Not in his America.

I knew. I'd been that ignorant too.

"What can be done?" My words still bit—more from desperation than from pure anger with him. Had I been in his place, would I have done what he'd done?

The ink embedded in my skin was an unarguable answer.

"I haven't figured out the sequence yet, Braxton. And now, with it out, a vaccination isn't going to be enough. We'll need the antibodies too." Looking back at me, there was agony in his wild eyes.

"Do you have that?" I felt anger growing harder on my face, because it was a dumb question and I already knew the answer.

Annyon shook his head.

"What the—" I cut myself off.

Annyon's voice shook right along with his fisted hands. "I thought I was researching it because of an external threat. Not—"

Not because we'd used it on our own people. The inhumanity of it rippled a shiver down my spine. Why would we consider using a lethal disease on any people? The darkness of a heart yielded to evil seemed to have no bounds.

I reached for his shoulder, feeling weak, now understanding the full crushing blow of what had been done. "Can you find it?"

He blinked, his mouth still trembling. "In such a short time..." His head shook slow as it hung downcast. Hopeless. "Only if one of them survives."

twenty-six

Hannah

Quinn held my hand while he led me through a labyrinth of dim halls. His long stride demanded a near-jog pace from my shorter steps, but I didn't mind.

"What will you do?" I asked, my heart squeezing with a faint trace of mistrust. He could be taking me toward death—turning me in to his mother. I wondered if they killed the Cloaked quickly or if they exposed them to whatever black death that was in the Quarantine and let them writhe in agony before they died.

Probably the latter.

"Exactly what you said." Determination

wrapped his words. "I'll expose this to everyone. It won't be hard."

"It won't?"

We stopped at a closed door, and Quinn looked down at me with a small tilt on his lips. "You don't get the kind of education I've gotten without some secrets mixed in."

I held his look, less worried now about myself and death waiting for me on the other side of that door, and more about him. "Quinn, you realize—"

"I know the cost, Hannah." He released my hand and traced the line of my jaw with one finger. "With privilege comes responsibility, right?"

"That's what your mother said," I whispered.

"Maybe one of the only honest things she's ever told me."

Confusion rose up in my chest, and I felt the need to probe into this deep resentment he carried. Everything I'd witnessed in their home, until Charlotte pushed me toward the Pride, seemed picture perfect. Nothing had seemed amiss between mother and son.

"Those dreams—" I studied his eyes as I spoke. A storm lingered there. "What did they tell you?"

He held my gaze. Yearning seemed to cry out to me—he wanted me to hear, wanted someone to understand. To believe. But he pushed it away. Swallowing, he broke our connection and turned toward the door. "It's not your burden to carry."

With a hand to his shoulder, I pulled him back to face me. "I'm willing to anyway."

A sad, tender smile eased over his mouth, and then he bent to brush my lips with it. "I know, Hannah. But I don't want you to. Not right now anyway. This is more important, and after it's done..."

After it was done, the veil would be torn and Quinn's life would be crushed. Unless Braxton and I could get him away.

Quinn punched in a code on the unmarked door and pushed against the handle. It gave way, and we entered a room full of computers and screens and modems. It looked like the technology housing center for the school. But clearly Quinn knew it to be more.

"Give me the All-In-One."

Handing it over, I stood feeling useless and awkward. "What will you do?"

"Load it to the central broadcasting network. Everything that comes from there has been previously filtered by the officials, so it will slide through without censorship. It also has precedence—anything being broadcast from the CBN will override whatever is being played on the other networks. Anyone who is watching anything right now will see it."

Adrenaline spiked, making my arms and legs tingle. "How long will it take?"

"Almost uploaded." He glanced to me, his resolve steady. "I'll need to do a voice over. Probably an intro, so that they can see my face, know who's speaking. After that, once it's sent to the CBN...just a matter of minutes."

"Quinn..." My hands shook as if I'd just realized the full import of what he was doing. I'd known, but now? Now it was real. Swallowing, I put my hand over his. "Maybe they only need the video. Maybe you don't need to show your face, to speak."

He shook his head. Decisive. Unswerving. "You know that won't do anything. The Party will blame it on the rebels, just like the fires. The orphans. The unrest. It has to come from me. That's why you came." He paused, settling a meaningful look on me. "Isn't it?"

I blinked, an uncomfortable burn glazing my eyes.

"It's okay, Hannah. You were right, and I'm willing. For once in my life, I can determine my own path, do what I know is right, and not just for face value. This is my choice."

"But you don't even know us—the rest of the Cloaked. The Uncloaked."

"I know you." He stopped, his expression hardening. "I remember finding you at the edge of the forest. I couldn't fathom why you'd be afraid of me. And yet, part of me knew... The rise in orphans, what I knew of the Den, what I suspected of the Pride, the house fires..."

He blinked. Swallowed. "Patrick Luther."

"You knew Pastor Luther?"

"Only of him. I used to listen to his sermons. In secret. When he died—"

"He was murdered." I nearly hissed, accepting, maybe for the first time, that Braxton had been telling the truth.

Quinn nodded, and his chin quivered. "I'd been suspicious. The man I listened to, though passionate, couldn't have been what they said he was. He couldn't have done what they accused him of doing. Killing those people in their sleep. Setting fire to their house. It didn't make sense."

That night replayed in my mind, and tears flooded my eyes. Quinn's thumb traced a trail beside my nose. "You knew him?"

I nodded. "That family he was accused of killing?" My bottom lip trembled, and I paused to regain control.

Quinn stood quietly waiting for me to finish.

"It was mine. And you're right—Pastor Luther didn't do it."

Truth washed over me with a fresh, horrible blackness. How had I not seen what was real? How had I convinced myself that Braxton, Eliza, and my parents had been wrong?

Quinn pulled me against his chest, one solid arm locked fast around my shoulders. "We will end the lies today."

* * *

Braxton

Walking beside Annyon through the halls of the hospital, a gathering near a break lounge caused the hair on my neck to rise. Like bugs to a lightbulb, whatever was on the central television was drawing a growing crowd. Annyon moved toward the group, but I gripped his forearm and sent him a warning glance.

If Hannah had succeeded...

A voice rose from the television, stirring a chilled hush among the crowd.

"You know me from my mother. You know my position within the Party. The hopes they have yoked upon my shoulders. But there is so much you don't know, and I must show you. I must give you the truth. With it, you can choose what you will do. For now, my responsibility is to pull back the lies hiding behind our pretty words. For now, I must tear the veil."

Quinn Sanger. Near unbelief swirled dizziness through my mind. He'd done it.

Hannah—she'd done it. And we couldn't stay. A spike of determined adrenaline cleared the fuzz from my head. He would be a death target, and Hannah would be easily recognized by Charlotte, making her a bull's-eye as well.

"What's happening?" Annyon whispered, still leaning to catch a glimpse.

"Our world is about to rip in half," I said. "And we can't stay here to watch."

His eyebrows gathered, suspicion in his scowl. "What have you done?"

"Hopefully, exposed the truth." I tugged him toward an exit. "Which means my visit to DC is about to come to a fast end."

Annyon stopped short of the door and glared at me. I didn't have time to convince him.

"Stay if you want. It's your conscience. Your life. I can't be here. I have people depending on me."

"What will you do?"

A long pause settled between us, and I gave him a hard look. One that felt like something my father would have given me when I needed to make a tough choice. I hoped that today Dad saw me. That he'd be proud of the man I was trying to become.

"You have to choose, Annyon. I can't decide who you'll be. But I don't have time to wait either. So choose right now…"

He glanced back to the group. Then toward the direction of the lab. His work, his life…

Then he nodded. "All right, little brother. Let's go."

"You can't look back," I warned. "There are too many other lives at stake."

Again, he nodded.

It was good enough for me.

* * *

Hannah

The purposeful energy I'd sensed earlier that morning had exploded into a rage of chaos along the streets.

It had happened. Quinn had done it, and now he and I were running for our lives.

#success

I'd had the message ready to send before Quinn uploaded the final version of the video, but I hadn't wanted to be premature. Now I desperately hoped Braxton was ready for us. That the coin he carried would actually work. That we could get Quinn out alive.

With an iron grip on his hand, I jerked Quinn into a back alleyway five blocks from the

National Mall. If Jude had planned precisely, if Tristan and Braxton hadn't failed in their jobs, we'd lift off a platform near the water, the coin Braxton carried shelling us in the same kind of cloaking technology that Jude had created for the Refuge.

There wasn't anything close to a guarantee with that plan. Jude hadn't actually tested the coin on something in flight. The fear of failure sank hard and cold into the deepest part of my gut.

God, please be with us...

"There!"

A shout behind us ripped the prayer from my mind, sharpening that fear.

Our pace somehow increased, though I thought I'd already been running at my maximum speed. Quinn kept up, his hard but steady breathing telling me he'd trained every bit as much physically as he had studied.

"Where are we going?" he asked.

"There's a chopper waiting for us on a paddock near the water, on South Capitol Street."

Quinn squeezed my hand. "I know where it is." He tugged me down another street. "But it's still over a mile from here, and they don't allow commercial flights."

"It's been arranged. I don't know how or any of the details. I just know that's the rendezvous point."

A clog of transports blocked the cross street in front of us. The constant blare of horns shattered the early morning air.

"Stop those two rebels!"

The shout behind us prickled gooseflesh along my skin. Whoever was following us was getting closer, and he was likely armed.

Quinn tugged me forward again, into the congestion of creeping vehicles. Closer, the blast of horns, now directed at us, jarred my thoughts, clouded my judgment. I didn't see the curb as we left the street, and my misstep sent me tumbling forward. Pain jolted in my shin, radiating down to my foot and up into my thigh. Quinn's hand tightened on mine, and he pulled me up against him, one arm wrapping around my waist to support me.

"We have to keep going, Hannah. I need you to keep moving."

I nodded, desperately keeping step with him, working to block out the pain that spiked every time my right foot struck the ground.

The noises around me faded. My vision tunneled. I heard only the throb of my heart, the whoosh of my labored breathing, the encouraging whispers Quinn dropped to my

ears as he struggled to run for the both of us.
"Hannah!" Suddenly support slipped under
my left arm as well. "What happened?"
I glanced, catching Braxton's profile next to
me. "Just tripped."
"Are you a part of this?" Quinn asked, his voice
drifting over my head.
"Braxton Luther," Braxton said, both still
moving at a pace I struggled to match. "Yes. I'm
supposed to get you both to the Refuge."
"And your friend?"
In my fight to keep up and my tunnel vision,
I hadn't noticed anyone else.
"My brother. Annyon."
That hadn't been part of the plan.
"We've got to go faster." Braxton kept talking.
"That official behind us is closing. Much closer,
and he'll fire."
So he was armed. Just not willing to shoot
haphazardly into the street. Probably wise,
considering the pandemonium Quinn's video
had unleashed.
"Hannah can't," Quinn said. "The gash on her
leg—I think she's broken a bone."
The helipad broke into view just as I felt
Quinn look back. His silence after that glance
sent a razor of warning through my brain. I
didn't like the feeling, and panic stirred a storm

in me.

"Keep going. I can keep up. Just keep going."

"No." He didn't stop, but there was resolve in his tone. "They're after me. They don't know you. Any of you."

"Quinn, don't!" My voice caught, and I glanced up to him. "We're almost there…"

His eyes connected with mine for the smallest of moments, and then he looked to Braxton.

"You won't have time to get off the ground. Get her to wherever it is safe. Don't let her look back."

"No!" I screamed.

With a grip on his shoulder, I fought his sudden change in direction. He covered my hand, squeezed, and then let go, his shift in momentum ripping away from me.

The world blurred into a hot, watery mess as I watched him run toward the people chasing us. Away from me. Vaguely, I felt the punch of Braxton's shoulder meeting my gut, and then the ground beneath my feet was no more. I continued moving away from Quinn, aware only of the tearing in my heart.

He ran until they caught him, the butt of a weapon shoved hard into his gut. On his knees, he looked back toward us and then fell forward to the ground. The weapon lifted into the air, and I knew where the next blow would land.

I shut my eyes. I couldn't watch anymore.

twenty-seven

Braxton

I stared at the message on my All-In-One. *#success.*

The message had been repeated back to us, along with the numbers 61855. I tipped the face of the screen toward Tristan, knowing he knew the code better than me.

"Free." Tristan's deep voice held a reverent relief alongside a strong sense of sorrow.

Jude had succeeded. We played the distraction, and he'd exploited the weakness in the invisible fence guarding the captives. He'd set them free.

Blinking away the warm moisture in my eyes,

I tipped my head back and let it all soak into my heart. Eliza—had she survived? Had they brought the sick ones out too?

Heavy questions, but at the moment, the weight of what we'd just done—of what Hannah and Quinn had done, pressed harder.

Silence gelled us as we sat on the shielded transport. A pair of sellouts, given a chance at redemption. The price had been steep. Hannah stared forward, unblinking. Unmoving.

I knew the ripping that burned in her heart. She'd made the ultimate sacrifice. I wanted to be proud of her, but everything in me just ached. Her heart was broken. Quinn had been exactly who she thought he was, and she'd risked everything for all of us. For the Uncloaked and for the Cloaked. With one bold act, she and Quinn had torn the veil.

Now they were torn apart.

When I'd submitted to the seal, I'd deluded myself into thinking that my actions were noble. I was protecting what I loved. But now, in the cold, thick silence that sat between Hannah Knight and myself, and the replay of everything that had happened that night reeling through my brain, I knew I'd just witnessed real sacrifice. For others. For the good of the people. For the hope of a nation that was in the labor pains of new birth.

Just like me, Hannah Knight had been called, despite her wayward path, for such a time as this.

I settled a look on her, keeping my focus on her face until she was compelled to look back at me. When she did, her eyes were distant, chilled, and a little wild. Expected, considering that the boy she loved would probably be dead before sunrise.

I gripped her hand and squeezed. "You were right about him. He was good."

She scowled. "Is. He *is* good. And this is not over yet."

No, it wasn't. The battle was just beginning. But I knew beyond all else that was not what Hannah meant.

I didn't know what Jude would think of that, but it didn't matter. Beyond all odds, I'd found Eliza. I'd be a total hypocrite to deny Hannah the same slim chance.

And after all that had happened since that fateful election three years before, I knew one thing for certain.

I was done being a hypocrite.

* * *

REFORMATION CAMP

Eliza

Reality felt like a distant stranger. I could not grasp it. The fever roasted through my body, and instinctively I knew I was close to death.

I welcomed it.

The pox that had ravaged my body burned like a sandpapery tongue of savage fire. They left nothing of me to mercy.

So many others had already died. The agony in their quiet whimpers a torture to my soul. How many nights had I lain, silently begging for God's mercy in death on the behalf of my fellow prisoners? Every time a tortured victim stopped their pain-riddled moan, I breathed a praise for their released soul.

Now it was my turn. I was so thirsty for the end.

But light suddenly ripped into our dark existence. Disoriented as I was, I could not make sense of the piercing white that blinded my sore eyes. Maybe I was dying. Now. The light was coming...

Shouting jarred my hearing. That couldn't have been the death I ached for. It wasn't the praise, the welcome kind of shouts.

"As quickly as possible!" Panic riddled the voice that rang through our cold shelter. "As many as you can. The next transport will be here any minute, and we don't know how long the Party will be distracted."

Not dead. Hardly alive either. The cruel in between. I tried lifting my head. Forms draped in the hazmat suits our unmerciful captors wore when they came in to "care" for us scurried around the space, lifting bodies. Carrying thin wisps of humans, the shells of what remained.

My mind could not make sense of it.

But the scurrying continued. A trace of fear pressed into me when a hazmat-clad stranger leaned over me. I pushed it away, the fear being unreasonable. What else could they do to me?

Angel of mercy, please come...

"Don't be afraid, sweetie." The lips behind the mask moved, and as if delayed, the voice registered moments after. "We're here to help. You are free."

I tipped my head back, waiting for a sense of relief. Of joy.

Neither came.

Free for what? Shame followed the ungrateful thought.

"Thank you," I mumbled, summoning the goodness to feel it.

Soft, like a gentle push, my spirit seemed to untangle from the dark place that had longed for death.

"Thank you," I whispered again. The feeling, though tender and small, poked through the wasteland of my soul.

"We'll take care of you," the gentle person said. "But the ride will be difficult. Just hang on." The rumble of an engine met my spine as I was placed into the hollow of a large van. After securing me, hands and feet inside, my rescuer closed the double doors at the back. Sudden movement provoked a surge of nausea in my stomach, and by the groans around me, others felt the same. A few heaves sounded around me, but I didn't smell the taint of puke within the van.

We had nothing in our stomachs to throw up.

A left turn, and then shortly after, a right, and then the steady velocity of our carriage continued straight. None of us spoke. I wondered if they, like I, struggled to believe this to be real. Perhaps the Party had thought of a new way to torture. They would make us well, only to be turned out again. Maybe completely naked this time. Chained to the walls.

I blocked out the darkness of my thoughts.

A hum from outside hung overhead, the strength of its buzz growing with every passing second until it became a roar. Suddenly a thunderbolt-like crash cracked the sound waves around us, the booming loudness shaking the earth on which we traveled. Another boom shattered the air, making my ears ring with a high-pitched squeal.

We held our breath as the van still trembled along the quivering road.

And then...silence.

I became certain in that eerie space. The camp had been erased.

THE END

Look for the conclusion of The Uncloaked in Charging the Darkness.

* * *

Thanks for reading! Please add a short review on Amazon and let me know what you thought!

About the Author

J. Rodes lives on the wide plains somewhere near the middle of Nowhere. A coffee addict, pickleball enthusiast, and storyteller, she also wears the hats of mom, teacher, and friend. Mostly, she loves Jesus and wants to see the kids she's honored to teach fall in love with Him too.

www.authorjenrodewald.com
fb.me/authorJRodes

Made in the USA
San Bernardino, CA
16 July 2017